CLEO BROWNE

Wire

Devil's Rose MC Book Two

First published by Meihana Pinker Ltd 2024

First edition

ISBN: 978-1-0670014-5-2

This book was professionally typeset on Reedsy.
Find out more at reedsy.com

Trigger Warning

This book deals with a badassery in all its forms.
Please be aware that in order for these characters to be badass,
this book contains content that some readers may find
disturbing, such as graphic descriptions of violence and
torture, R18 sex scenes, and badly timed strippers.

Hey Readers!

Thank you for being here! This book was a little different for me to write. I thought I was clever and could write a book where we go back in time a little to see the beginning of Wire and Remy's relationship, and the events that happened in August's book from their point of view. It turns out that it was a lot harder than I thought and I almost died in the midst of this from a writing induced conniption. However, I persevered because this couple's story wormed its way into my heart.

I hope they worm into yours as well.

Prologue

R *emy aged 4*

I run as fast as I can, down the short hall into my bedroom before hitting the ground. The brown carpet scratches my knees when I crawl into my hiding place. I have Paprika in my arms; she's my stuffy that Daddy got me. Sometimes he picks me up and takes me for rides on his bike.

Mommy is screaming so I curl up even smaller and close my eyes. When Mommy has her friends over I have to stay in bed and not get out. Sometimes she makes screaming sounds but she told me it's because she's having lots of fun.

"Rem? Remy, are you here?"

"Sunny?" Unscrunching my eyes I peek through the flaps of my tent. My daddy got this for me too. I like hiding in here with Paprika when the men come. A big blue eye peeks through and then Sunny is crawling into my tent with me. I scrunch up small so she can fit. She's bigger than me. Like really big. She goes to school.

Mommy starts screaming louder now and she's saying lots of bad words. I don't know what's happening, but if Sunny is here, my daddy must be here too. I snuggle into Sunny and she puts her arm around me and squeezes me tight.

"It's OK Remy. Dad's come to take you home. You're going

to live with us now."

Remy aged 9

"Come on Remy, Dad gave us money to go to the mall," Sunny is smiling huge at me, waving a wad of cash. I don't want to go to the mall, but I heard the men talking about "club business".

I know that means me and Sunny have to hang out somewhere else for a while. When we were younger some of the club girls would look after us. Well, they'd look after me. Sunny said it was because they were trying to become Dad's Ol Lady. It didn't work. After I grew out of being little and cute they just ignored me until Sunny could take care of the both of us. Sunny told me that both our moms were club girls. Sunny's mom left her with Dad straight after she was born. My mom kept me for a little while until Dad got sick of her leaving me by myself all the time. Then he came and got me and I've been with him and Sunny in our trailer at the clubhouse ever since. It's not too bad except when we have to be out for a long time when I'd rather be reading my book.

"Come on, bring your book. We can get smoothies and sit. You can read and I'll do schoolwork."

I smile up at my big sister. She makes everything better.

Remy aged 11

"Rem?" Turning to the sound of my name being called, Dad is heading my way, his face crumpled. Sighing, I know that club business is about to happen.

"Rem, there's some shit going down, I need you to not be

here. Is there anywhere you can go for a few hours?"

I gather up my books and nod up at my dad. It's not his fault that stuff goes down all the time. Usually when this happened Sunny would take me somewhere with her. We'd hit the mall, go to back-to-back movies, or even hang out at her friends' houses. Since she's seven years older than me it was up to her to look after me. Now, she's busy working her butt off at community college.

"I'll go to the library. It stays open until late and I have some things I can do there," Dad looks at me with soft eyes and kisses me on the top of my head.

"Thanks Rem. I'll send Chase to pick you up when we're done." Nodding, I let out a breath. Chase is one of the nicer prospects we have around here. I've heard that he's having his patch-in party at the end of the week and his new name will be Savage. That's what they should name the other prospect, Carter. He's nasty and goes out of his way to mess with me. He stands too close and tries to touch me all the time. He sometimes tries to get me to go places with him. Chase caught him one time and broke his nose. He's pretty much left me alone since but he gives me filthy looks or tries to corner me.

"Don't forget, stay inside the library until Chase comes, baby girl."

Remy aged 13

"Well, you're back again huh, Miss Remy?" Miss Shawna's eyes light up. I love coming in when she's on.

"Hey Miss Shawna, yup, back again!"

"Well, that's just fine with me. I have something a little special that's just arrived. I thought to myself, 'Miss Shawna, who is a good kid you would trust with this here thang?' and you

3

were the only one! So, come on child. Lemme show you what we got," Miss Shawna books it through the library, heading to where all the community computers sit, her ample body jiggling under her colorful long skirts and scarves and things.

"Ta daaaaa!" She waves her hands around like those women you see on TV game shows, my gaze following her hands.

"Is that a gaming computer?" It's beautiful. I've been coming and hanging out at the library for the last couple of years. After reading all the books that took my fancy, I started to gravitate more towards the computers and the cheap internet. Whenever there was bad stuff going down at the clubhouse, which seemed to be all the time, Dad would send me to the library with $20 and a cellphone top-up so I could let him know when the library was closing.

"It sure is, sweet thang. It's loaded up with that game that all the kids are raving about these days. AND you can chat with other gamers online." She gives me a pointed look and I know what that means. She's been encouraging me to get out there and make some friends, but it's hard when you belong to the Death Riders MC. Most of the kids at school just ignore me; the ones who don't ignore me call me biker trash and wreck my stuff.

"Look, child, online friends are just as good as real-life friends. Unless they're 50-year-old men pretending to be kids. Watch out for those creeps, OK?" I nod up at Miss Shawna and try not to giggle. "OK, well, take a seat and get to it girl, I think you might surprise yourself." With a smile she swans off in a blur of color, whisper yelling at some kids to keep it down.

I wiggle the mouse and the screen comes to life showing the opening graphics of the game - Shadow Wrath. I've heard the kids talking about it at school. The start-up screen asks me for my gamer tag, what I'll be known by in this world. Thinking about my name, Remington Wright, I decide to do a play on words. Beretta_Penn. That sounds pretty cool.

I click through to the next screen and realize it's some type of role-play game. Maybe in the Shadow Wrath world, I can be confident and outgoing and maybe even popular. Someone different from who I am in this world.

I want to be the opposite of myself so I choose a huge troll avatar. I give him long black hair and a nose ring. I finish up with spiky armor and then my avatar gets dropped into the village where my campaign is going to start. A flashing box in the corner of my screen catches my eye so I click on it. A message pops up from an elf character with a single word:

St_Margarita: Hi.

Chapter One

St_Margarita: Hi.
Beretta_Penn: Hi.
St_Margarita: Wanna campaign together? I need a troll.
Beretta_Penn: K. Let's go, Elf.

Wire

"Church!"

Marx's bellow sounds out down the hallway, snapping me out of my work, which is probably a good thing. I've been sitting in my fancy office chair for far too many hours. Even though the MC sprung for the most ergonomic chair we could find, I don't think it's meant for a 6'3 250 lb man to sit in it for hours on end.

"Boooooooo!" comes drifting out of my closet. On my way past I open the door and peek in, finding Chewy sitting on the floor cross-legged. "When do you think I'll get an invite? I have so many good ideas for new businesses and ways to really enhance what we've got going on. Not to mention I have the best critical thinking skills of everyone here."

Shaking my head at her, I roll my eyes, "Maybe one day Chewy Girl. But not today," I smirk as she boo's me again and I gently close the door on her. Who knows how long she'll be in there? Of all the places for quiet time, she commandeered my closet. Not that it bothers me. I'll do anything I can to help my brother's Ol Lady feel calm and happy.

My "control center" is the furthest away from Church, so I have to leg it down the hall to get there in time. Thanks to Fox and Nitro always being late, we now get fined for being the last one in.

Meeting Rider in the doorway, I shove him to get in first, falling into my chair as he trips me up. He may be one of my closest brothers, but he's still a fucker. He smirks as he takes the seat next to mine. We're just a small MC. At present, we have a dozen members and two prospects. Obviously, they aren't allowed into Church just yet. I would imagine one is on gate duty and the other will be tidying the bar, ordering supplies. All hell would break loose if we ran out of booze.

Seated around the large oval table we use for church, I see as per usual, we are waiting for Fox and Nitro. No surprise. They both work off-site in one of the garages in town and if they're not doing that, they're busy fucking a bunny. We all know they won't leave before getting their rocks off.

"I'll give them five minutes and if they're not here, I'm locking those fucking doors," Pres growls out.

I don't know if he's noticed this yet or not, but there are looks of glee going around the table. Marx sits at the head as Pres. One of my best friends, Rhodie, sits next to him as our enforcer; Rider on the other side as our SAA. I'm the secretary given that I'm always on my computers and have apps out the ass keeping track of all our shit. The rest of the brothers are dotted around the table, eagerly awaiting our last two.

"We're here! Shit, we're here!" Fox and Nitro come barreling into Church stinking of Whitney's perfume. The room erupts into laughter as we see Fox's soft cock hanging out of his zipper.

"Fuck's sake! Put it away, sit down and you're both fined $100. I swear to God you better be here early next time or else you're on toilet duty for the month," Marx seethes, then slams his gavel, getting business started.

I'm a little intrigued to see what this meeting is about. This isn't our usual church day, so something must have come up.

"Savage has asked a favor, and I want to run it by you all before we decide."

The brothers all sit a little straighter in their seats. A favor for the other MC could mean anything. Savage's MC, the Death Riders, has their territory two towns over, around two hours away. For the past few months, we've been allies, although it hasn't always been like that. Death Riders, until recently, have always been a 1% club. Our MC, on the other hand, has always been a safe space for ex-military men to find solace and brotherhood.

"What's the favor?" Switch booms out, making me shrink into myself a little. The guy is so fucking loud. I feel sorry for his patients when he's working at the local hospital. There is no confidentiality when that bastard is yelling your diagnosis at you.

"Savage doesn't have a computer tech. He's been using Wire or Chewy for all background checks, security, and shit." Marx answers, nodding in my direction. "He wants to send us one of his to learn the ins and outs. This will affect you, Wire, and maybe even Chewy, because we all know she won't sit this out."

Chuckling goes around the room, everyone knowing exactly what Chewy is like.

"Who's he sending? I'm not having any random fucker near my Ol Lady," Rhodie grits out. And with good reason. Ol Ladies are fucking special. I don't have a woman, but if I did, I wouldn't want any random fucker near her either. It may make us sound like cavemen, but fuck it. We don't care.

"You know his stand-in VP, Flack? His daughter." Eyebrows raise at this.

A few months ago, Savage staged a coup and got rid of the old Death Riders' Pres. He's making steps to go straight, and he's been working hard on that even though half his crew tried to shit all over his plans. He cleaned house with support from the original VP, Flack, who agreed to stay on until Savage could replace him.

"Wire, what do you know about Flack?" Marx turns his dark gaze to me. Tapping away at my ever-present laptop, I pull up the personnel files I have on all the members of the Death Riders. There was no way we were going to ally ourselves with another club without doing some research on them.

"Paul 'Flack' Wright. Legacy member. His father was a founding member back in the day before the club turned, so I can see why he supported Savage's decision to go legit. Has two daughters, Sunny and Remy. Both raised by him. Sunny is a trained chef, heading the new restaurant the club has opened. Remy is a librarian."

Raising my eyes from my screen, I see all the brothers deep in thought.

"Remy. The librarian. Savage said she'd transfer to the library here, if we agree. She'd train with you and possibly Chewy around her shifts." Marx taps his enormous fist on the table. "What do we think?"

Rider clears his throat "I think let her. In the long run, it adds security to the Death Riders and frees up Wire to work on whatever shit it is he works on." The big bastard smirks at that while I roll my eyes and flip the bird.

"As long as it's a library woman, I'm sure Chewy will be fine," Rhodie adds with a nod.

"Dude, Chewy is fucking scary. It's not her you should be worried about," Rider laughs, the brothers all joining him.

"Shut it! Are we all in agreement?"

A chorus of "Yes, Pres" goes around the room. I join in with the rest of them. Rider is right. The less stuff I have to do for the Death Riders, the more time I have to work on my actual shit.

"I'll let Savage know to arrange it." Marx bangs his meat tenderizer that we use as a gavel because we didn't have one. We all leave church heading for the bar, grabbing our phones we dump in the box next to the doorway on our way out.

It's only 6 pm so I'll have a beer for now, unlike some of my brothers who are hitting the hard stuff. I've never been a hard partier. Even less since we've had shit going down. A lot of the club security comes down to me. Chewy usually steps in to give me a hand whenever she's around, which is most days after she finishes work. The woman is a machine and so open and free with her knowledge. I've learned so much shit, both legal and illegal, and it's all down to her. I'm much better at keeping the brothers safe and keeping shit ticking over thanks to her and some of her tech.

A hand grips my ass and I turn to find Whitney on me. She's been throwing herself at the brothers with more aggression since Chewy turned up and locked Rhodie down. She's barking up the wrong tree with me, though. Yeah I've tapped that a couple of times in the past, but I can smell the crazy on her. These days I prefer to head to town and pick up a bit of strange from one of the local bars rather than use the bunnies and give them any ideas. Gently pushing her towards Sniper and Judge, I untangle myself from her claws, giving my brothers a chin up when they drag her off in their direction.

I finish my beer by shooting the shit with Tank and Rider before heading back to my cave. I want to do a little research into Remy, so I know what to expect. Hopefully, this woman knows how to use a computer; it'll be a total ball ache to start from the very beginning.

"That was fast. Anything I need to know?"

Chewy is sitting at the station I set up for her, watching the camera feed from one of the garages we own.

"Yup, we have a trainee, Chewy."

She spins in her seat to look at me with her huge eyes. "A trainee? A baby hacker? A newbie? A probie? A computer prospe-"

I put my hand up to stop her. "Yup. A trainee."

"Who is it? What do we know about them?"

"Well, she's the -"

"SHE?" Chewy shouts, wide eyed. "The baby hacker is a she!? Shit, I gotta go, I have girl friend stuff to research. Rhodie!"

And with that I watch Chewy run off like her short ass is on fire. Letting out a sigh I take a seat in my comfy as fuck leather chair and look around what is dubbed "The Control Center". When I got out of the military and landed here Marx knew that there was no way I would be separated from all my "toys" as my brothers call them. So he did the only thing he could think of, he gave me the biggest room on the first floor to house everything. The control center takes up one whole side of my suite and with so many people coming and going, we sectioned off my bed and bathroom area with a dividing wall for privacy.

The new kid will sit between me and Chewy, that way they can get the best of both worlds. Chewy and I each have dual screens, with a larger almost wall sized screen. We can project anything on there and use our dual screens for searches, surveillance and in Chewy's case, early 2000's music videos. If I have to see or hear "Dirrty" one more time I'm going to set Chewy's workstation up in my closet, since she loves it so much.

Checking my video feeds one last time to make sure all is right in my world I pull up my search engine and type in one name. Remington Wright.

Remy

"Thanks Miss Remy!"

I wave the last of the kids and parents off before rolling to the side, getting up out of the beanbag I'm sitting in and tidying up the floor cushions. Mondays, Wednesdays, and Fridays are the days that I host the Afternoon Readers' program in the kids' section of the library. I've been working at Roxwell Library since I left high school. I knew community college wasn't for me purely because I had no idea what I wanted to study or do with my life. There seemed to be a world of career options and I just didn't know which one I wanted to settle on. The only thing I did know for sure was that if I wanted to spread my wings and have my own apartment I would need a job. Our old Pres, Hammer, pointed out how at home I felt at the library and maybe that would be something I liked doing. Luckily for me, Miss Shawna gave me a good reference for the children's librarian job when it came up. I like kids, books and the computers and I mean, I had spent the best part of my childhood at this library. I know this place like the back of my hand.

"What are your plans for your last night in town, Miss Thang?" Smiling, I turn to find Miss Shawna leaning on the early reader's bookshelf, her hip popped out, hand resting on it.

"Well, I'll be spending my time getting myself ready for my move." I chew my lip for a moment before Shawna's tutting breaks me out of my thoughts.

"You know I told you, child, the Rose Grove Library is full of good folks, and they're excited to have a new children's librarian for their after school programme. What you should do instead of fretting, is plan a big going away party and get drunk and dirty dance with some of those fine male specimens I see wearing the MC patch." She wiggles her eyebrows at me and I can't help screwing up my face.

"Oh, heck no Shawna! Those men are like uncles and brothers to me. Ugh."

She throws her head back and cackles, her ample bosom jiggling her many beaded necklaces. "Well, hopefully, Devil's Rose MC has better options for you." She moves closer to me, resting her hands on my shoulders, her warmth seeping into me. "Remy, take a chance. It's a new place, with new people. Heck, you don't even have to work at the library. You can do anything you put your mind to, child. You have too much light inside of you to hide it. So let it shine, girly. Show them the kickass woman I know and love, yeah?"

Her eyebrows raise, and she bends slightly so she can look me directly in the eye. She turns a little blurry in my vision and I sniff as I nod and pull her into my embrace. Her spicy cinnamon scent wraps around me, the scent that always comforted me when I was a kid and worried for my Dad. She pulls away, holding me at arm's length, and blinks the tears from her eyes before sniffing.

"Right child, keep me updated. Otherwise, I'll have to come down there and get all the tea in person. Maybe I will anyway?" A huge smile spreads across her face before she cackles and then pats me on the butt. "Get going. Talk soon. And shine, baby girl!"

I give her one last tight hug before gathering my stuff from the staff room. Taking one last look around my safe space, I take a deep breath and walk out the front doors to the staff parking. Throwing my stuff into the back of my little hatchback I head home. Not the studio apartment I've lived in for the past 7 years, but back to the Death Riders compound.

Dad and the prospects moved my stuff into our trailer last weekend, so I've spent the past five days lying in my old room, looking at all the posters I left behind when I moved out to spread my wings.

When Dad took me from my mother, he and Sunny shared a room in the clubhouse. But with me in the mix there were too many people crammed into the small space, so Dad got a trailer for us to live in. The reasoning being that he felt safer having his whole family living at the compound with all his brothers having his back, than out in some bad neighborhood in Roxwell. Which is funny given that the most dangerous thing in Roxwell, Texas at that time were the Death Riders themselves. Sunny and I shared a room until she moved out and I got to decorate my space with posters of boy bands and bookshelves to hold my collections of romance novels.

It seems weird that after spending my young adulthood trying to get away from the MC, I'll be moving into another. Not that growing up with the Death Riders was bad. But it wasn't always great either.

My whole life, the Death Riders have been on the wrong side of the law, much to my father's chagrin. He tried to shield me and Sunny from as much of it as he could, but we still saw stuff that no young person should see growing up. Sunny, more so than me. She protected me from a lot. Even so, I've seen enough of the brothers' franks and beans to last me a lifetime.

Driving back to the compound, I let my mind wander to the Devil's Rose MC. When Savage floated the idea of having one of the Death Riders learn from the DRMC hackers, I never in a million years thought he would choose me. I also never in a million years thought they would agree. But I guess with Savage's plan to turn the MC legit, the DRMC is happy to not only ally but offer support when needed.

Pulling up to the gates, the prospect waves me through and I see various men, some I call "Uncle" all giving me chin lifts or two-finger waves as I pull into a free parking space.

"Hey Rem! Last night in the princess room, huh?" Bones is one of the legacy members, like my dad. After Savage ousted Hammer, the old Pres, the MC split in two. Those who wanted to grow old without gun fights and the threat of prison, and those who wanted to get rich quick, no matter how dangerous or criminal. Hammer took a lot of the younger and more dangerous members. Death Riders MC is now a small MC, of maybe around ten members, the bulk of them older men looking for a quiet life.

"Yup, last night in the twin bed before I head off to Devil's Rose MC." I give him my most confident smile, but it doesn't stop him from seeing right through me. He stomps over and places his giant paw on my shoulder.

"Anything happens, you feel unsafe or anxious, or hell, even homesick, you call me. Anytime, OK Rem?"

I place my hand over his on my shoulder and give it a pat, smiling up into his craggy face, "Promise." He nods his shiny bald head at me and then leads me inside.

It takes a while for my eyes to adjust, coming into the darker common room after being out in the sunlight, but when they do, I gasp, my hands flying up to my mouth. All the MC brothers that I didn't see outside are all congregated in the main room under a giant pink banner that says "We'll miss you!" It's so incredibly sweet and hilarious because all these big, frowny bikers are standing under it looking a little sheepish. My sister is standing next to the Pres's Ol Lady, Nat, both of them with grins on their faces. I know this is all their doing.

"Surprise! It's your going away party!" Sunny yells and lets off a party popper. I blink the tears from my eyes and rush up to hug her before she passes me off to be hugged by men I've known for most of my life.

"Thank you for doing this, Remy. I know it's a big step for you." Savage smiles down at me before giving me a quick hug.

"It's OK Pres, it'll be an adventure. I'll learn as much as I can so I can help out around here."

His brows pinch a moment, "You know this isn't just about you helping out. You're one of us, regardless."

I smile up at Savage. "I know."

Even though I'm nervous, I'm also excited that Savage and

the MC thought of me, out of everyone here, to learn from the DRMC. I've always loved computers, ever since the day I logged on to Shadow Wrath at the library. Once Dad saw how serious I was about gaming, he surprised me with my very own laptop. Since then I've taught myself coding and very basic hacking skills. The chance to learn from real hackers is something I would never pass up, no matter how scary it will be. Before I can think too hard, I'm being pulled into my dad's arms. I wrap mine around his bulk, my hands not meeting.

"I love you, Remy girl. You watch your back and I'll take care of everything here, OK?"

I pull back to look at him. "You'll be careful, right? I don't want you to get hurt because of me."

"Psssh, nothing can hurt me, sweet girl."

I roll my eyes and snuggle back in for another cuddle, "Love you, Dad."

"OK, that's enough. You know you'll be doing this all over again tomorrow Flack, when we drop off Rem. Now back up, I have wisdom to impart," Nat's voice breaks through and I snort into my dad's chest before pulling back. I can hear him grumbling but he would never say a cross word to the Pres's Ol Lady. Mainly because she would kick his butt herself.

Nat pulls me to sit on the couch, tucking her long legs under her. "Right, there will be club bunnies there. You need to assert your dominance early, OK Remy Girl? Don't take any of their shit. If you need to beat a bitch, you beat a bitch."

I open my mouth to protest, but Nat holds her hand up, stopping me.

"I know you're a real sweetheart and you just want to love on everyone, but sometimes people need a backhand. You go in there shoulders back, confident as hell, and don't let anyone fuck with you. They do? You call me. Savage will have me there ASAP."

I may not want to beat anyone, but I give Nat my most confident smile before I wrap my arms around her.

"Thanks, Nat," I whisper. I'm going to miss my family here. They haven't always been on the straight and narrow. Heck, some of them were downright nasty men; but I knew who to stay away from and who to trust. Since Hammer left and took all the bad seeds with him, it's been a calmer place to be.

"You're welcome, sweet girl. You know how to contact me." We hug for a little longer before we both pull away, and I'm surprised to see Nat wipe underneath both her eyes. She breaks the moment by clapping.

"Right, let's party!"

Chapter Two

St_Margarita: *So, you're like, on here all the time.*

Beretta_Penn: *Yeah. I like to keep busy.*

St_Margarita: *What do your mom and dad think of you playing all day?*

Beretta_Penn: *Oh, I don't have a mom and my dad has a lot of stuff going on.*

St_Margarita: *Right. So no time for you then?*

Beretta_Penn: *Well what about you? You're always on when I'm on.*

St_Margarita: *I'm ignoring my mom and dad's fighting.*

Beretta_Penn: *Um, I'm sorry*

St_Margarita: *Why? It's not your fault*

Beretta_Penn: *............*

Beretta_Penn: *............*

Beretta_Penn: *There's a horde of orcs coming our way. I've never faced a horde before*

St_Margarita: *Stick with me kid, I'll show you all you need to know.*

Wire

"Ohhhh Wire!" Chewy's voice drifts down the hall. Since she's been here, she's gotten a lot louder. She never really had good volume control, but now it seems as if she's competing with Marx and Switch to be heard.

I lean back in my chair, bringing my arms up, hands on either side of my head, and then lean back, trying to get a good stretch going. Even though we went for slightly larger than normal office furniture, I still have the tendency to hunch.

"Ow! Dammit, who put that there?" I swivel my chair to see Chewy rubbing her elbow.

"Fire extinguisher again?"

"Nah, sweater got caught on the door handle. Anyhoo, guess who's here? The new kid. I saw them all pull in. Thought I'd come down here to chill out a moment. I'm a little overwhelmed to be getting a new vagina around here." She says in a bland voice, bouncing on her toes, curly hair wild around her.

"Um, you know that we have lots of vaginas around here?"

She waves me off. "Bunnies don't count. I mean a vagina with brains. And clothing. I'm betting I won't see this vagina peeking out of skirts or shorts. This vagina will have class. It'll be able to talk about coding and gaming and dress sensibly. A sensible vagina to befriend is what I'm after. I don't have any female friends yet. I have to make a good impression."

I squint at her and open my mouth to rebut that whole sentence, but she spins in place, bumps into the doorway, and then leaves.

"Come on Wire! We have to get to the vagina before it's

tainted by the rest of the brothers!"

Shaking my head, I get to my feet, do a few more stretches, and follow Chewy down the hall.

Entering the common room, I see Savage, his SAA Dex, and Flack. I've only met him once, but he's a nice guy. Nothing like you would expect from a man who lived through his MC's criminal years. He's reasonably tall, around 6ft at a guess. Solid with a ruddy, round face and an easy smile. Not the type of man who you think has seen action and I'm betting killed a few people.

They're meant to have brought his daughter with them today, but I can't see her. Neither can Chewy, by the way I see her head swiveling this way and that. Rhodie grabs hold of her and pulls her into his body. I can hear him murmuring to her about chilling out. He's rewarded with a squinty eye and an eyebrow raise that looks a hell of a lot like her brother Gus's.

Marx's whistle rends the air, quieting all the brothers who have congregated to meet the new person. It's not a pre-arranged thing. We're just nosey as fuck.

"Everyone, as you know, we're welcoming Flack's daughter into the fold to learn from the very best, Wire and Chewy."

"Just show us my new vagina, Marx, sheesh," Chewy mumbles under her breath. I watch Rhodie's head snap down to stare at her, but she's oblivious.

"Remy is special to us, so we are trusting you with her. Take care of her." Savage's comment leaves no argument as he stares at Marx for a beat, the two of them coming to some sort of unspoken agreement.

They both nod and then Savage turns and whispers something to Flack. Flack turns, and a blonde woman steps out from behind him.

She's taller than Chewy, which isn't hard given that Chewy is fucking tiny. I'd put her at about 5'5. Her straight blonde hair reaches her jawline, with bangs hanging in her eyes behind the glasses resting on her button nose. She has a heart shaped face and smooth creamy skin. She's beautiful in an innocent, sweet way.

From my research, I know she's a children's librarian, and she's dressed exactly as I would imagine. The usual boring librarian attire, but more colorful. Conservative and a little dowdy. All topped off with a book shaped brooch pinned to her ample chest.

"Hi, um, I'm Remy," she whispers out.

I'm not sure what we expected, but it was not this woman. This small, timid, whispery woman somehow grew up on the compound of a 1% MC. It just doesn't seem to compute. Well, not to us. Chewy, on the other hand, has bounced over and started info dumping about vaginas and hacking. Remy has a shocked look on her face, but she smiles and nods at Chewy anyway.

"Rhodie!" Marx whisper shouts, gesturing at his brother's girl. Rhodie just sighs, then grips Chewy around the waist, lifting her and carrying her back to where he was standing.

"Right, well, welcome Remy. You'll be with Wire –" I step forward, giving her a two finger wave and smiling to make her feel a little more comfortable. Her gaze swings toward me and I'm startled by her eyes. At first glance, she didn't seem to resemble Flack at all. Now though, I see she has his icy blue eyes, framed by sooty brows and lashes, that seem to be out of place with her pale skin and dirty blonde hair. "– and Chewy. The tiny woman yapping at you before." She blinks owlishly at me for a moment before looking at Chewy, who is doing her big goofy wave.

"Hi," she smiles and waves back.

I hope this woman had a louder voice hidden away somewhere because there's no way we'll ever hear her otherwise.

"OK, well, the prospects have all your shit, so I'll get Chewy to show you to your room, and then around the compound while I meet with your Pres and Dad, OK?" I notice Marx has gentled his voice so as not to scare her. She nods up at him and Chewy barges past me to get to Remy. For a woman who until recently had very few friends, she now takes to new people as if she's on a personal mission to befriend as many as possible.

"Great. Another person to share my woman with," Rhodie grumbles next to me.

"Don't be a pussy. It'll be good for Chewy to have a girlfriend. I mean, what if she wants to talk about pe-" Before he can even finish his taunt, Rider starts gagging.

"That joke backfire on you, brother?" I smirk over at him while Rhodie has a big grin on his face.

"What was that you were saying, brother? When Chewy wants to talk about.... Periods?" Rhodie says the word period loud enough to be heard over Rider's gagging, which makes him gag even more violently.

"Eurgh - fuck off! - eurgh" Rider stumbles out of the room as me, Rhodie, Fox, Nitro, and Switch all laugh our asses off.

"He's still upset after Chewy went into detail about her IUD," Rhodie chuckles.

"Who the fuck gave Chewy explosives?"

I squint at Fox for a moment before Switch practically yells in his face.

"IUD contraceptive, you dumb ass! You shouldn't be fucking if you don't know that." With a disgusted look on his face, he stomps over to the bar, leaving the rest of us to taunt Fox.

"Right, better get back to it before Chewy shows Remy around my control center. There are rules for how things need to be done. And no offense, brother, but your woman isn't interested in any rules other than her own."

Rhodie doesn't even answer, he just smiles softly when he thinks of his woman. I would tease him, but it's good to see two people I love, happy. Clapping him on the shoulder on my way past, I head back to the room I spend the bulk of my time in. If I'm not here, I'm in the gym or the common room. It's a pretty small existence, but it's what I needed after getting out of army intelligence. Posted to the team Rhodie led, I was in charge of feeding them info in real time. After too many missions, I needed to see some good in the world. Coming home to my mom and sisters, and then joining DRMC helped me get out of my head.

My ass just hits the leather of my seat when Chewy swans in, Remy following behind, standing awkwardly in the room.

"Hey, I set you up a workspace. You're in between me and Chewy."

Her eyes get large and a blush stains her cheeks.

"Oh wow, thank you so much. You really didn't have to. I would have been fine with my laptop," she looks around my room before pointing to a random swivel chair in the corner, "Over there. I could sit there. I don't want to be any trouble." She wrings her hands, and I can see she's getting uncomfortable by the way Chewy is staring.

Before I can say anything, Chewy starts up. "Why would you think you were trouble? And why would you sit all the way over there? You can't learn if you can't see. Take a seat." She waves at the chair between us and Remy creeps, literally creeps, over to her workstation. She gingerly takes a seat before letting out a breath and giving me and Chewy a smile. Yet again I'm left wondering how the fuck this woman was raised on an MC compound.

"You're really shy for an MC kid, huh? Like, I would have expected you to be like Rhodie and Marx. They're MC kids. Oh and Rider, huh Wire?" Chewy finishes her sentence by gesturing to me, but not making eye contact as it "wigs her out".

"Oh, um, well, I guess I was happy just to read or play games on my laptop. My sister did a lot of the talking for me, or my dad."

"Close to your dad, huh? Cool, cool." I try not to chuckle at Chewy's small talk. I know she's trying and Remy is nice enough to engage with her.

"Yeah, I love my dad. He's one of my best friends, but I guess all dads are like that."

"Dunno. Mine was murdered."

Remy looks mortified, and her panicked gaze swings to mine. I shrug. "I can't help you there. Mine left when I was 13."

She starts wringing her hands again. "I'm sorry."

"Bah, not your fault. You didn't murder my dad or make Wire's bail." Chewy waves her off as if it's nothing. Remy's eyes get huge and I want to see what she does to get out of this situation. Mainly because living here and working this closely with Chewy, there will be many more of these types of situations. Her eyes dart everywhere but to me and Chewy and I watch her swallow a couple of times before deciding what to do next.

"Well, um, shall we do this then?" She gestures toward her computer and Chewy nods emphatically.

I smile at her. "Stick with us kid, we'll show you all you need to know."

Remy

I want to die. Or at the very least, have the earth swallow me up. I'd even take being abducted by aliens at this point. Big blue ones with vibrating peens. Not even half an hour in and I've put my foot in it. Luckily for me, Tuesday, or "Chewy" as her property cut states, seems to take this all in her stride. She is a highly unusual woman and I'm wondering if she may be on the Autism spectrum. I have had enough kids with ASD visit me at the library to recognize the signs.

I didn't only make the faux pas with her dad, but also with Wire's. Ugh. I want to slap my own face. He was nice, though; he didn't make me feel bad. Just smiled at me. And what a smile it is, holy moly.

When I first walked into the common room, I faced a wall of hotness. I don't know what they're feeding the men in Rose Grove but butter my buns and call me Sadie; they are hot with a capital H. Far more impressive than where I came from, although that could be purely because these men are younger and I didn't grow up with them.

Marx, the DRMC Pres, made the quick introductions, and if I can remember them correctly, there was Rhodie, Chewy's Ol Man. He's also the enforcer and Marx's blood brother. Then there was Rider, the SAA, Judge, the road captain, Tank, and

Sniper. I met Switch, the MC medic when Chewy showed me to his clinic room, and Fox and Nitro in the garage out back. There are a few others I'm yet to meet. Squeak lives in town with his wife and kids and isn't as active a member as the others, and Mad Dog, Rhodie and Marx's father is travelling around with his Ol Lady. Chewy said that the ones that are here make up the bulk of the MC. Well, them and the man sitting beside me.

When Wire stepped forward and gave me a two-fingered wave, I almost swooned. This man, wooowee! Tall, broad, and so very handsome. His brown skin almost shimmered under the fluorescent lighting of the common room, and his hazel eyes shone with intelligence. It's the only way to describe him. If that wasn't enough, the man's hair is beautiful. Dark brown, shaved close on the sides and longer ringlets on top that were pulled back with a band. He is breathtakingly beautiful. He is also nice, which is a double whammy of hotness.

I shake my head and try to concentrate. I'm here to learn. Although that won't stop me panic messaging Saint_Margarita, or Mags, as I like to call him, to tell him about my mortification.

We've messaged every day since we met playing Shadow Wrath. He's my best friend and has been since I was 13 years old. We know each other's deepest darkest secrets, which some might find odd given that we've never met or even spoken in real life, but I don't care. Chatting to Mags is like confession. The faceless person on the other side doesn't judge me on my looks or behavior. Just like I don't judge him. I've heard enough bad sex and crazy girlfriend stories over the years to last me a lifetime. Likewise, he knows all about my failed prom night and my overprotective uncles.

"So, once you're set up, we can get into the security crap. We've run background on you and you've passed, but as you know, you may deal with some sensitive stuff, so you need to be aware of that." I nod at Chewy and try to ignore the fact that she's staring at my nose. I'm guessing she doesn't like eye contact too much.

"Marx wouldn't have let you come here if you were a risk, Remy. Me and Chewy just like to know that whatever we come across here is kept tight, you got me?" Wire's smooth voice rolls over me and I can feel myself blush again.

"Yup, got it. I grew up with a 1% club. Trust me, I know how to keep my mouth shut. Unless you're concerned I'll be telling all your secrets to the little kids of Rose Grove. They're the only friends I'll have anytime soon." I smile at my bad joke, and relax a little when Wire smiles back at me.

"Don't worry. We're friends now. I'll plan a girls night for us in the next few days once I figure out what that entails," Chewy says in her matter-of-fact voice. Shocked by this, I catch Wire's smirk as he shakes his head and taps away at his keyboard. Well, okay then. Looks like I'm having a girls night.

"Knock knock," a gruff voice sounds out and all three of us spin in our chairs to see Marx step into the room. His big body fills up the space. "Hey Remy, the Death Riders are about to head off if you want to say goodbye," I smile up at the huge man before looking back at Wire, who gives me a head tip.

Getting to my feet I head back the way I came, only stopping to let Fox and Nitro pass me in the hall. I think those two must be best friends or something. They seem to always be together. I would have thought they were related or blood brothers were it not for the fact that Fox is taller, lean and blonde, to Nitro's shorter, stocky and dark.

Stepping into the common room, I see my dad leaning toward Savage, a frown on his face, before Savage grips his shoulder and nods in my direction. I've always hated interrupting them in the middle of business, so instead of moving straight away I wave to them both, then slowly walk toward them. Obviously, whatever has gone on has passed as my dad meets me in the middle of the room, sweeping me up into his big arms.

"You be good, Remy girl. Call me every night to tell me what you learned." His gruff voice rumbles through him.

I roll my eyes and wait for Dad to put me back on my feet before agreeing to anything.

"Dad, I'm 28. I'll be fine. But you call me if you need anything or can't find your glasses. Also, tell Sunny to call me. And you be good! Stay out of trouble, otherwise I'll drive back to Roxwell and kick your behind!"

Dad just smirks down at me, before dropping a kiss to the top of my head and wrapping me in his bear hug once more.

"Love you Remy girl,"

"Love you too, Dad." We let each other go and I walk them all out, before waving them off in the cloud of dust. Turning back into the room, I'm faced not with a wall of biker hotness, but what seems to be a wall of bunnies.

"Who the hell are you?" sneers a tall blonde with hair so high it can't be real. She also has the thickest eyelash extensions I've ever seen.

"Whitney, just back off, yeah?" An incredibly deep voice calls. I'm guessing it's the prospect behind the bar.

"No! I want to know who this bitch is!" She doesn't even turn to look at him, just eyeballs me as she stabs a long, pointed red fingernail in my direction.

I almost want to sigh. I've dealt with bunnies all my life. I know Nat gave me the "talk" about asserting my dominance and "beating a B" but I've never been that way inclined.

29

Instead, I turn and address the girls standing with Whitney.

"Hi! I'm Remy." I smile and wave. Whitney, and a woman I'm guessing is her bestie scowl at me. But the other two girls smile and wave back.

"Don't smile at us, bitch! You better walk away. All the men here are taken, so get out of here skank." She shoos me away with her hand.

I paste my biggest smile on my face and lean in a little. "I'm not going anywhere. I'm here to stay. In my own room. With my own bathroom." I tap my bottom lip as if I'm thinking, "Let me guess? You share a room, right?" Behind Whitney's back I see a small brunette shake her head at me. "Oh you don't live here? So you're not real bunnies are you? You're just hangarounds. Wow, so then men you say are taken, don't even let you stay here? Tell you what, I'll think of you in your apartments somewhere in town when I'm stretched out in my big bed. In my very own room here at the compound." I straighten up and smile at the dark-haired bunny. "Right, I have places to be, and it's not riding brothers for rent money either."

I walk past the bunnies with my head held high, faking confidence even though my hands are shaking. It's not in my nature to be nasty, but sometimes bunnies need to be put in their place. I'd rather we all just got along.

Whitney's nasally voice follows me down the hall to the Control Center of the MC. Well, that's what Chewy calls it. I think it's just Wire's room. Or suite more specifically. It's a large room, with one side dominated with a large screen on the wall. Under it sits a desk that runs the length of the room. Wire's station is set up closest to the door, Chewy's on the other side and mine in the middle. There's a large dividing wall that cuts the room in half, so I'm guessing his bed and things are on the other side. I didn't have a good look, because it's not my business. All I know is that the whole room smells like him, all woodsy, spicy, and masculine. Even though the man may fluster me, his scent settles all my nerves.

I wonder if Mags wants to hear about it? He hates when I girl-talk with him. But he owes me after I saved his ass time and time again by giving him girl advice. There was a time when I used to think that Mags and I would meet up and fall madly in love.

I'm snapped out of my thoughts when I walk into Wire's room to him and Chewy clapping.

"Um, what's going on?" I look around, trying to figure out what the heck they're doing. They're both kinda weird, in the usual way of computer geeks.

"Celebrating you putting Whitney in her place. And you didn't even use any curse words!" Chewy cheers. "I never even thought to take her out that way. I just threatened to kick her in the cunt," she shrugs.

My quick inhale of breath at Chewy using that word has me choking on air and coughing for a moment.

My eyes water and I croak out "Um, thanks?"

They both smile at me as I take a seat and wake up my screen.

"I know it's a lot, but you're doing fucking great, Remy," Wire whispers. I let his words settle inside me, building up my confidence. This may be the furthest I've ever been away from home, but I can do this. New home, new job, new somewhat crazy friend, new me.

Chapter Three

St_Margarita: *Why don't you curse?*
Beretta_Penn: *Why do you?*
St_Margarita: *I asked you first.*
Beretta_Penn: *My dad wants me to be different to my mom.*
St_Margarita: *Fair enough. She sounds crappy*
St_Margarita: *........*
St_Margarita: *Do you want me to stop cursing?*
Beretta_Penn: *Do you want me to start?*
St_Margarita: *Nah, I like you all prissy like this.*
Beretta_Penn: *And I like you all angry yelly like this.*

Wire

"Church!"

Marx's voice booms down the hall and it's crazy to think that Remy has been here for a week already. All my fears that I would have to start from scratch with her have been completely unfounded. The woman is a machine when it comes to learning. I thought it was going to take a lot longer to get her to the level she's at now. She works shifts during the day at the local library, meaning we can only train for a few hours here and there, but she's killing it.

Standing, I stretch my arms up over my head and hold them there. I can feel my shirt has ridden up a little.

"Have fun at church!" She smiles up at me, freezing when her eyes hit my exposed midriff. She bites down on her plump bottom lip and her face turns bright red before she spins back to her screen, staring at it so hard I'm sure she's going to burst a blood vessel.

"Thanks Remy. Oh hey, I have a name for you. See what you can find for me, yeah?" I try to hold in my laugh when she nods and doesn't move her eyes from the screen, even when I slide over the slip of paper with the name on it. I'm sure she's not blinked yet either. "Cool, I'll see what you've got for me when I get back."

"Yup. Sounds great! I'll be right here. Eyes on the screen." She gives me a thumbs up behind her back, still not turning. I snort and head out the door, but not before I take a quick peek behind me to see Remy lightly bumping her head on my desk.

I'm glad to see that my abs have an effect on her. This whole week the quiet librarian has been doing something weird to me. I'm not sure whether I want to spend time with her because she needs protecting, and with three sisters, I'm just that type of man; or whether there's something about her that draws me to her.

I asked my best friend Retta what she thinks, and she said maybe I need to get laid. But then she said some interesting shit. She asked whether seeing Rhodie happy is giving me ideas. Well, she didn't mention Rhodie by name, of course; we don't share those types of details. Which is weird given that we've

33

been online besties for years now. So long, in fact, that when we outgrew Shadow Wrath (although who really outgrows that? I still sign on now and then), we moved over to messaging. Even though it is in my power to find out exactly who Retta is, I have no urge. She's just this comforting presence that has been in my life since my dad left and I became the man of the house; when I went on tour and since I've been back. We have messaged every day and I don't see that changing anytime soon. I can say, hand on heart, that outside of my family and the MC, Retta is the only other person I love. I know it doesn't sound like she's that far up the ranks, but no other girl has ever gotten this close.

"Yo, you gonna stand there all day looking simple or you gonna get in there?"

"You're blocking the door fucker and I don't want to be fined again!"

Both Fox and Nitro stare me down to move out of the way, but I can see Rider is coming down the hall, so I decide to fuck with them. I know Rider will have my back.

I take a look into church and see they're waiting on us four. Marx is going to fine these two fuckers if they're the last men in the room.

Rider slides along the wall to position himself behind them. In a coordinated attack we both pants them, then shove them further down the hall before running into Church and slamming the door behind us. We cackle like little girls as we find our seats and listen to Fox and Nitro grumble about our dirty tactics.

"Fuck sake, you two! What did I tell you? You're both on toilets for the next week." Marx shakes his head in disgust before banging the gavel getting this shit started.

"Wire, report on Remy. I have Savage wanting progress on how she's doing."

"She's awesome. I've never met anyone who can learn as fast as she does. Well, other than Chewy, that is. They also get on really well, so that's a bonus." I look around the table and see brothers nodding.

"Yeah, she's a real sweetheart. Not imposing or a pain in the ass. I like the girl." Sniper adds, which is pretty high praise from the grumpy bastard.

I've noticed over the past week that although Remy sticks to herself, she's happy to chat to the brothers during meal times. I've also noticed that she gravitates towards the quieter brothers like Tank and Sniper. Which irritates me for reasons I'm not going to think about.

"Chewy can't stop talking about her. Apparently, she's a lot more interesting than I've noticed. Between her and Ana, it seems Chewy has gotten herself a girl gang," Rhodie begrudgingly says, but we can all see the smile he's trying to hide. Whatever Chewy wants, if it's in Rhodie's power, he will give it to her. Chewy wants female friends? Rhodie will do whatever he can to ease the way forward. I heard them practicing small talk topics the other day.

"Good. Thank fuck she's getting along well. The last thing I need is to have another catty bitch in my clubhouse." We all nod. Having the bunnies is bad enough. "Rhodie brings me to my next point of business. I'm sure you all know that Gus married Ana last week."

We all start pounding our fists on the sturdy wooden table we're sat at. Gus is Chewy's eldest brother and an all round good guy. I'm sure Marx would give him a patch if he thought Gus would accept it. As it stands, Tombs Security is another

35

ally we've gained, thanks to Chewy.

"Yeah, who didn't see that coming? Anyway, Chewy approached me saying they've been tailed a few times. Not sure who it is yet, so stay alert."

Shit. It could be anyone. Ana is part of the Bartashev Bratva, and Gus helped us shut down a trafficking operation.

"Because of the shit that went down, Chewy has asked us to put our own tail on her brother and new sister-in-law. Gus and Ana have been court ordered to camp out at the weekend. Don't ask me why, I have no fucking clue."

I have a clue. With the speed of the marriage and the fact Ana is on a working visa, I'm guessing they've been court ordered to complete couples counseling to secure a green card.

"I need someone to tail Gus and keep an eye on him. We all know he won't want any of his siblings to shadow them. I told Chewy I'd have a brother do it. I know you're busy Wire but I'm thinking you and Remy? Gus and Ana don't know Remy, might be easier for her to get close. Before you get your panties in a wad, Chewy has offered to run your usual security ops."

My blood pressure eases when I hear that Chewy will take on my jobs while I'm away. I hate leaving my station, especially unmanned, but I have ways to do my checks on my watch and phone, so between Chewy and all my tech, it should be OK.

I roll Marx's request around in my brain for a moment and I can't find a flaw in his logic. Not to mention Remy's so quiet you almost forget she's there.

"Yeah, I'm sure we can do that. We better ask her, though. She may not be the camping type." I shrug my shoulders. I know little bits about her, but not much. When we're working together, that's what we do. Work. We get so engrossed in what we're doing, there isn't much small talk.

Marx yells for the prospect to bring Remy to church, and when she steps over the threshold, I can see she's shitting herself. She looks to me for reassurance, which makes me feel 10 fucking feet tall. I give her a smile to let her know everything's fine. She nods her head and creeps further into the room.

"Um, you called for me, Pres?" The poor girl looks like she's shrinking into herself.

"You're not in trouble, Remy," Marx softly says, earning a lot of raised eyebrows. Our Pres is gruff and growly. He's not this teddy bear in front of us. "I was hoping to send you on a stakeout. You'd partner with Wire. There will be camping involved."

She scrunches her eyebrows together before nodding. "Yes, I can do that. Thank you, Pres, for trusting me with this. I won't let you down." She nods emphatically, and we all watch as she pulls her shoulders back and stands tall.

I'm sure all the brothers are feeling the same thing I am. She may be small and shy, but without a single question, she accepted Marx's orders. She trusts and respects him, and by extension, she trusts and respects us. That sort of thing goes a long way in our eyes.

"Thank you, Remy, I know you'd never let us down. You can go back to what you were doing." Remy smiles at Marx and gives us all a little wave before leaving and closing the door gently behind her.

"I have no idea how the hell that girl grew up with the Death Riders and came out that fucking sweet." Switch shakes his shaggy ginger head back and forth, voicing what we're all thinking. Flack obviously did a fucking great job at shielding her.

"To my last point of order. With this shit going down with Gus, we need to be vigilant. We've been waiting for the fallout from shutting down Kraykowski's operation, and nothing has happened. This puts me on fucking edge. Keep your eyes and ears open, have each other's backs and report back anything you hear on the streets. They'll be the ones to know if shit is going to hit the fan."

We all nod. I know for a fact there haven't been any murmurs on the dark web, and that is suspicious in itself.

"OK, that's it. Wire already sent out his report, so you all know how well our businesses are doing. We may even have to look into buying another one, keep the tax man off our backs. Bring me any ideas you have. Right, get out of here, fuckers." Marx bangs the gavel and I head back to the control center, eager to brief Remy on our mission.

Remy

I was shocked to my core when Marx asked if I would be open to doing a stakeout. I'd only been here a week and by anyone's standards that's not nearly enough time to garner anyone's trust, but trust me, they did. After the initial shock wore off, pure blind panic kicked in. What if I fluffed it? What if I got us found out or put everyone in danger? I didn't want to freak out and look weak in front of the DRMC. These men were counting on me. So instead, I panic messaged Mags with a story about my boss wanting me to keep an eye on a dodgy coworker. He then spent the next hour talking me down. I have no idea what I would do without him in my life, and I never want to find out. As a kid, I only had Sunny to talk to about things that worried me. Once I met Mags, the number of people I could go to for advice doubled. I never went to my dad. He had other things to worry about, like not getting shot and leaving me and Sunny as orphans. Sunny never knew her mother and I haven't heard from mine since my dad took me. Heck, with Hammer in charge, he would have sold me and Sunny to the traveling circus or something. Thank god Savage got rid of him and turned things around.

I'm snapped out of my thoughts by a small voice. "Miss Remy, I've finished." Jovie smiles up at me with her gap-toothed smile and crooked pigtails and I grin back at her. Even though I've only been here at the Rose Grove Library for a week, I know Jovie is going to be my favorite kid. She's been here every day. I've never seen her parents, but she spends a lot of time just hanging out. She's quiet and polite, no trouble at all, and if I'm being honest, she reminds me a little of myself when I was a kid. I had Miss Shawna, and I guess Jovie has me.

"Great job Jovie! Tell me what you liked best about the story."

Looking at the cover, there's a large dinosaur on the front. I smile at that. It's one thing that stood out to me when I first met the little girl. Where all the other girls her age, of which I'm guessing she must be around 6 or 7, were busy in the fairytale section, Jovie seemed to delight in the dinosaur story books.

"I liked how the big dinosaur protected the little ones. Big things should always look after little things." She nods up at me as if that is an absolute fact.

"I agree. Animals, people, dinosaurs. We should do our best to look after them all." She beams up at me with her slightly grubby face and clutches her book to her chest before wandering off to the beanbags and the rest of the kids in my after school programme.

I take a peek at the clock on the wall and realize it's time to tidy up before the dance party and then pick up time. And by dance party I mean the quietest dance party ever given we're in the library and all. I like to end by doing something physical because the kids have spent an hour sitting down, and it's good for their little bodies to move.

"Macaroni Cheese,"

"Everybody freeze!" They not so quietly answer in reply.

Once all eyes are on me, I quietly let them know that it's time to tidy up so we can have our afternoon dance party. They jump up and bustle around, haphazardly putting their books back on the shelves and very unhelpfully kicking the beanbags out of the way. I introduced library dance party on Monday, and since then it's been a hit with my kids.

They gather in the empty space in the children's section with "Airplane arms" to space themselves out. I pull up "Firework" by Katy Perry, the message telling the kids to let themselves shine, the opening notes gently playing. We jump and twirl and boogy until we're all breathless. By the end of the song we're all a little sweaty, puffed and red faced.

I catch sight of Jovie's face, her eyes wide, staring at someone over my shoulder. Spinning, I notice it's Wire, looking larger than life surrounded by kid sized furniture. I also notice that some parents have arrived to collect their kids. At least four moms are staring at Wire like they want to snack on the man, and I really can't blame them. Wearing his cut over a dark blue henley, worn jeans and his boots, hair tucked into a beanie, he looks less like a snack and more like a buffet.

"OK friends, thank you so much for hanging out with me today. I will see you next week!"

I offer high fives to the kids, their sticky moist hands slapping mine. Turning to high five Jovie, I notice she hasn't moved, still in the same spot staring at Wire.

"Jovie, sweetie, are you OK?" She turns her large brown eyes up to me and she looks terrified. Squatting down in front of her, I gentle my voice. "Hey, it's OK. That's my friend Wire. He is here to pick me up. We're going camping." I offer her a smile and she wrings her hands for a moment.

"So he's not a bad man?"

"No sweetie, Wire is a nice man. He's my friend." I turn to look at him, his gaze bouncing around my face and he must see something written there because he shifts his gaze to Jovie and softens his stance a little. He smiles softly at Jovie and comes closer, squatting down when he's within arm's length. "Wire, this is my friend Jovie, Jovie, this is Wire."

"Hi Jovie, it's nice to meet you. I like your shirt. Brontosaurus, right?" He offers her a smile and holds his huge fist out. She eyes him for a moment before gently tapping his fist and offering a small smile.

"Yeah, they're my favorite." She smiles wider before she high fives me and races off into the shelves. My eyes follow her as she leaves. Something about the way Wire looks unsettled her.

"You ready to hit the road, Remy?"

I shake off my thoughts and nod at Wire.

* * *

"Can I ask you something?" Wire's smooth voice breaks through the comfortable silence in the car. Well, not totally silent, the radio is turned down low, playing some song I can't quite hear enough to work out what it is.

I turn to look at him before nodding.

"How come you're completely different at work?"

My brow furrows. I'm not sure what he means. "I'm just me."

He glances at me before speaking again. "At the library, with the kids, you're confident and assertive. At the MC, you're timid and go out of your way to not be seen or heard. Sort of invisible."

Instead of answering straight away, I look out my side window and pause to think.

"Um, when I was younger, my mom would tell me to make myself invisible. Then when I moved into the clubhouse, there was always club business happening and angry men stomping around, so it was easier to stay quiet and out of the way than get into trouble."

Wire hums a little before his brow furrows. I've noticed he does this a lot when he thinks. I've also noticed that his perfect dark brows look as if they've been lovingly manicured, which is completely unfair given that I have to pluck mine into submission or else sport a unibrow.

"How come your mom wanted you to be invisible?"

I blow out a breath "When I was little my mom would have a lot of .... friends come to visit. As soon as I was old enough to understand, Sunny told me that Dad found out Mom was working as a hooker. He took me away as soon as he arranged a cage and a car seat." I look down at my hands and examine my short, purple fingernails. I may not be the flashiest or the prettiest of women, but I do love painting my nails.

Wire is eerily quiet and when I take a chance to peek over at him I notice his sharp jawline is tight and he's gripping the steering wheel so hard his dark knuckles are almost white.

"So, she entertained her Johns in your home and you had to hide?" he grits out. The anger showing on his face should frighten me. However, something tells me he's not mad at me, but at the situation.

"Yeah. My dad bought me a teepee tent thing. It was a Rug Rats one." I smile at the memory. "I would hide in there and wait for her friends to leave. It was my special fortress." Unfortunately, when my dad took me away that day, he forgot to pack it up and bring it with us.

"How old were you?"

"Four."

"And how long had you been hiding in your little tent for?"

"For as long as I could remember," I whisper back at him.

His brow furrows again. I can see something working behind his eyes. Whether he's trying to tamp down his anger or trying to find the right words, I'm not sure. He opens his mouth before closing it, then blowing out a breath.

"You don't have to hide anymore. I liked the Remy I saw at the library. If you want to be that Remy at the clubhouse, then be that Remy. No more hiding, OK?"

"OK."

Chapter Four

Beretta_Penn: *Girls suck.*
St_Margarita: *Ah yeah, why do you think I like them?*
Beretta_Penn: *You're a pig.*
St_Margarita: *Yeah, and you still talk to me. So, how was prom?*
Beretta_Penn: *Awful. The girls laughed and pointed at my dress.*
St_Margarita: *Those fuckers! What did your date do?*
Beretta_Penn: *Nothing. Just told me to ignore them. Tried to get me drunk.*
St_Margarita: *He didn't try anything did he?*
Beretta_Penn: *Twiddled my nipples and then couldn't get it up. Blamed me instead of all the shots he had.*
St_Margarita: *Are you OK?*
Beretta_Penn: *Yeah. Looks like I'll stay untouched for a while longer.*
St_Margarita: *There's no hurry babe. Wait for someone special.*
Beretta_Penn: *Oh yeah, like you did?*
St_Margarita: *Hey! Kelly's boobs were VERY special to me.*
Beretta_Penn: *You're gross.*
St_Margarita: *You love it.*
St_Margarita: *Do you need me to beat someone up?*
Beretta_Penn: *You'd do that?*
St_Margarita: *Hell yeah! I've got your back. Always.*

Beretta_Penn: Thanks Mags. I've got yours too. Always.

Wire

"Can I ask you something?"

I crack my neck before looking at Chewy. Remy is still at work and I think that Chewy's question will be a good distraction for me. Since I saw Remy in the library with her after school group, I've been out of sorts. The woman I saw there is so different from the one I see here. At the library she was confident, but quietly so, if that makes sense. There is definitely a lot more than meets the eye with Remy. I mean, I don't think she's ever going to be outspoken and loud, but her differences make me think about her all the damn time. Something has been drawing me in and I think it's because I've never spent any significant amount of time with a woman quite like her. The club bunnies are all outgoing. Chewy is, well, Chewy.

Even the women I grew up with are the opposite in personality. My momma raised me and my three sisters on her own when my dad left. I was 13 and old enough to see that the pairing between them was never going to work. Dad was trailer trash from the wrong side of town, Momma was from the hood. Both of their families hated each other. Momma's family hated that she was with a white boy, Dad's family hated that he was with a black girl. What united them in the beginning was the fact both of them were bottom of the heap and wanted a different life. They fell in love and had my sister Eve, then me, then Zoe and Jade.

45

My Momma is a strong woman and as I've grown older, I've realized that was something my father couldn't deal with. My mother didn't need him. She's successful in her own right, and when he would gamble away his money or forget to take the girls to dance or forget to pick me up from basketball, well, that just led Momma to doing it all until his role became redundant. He moved on to another black woman, but one who made him feel important and needed. Now they both drink and gamble their days away, blissfully happy in their dysfunction.

"Wireeeeee, you with me? Or are you dreaming of Retta?" Chewy makes her voice all high and bats her eyelids while she swings in her chair. Hanging out with Rider has turned her into a smart ass.

"Yeah, I'm with you. And what do you know about Beretta, anyway?" I squint at her. I haven't really told anyone about her. She's my friend. My conscience. My lifeline during all the times things went to shit.

"I know that you have to message her every day otherwise you get really pissy."

"Well, she's my friend. And I enjoy talking to her."

Chewy shrugs "OK. Anyway, I need advice on something."

I smile at her, loving the fact that Chewy doesn't pry. I've answered her question, and that's sufficient for her. Unlike half of the nosey assholes that make up the MC. I circle my hands in the universal sign for "get on with it."

"I'm having a Girls' Night tonight. I read snacks will make a successful evening. So are we talking Doritos and dips or, like proper canapes? Or an actual meal? Also, should the pillow fight and nail painting come before or after the food?" She looks at me for a moment before her gaze flitters off to something more interesting.

"Umm, well, judging by what I remember of my sisters' sleepovers, I think chips and dips are fine. And maybe chocolate and ice cream, that sort of thing. I'm not sure any of my sisters had pillow fights, though. But they definitely painted their nails." I can still remember the fumes wafting down the hall to my room. "I also don't think there's any real schedule either. Just play it by ear." I shrug at her and then remember to do some stretches when my neck twinges.

"Right. I can do that. I'm going now." Chewy abruptly stands, shoves her feet in her shoes and leaves, exactly as she said she would. She's such an odd little thing, and I love everything about her. In a little sister type way. Rhodie would murder me otherwise, and I'd never do that to a brother.

Checking the time at the bottom of my screen it's pretty much beer o'clock, and seeing how my concentration is shot, I may as well go see what my brothers are up to. I put on my screen saver and then switch all alert notifications to my watch. That way, I can keep my finger on the pulse of everything that I'm monitoring. There's always shit to keep an eye on. After the whole Kraykowski bullshit, I want to make sure that there aren't any new players in the skin trade. I also need to keep all channels open with the Russians, as well as any informants we have. We pissed off a lot of people when we shut down that operation. It's only natural that someone will want to take a swipe at us.

Heading down the hall, I dodge Whitney and stomp my way to the bar. Lifting my chin at the prospect, he hands me a beer without a word, nodding once before going back to wiping down the bar. Takoda has been with us for around a year now and he's tracking to be one hell of a brother.

"Finally made it out of the cave, huh?"

"Shit Switch, speak a little louder." I grimace as I stick my finger in my ear and jiggle it around. There has to be a medical reason why he's so fucking abnormally loud. Has to be. He doesn't answer me, just flips the bird and goes back to yelling in Sniper's face. That there is one weird ass friendship. Opposite ends of the spectrum. A hand lands on my shoulder and Tank maneuvers his way next to the bar.

"Brother," he nods before taking the beer Takoda has placed in front of him. "Where's Remy? You should have invited her for a drink."

I can feel my brows pulling down. What the fuck does he want with Remy?

"Yeah brother. She's a lovely girl. It'd do her good to get out more. She's only ever out here for meals, then she creeps away again." Sniper says, while Switch nods solemnly next to him. I clench my teeth, thinking about all the meals she's had with these fuckers. I have no idea why it pisses me off to see her with them giggling and smiling.

"She was getting organized for Chewy's Girls' Night," I let them all know. I may or may not have also given them all the hairy eyeball.

"Good. It'll be good for her to make some friends. She's a real sweetheart, and I don't like the thought of her sneaking around here like she's unwanted. She's like a ghost, almost." Tank continues on.

Taking a sip of my beer, I let the flavors burst on my tongue and as much as it pisses me off, I can't help but nod and agree with them.

"Her mother taught her to be invisible when she had a John visiting." This comment is met with a series of "What the fuck?" I nod, "Yeah. She hid in a Rug Rats teepee that Flack got her. Soon as he found out her mother was not only prostituting, but doing it at home, he picked up Remy and she never went back."

The brothers all nod and grumble out agreement that Flack did a good thing. We drink in silence for a moment before an impossibly deep voice says, "Fucking loved Rug Rats as a kid," We all spin to look at the prospect.

"Fucking hell! And I thought Tank's Barry White voice was smooth and sexy! Damn kid, you could drop panties just by saying hello!" Switch says, all of us laughing along with him, the prospect's face turning a dark shade of red.

"Anyway, I'm glad she's off with Chewy for the night. Even if Chewy is fucking weird sometimes." Tank's smooth voice says. I notice he's tried to deepen it to compete with the prospect.

"That's my Ol lady, you fucker!" Rhodie's voice grits out as he storms over and cuffs Tank around the head.

"Oh, like you haven't noticed?"

"Of course I fucking have! She owns a tank full of dick fish that she's hand reared as if they're her own babies. But still, she's the best thing to ever happen to me, so keep your mouth shut, Tank."

Switch decides it's his turn to fuck with Rhodie, so he says, "Oh, you're just pissed because you're stuck here while Chewy is having a Girls' Night and you're not allowed to go. Pussy whipped by the ole ball and chain, huh?"

"I am not pussy whipped, and she isn't a ball and chain. She doesn't weigh me down, she lifts me up. She's the wind beneath my wings, fucker."

He swipes his beer off the bar top and downs half of it in an effort to calm down while we all piss ourselves laughing. We continue to shoot the shit until our drinks are done, then

I decide to ditch and head back to my room. Partly because I want to message Retta, to see how she's getting on. But mainly because I could see Whitney had her tractor beams on and was looking like she was headed my way. No, thank you. Fuck, my momma would have a damn heart attack if I took Whitney home. Not that there's anything wrong with her or what she does around here. Women can do what they like with their bodies. The problem with Whitney is that she's vicious and conniving. But she has a mouth like a hoover, so the brothers keep her around.

Instead of sitting at my desk, I grab my laptop, kick off my boots and lie down on my bed, with my top half propped up on pillows for the ultimate in comfort. I pull up mine and Retta's message threads and marvel at how many messages we exchange.

Our last messages were her telling me she accidentally happened upon a bunch of swingers at her new job. I have no idea how, given that I'm pretty certain she works with kids. Perhaps some of her coworkers are swingers. They seem to be everywhere these days. Shit, Gus and Ana were accidentally camped next to some. I even saw the guy's dick.

St_Margarita: Hey you, what's happening tonight? Did you end up talking to that quiet bunch at your work?

She had told me she was finding it a little tricky to fit in at mealtimes. I suggested maybe she wants to look out for a quieter group to eat with, people a little more like her. I know from all the years talking to her she's a bit shy, and not very extroverted. Hell, that comes through her messages.

Beretta_Penn: Yes! It totally worked! I have a group that I've infiltrated and we eat together now. They're really sweet. I think I've convinced them I'm cool Your magic advice worked!

St_Margarita: What did I tell you?

Beretta_Penn: All hail the wise one. I bow at your feet!

A snort escapes me. Fuck, we're geeks.

Beretta_Penn: OK, so I need your advice. One of my coworkers invited me to her house for a get together thing. What do I take? Are chips OK? She said to wear pajamas so we can be comfy and relaxed and stuff but usually I just wear an old shirt of my dad's and shorts. Is that OK?

That is not a visual I needed. I don't know what she looks like other than the comments she's dropped over the years about how annoying big boobs are or her soft belly or whatever. So I have a vague idea. Anyway, not knowing what she looks like has never held me back from fantasizing about what it would be like if she were here with me. Which is a total ass of a thing to be thinking about my best friend. So I answer her as she would expect her guy bestie to answer her.

St_Margarita: I thought girls wore lingerie to girls' night parties?

Beretta_Penn: You're a pig. I'm not sure how you manage to lure poor, unsuspecting women to sleep with you.

St_Margarita: What can I say? It's a gift.

St_Margarita: Anyway, I think go in whatever you feel comfortable in. And then message me tomorrow with all the sexy details.

Beretta_Penn: Yeah, yeah. Chat later x.

I flip my laptop closed, toss it beside me and lay back with my eyes closed. An image of Retta flits through my mind. Well, a faceless woman shaped image. What would it be like to hear a real laugh when I offer shitty advice? What would it be like for her to roll her eyes at me when I make a computing pun? Maybe it's time me and Retta met up for real.

Remy

I'm sitting in my car outside of a cute little cabin and I know that this has to be Chewy's house. I mean, I know it is anyway; I followed the very precise instructions she gave me. But even if she didn't, I would know that the Marvel themed garden gnomes belonged to her. Although I'm not sure if she or her brothers arranged them into rude poses.

Blowing out a breath, I look down at what I class as my pajamas. I had a slight freak out when Chewy said it was a pajama party, because I usually just sleep in an oversized tee that belonged to my dad, and a pair of soft shorts, but Mags assured me it'd be fine. Well, actually, he didn't, but he didn't say that this was awful either, so I'm going with it. I grab my snacks - Cheetos, Milk Duds and a tub of cookies and cream ice cream that's left condensation all over my seat - and juggle that all while getting out of my car, kicking the door closed with my foot, and then carrying it up to her front door.

Before I can get the tub of ice cream securely in my armpit, the yellow door flies open and Chewy stands there in a Loki onesie.

"Hello! This is my house. You can come in. I have Girls' Night stuff planned." She spins and her curls fly around, almost hitting me in the face. I follow her and then almost crash into her when she spins to face me abruptly. She puts her hands on my biceps to steady me before pulling her hands back as if she's been burned.

"Whoops, soz. Bring your snacks. You can put them on the coffee table with the rest of the heart attack inducing food that we shall feast on."

She moves to the side and I see her house is fully open plan. From where I'm standing, I can see the kitchen to my left and the living area to my right. It's definitely Chewy's house. Bright colors and Marvel themed bits and pieces are everywhere. Is that a Marvel dinner set? There are an abundance of cushions and throw blankets, and a huge fish tank takes up one entire wall of the living room.

"It's a lot, huh?" I spin to see Ana thankfully wearing similar clothing to me - sweats and a shirt that looks like it belongs to some New Zealand sports team; sitting in the comfiest looking armchair I've ever seen in my life. Poofy, soft and cream colored with a furry throw.

"Oh, um, hi Ana!" I can feel my cheeks heating. It was only a few days ago that she pulled me from her tent when she thought I was an intruder.

"Remy, look, I am so, so sorry about pulling your hair. I still feel incredibly shitty about that. Can we please start again?" The look on Ana's face is so hopeful, there's nothing I can do but smile and nod.

"I'd like that. I'd also like to be less embarrassed every time I see you."

Ana throws her head back and laughs before raising her hand. "Dude, same!"

We smile at each other for a moment before Chewy reminds me I'm still standing with an armful of snacks. I can feel my cheeks heating again, but I tell myself that these women aren't judging me. I settle on the couch next to Chewy and unsuccessfully hold in my groan when I sink into the plush fabric.

"I know, right!? It's like sitting on top of a pile of babies or something. It's so soft! I almost orgasmed when I sat down."

Ana pops the cork on the bottle of bubbles, holds up a glass and tips it in my direction with her brows raised. I don't normally drink, but I also don't normally attend girls' nights either, so what the heck! I nod and thank her when she hands me my glass, taking a little sip and letting the bubbles fizz in my mouth and tickle the inside of my nose. I take another dainty sip and then try not to spit it out when I see Chewy throw it back in one go.

"Yeah, that hits the spot."

Me and Ana share a look and try not to smile too wide. I turn back to Chewy and take in what she's wearing.

"Do your pajamas have feet attached?" I stare down at where her feet should be and they are most definitely covered.

"Yup. Rhodie bought these from the big kids' section because he was sick of me putting my cold feet in his lap when we're relaxing on the couch. He has Thor ones without feet attached. And we only wear them when we watch TV in case my brothers or Pops visit. We usually sleep naked because we go to sleep after we fuck." Chewy states proudly.

I'm not sure what to say, so I look at Ana, whose eyebrows are currently making out with her hairline. And then she snorts and bursts into giggles.

"Um, well, they're um, they're nice TV watching pajamas." I say, just because, well, someone had to say something.

"No. Nope, you're not doing that. You, my dear Remy, are going to loosen up. No quiet timid Remy here. You want to laugh at Dayz being so fucking short she can fit kids' pajamas, or the ridiculousness of Rhodie dressed in Thor PJ's to please her, you laugh. It's hilarious." Ana says, before giggling again.

Chewy blows out a breath. "She's right. It is actually hilarious. Here, I'll show you,"

She taps a few things on her phone screen and then the huge TV on her wall that was disguised as a Van Gogh painting comes to life. Suddenly, Van Gogh is replaced by a picture of Rodie in the smallest Thor onesie I have ever seen.

The bottom part comes halfway up his legs, showing enough calf to make an Amish woman blush. The zip doesn't go all the way up due to how wide he is, a large expanse of tattooed chest on display. The tightness of the zip being done up halfway makes his pecs look like they're in a push-up bra. The most horrific part, however, would be the way the center seam has lifted and separated his franks and beans, creating the most obscene moose knuckle known to man.

There are so many reactions to what I'm seeing that I can't settle on one. Neither can Ana, who is staring open-mouthed. She swallows, then opens and closes her mouth a few times.

"What in the fuck am I seeing?! Why the fuck is Shit Stain dressed like a fucking steroid-taking Peter Pan reject?"

A scream erupts out of me and before I know it, I'm across the room on Ana's lap, heart beating out of my chest. Ana is also screaming blue murder at the elderly gentleman that is standing in the doorway with his hands on his hips. Chino's pulled a little too high, polo shirt and comfy looking walking shoes. His white hair is slicked back, and he has to be related to Chewy because he looks a lot like her brothers, just old.

"Shit, sorry girls. The door was open. I wanted to make sure you were all safe." His gaze swings to mine and he steps forward, hand outstretched. "I'm Dayz's grandpa. Everyone calls me Pops."

I take his hand. Rough calluses from probably years of hard work scrape across my much smaller palm. He squeezes my hand a moment before looking around the lounge. "Oh, chips"

He then sits where I had been sitting, grabs a bowl and pops a chip in his mouth.

"So, why are we looking at the outline of Rhodie's dick in that spray on outfit?"

Chewy rolls her eyes before snuggling into her Pops "It's Girls' Night. I was showing the girls Rhodie's PJs."

"Well, it's giving me heart palpitations. You better get that shit off the tv before I have a heart attack and die."

A little snort escapes me, catching his attention. He gives me a wink and a smirk.

"So, girls, what are we doing?"

* * *

I don't know how it happened, but I'm four drinks in and about three sheets to the wind.

Chewy is now sporting fingernails of every color. Ana painted my toes as bumblebees. The soundtrack to Saturday Night Fever is playing, and we are all staring at Pops as he performs John Travolta's dance moves.

"You know, he's actually rather good at that," Ana mutters under her breath.

I nod at her. I can't possibly look at her because my eyes won't let me. Somehow, the old man's hip movements have hypnotized me. Either that or it's the wine. I take another sip and try hard not to sway.

I never knew I was such a lightweight. It's a little embarrassing. I'm the daughter of the Death Riders' VP. I feel like I should be way tougher. Which I voice, loudly.

"I need to get tougher. And cooler. And drink more so I can build a constitution."

Chewy leans toward me, peering at me with only one eye open. "I feel like you need a bigger voice. Do you have a bigger voice in there?"

She pokes me in the chest, then moves her finger to the side slightly and pokes me again in the boob.

"You have a great rack, Remy." Tuesday says, poking me again. "Ana, you have a great rack, too. But Remy's feel different to yours. Poke them."

Ana rolls her eyes before she leans over and pokes my other breast. She then frowns and pokes her own breast, then mine again. "You're right. They're so firm! I bet her nipples point straight forward. Or up. Do your nips point up, Rem?" Ana's head is tilted sideways, her eyes narrowed.

"Um, no, they point straight forward, I think." I look down at my chest. I can't say I've ever paid that much attention to them.

"Ugh. Lucky bitch. Mine point down. And are huge. Big hubcap nipples. Pointing down like sad dog noses." Ana sadly shakes her head, swipes a bottle of wine off the table, flops back in her chair, and pours herself another glass.

"I'm sure they're fine. I bet Gus likes them." I offer. She's such a nice lady, she shouldn't be sad about her dog nose nipples.

A smile spreads across her face. "He may be titmatized by them. He stares at them a lot."

"Listen, girls, when you're with the right man, he will worship every inch of you because it belongs to the woman he loves." Pops says in his rough voice before sitting himself down next to Chewy.

I think about his sage advice. I wonder if Mags thinks about me in any type of way? I know I think about him a lot. I wonder what it would be like to meet up? Would he think I was cute? Or would I be a letdown because he's expecting someone else? Someone hotter?

"Who's Mags?" Ana asks. Whoops, I must have said some of that out loud. I look up and everyone is staring at me. Well, not Chewy. She seems to be frowning at the window.

"Um, Mags is my childhood friend. My first non-related friend. We met gaming online when we were 13 and we message every day. Whenever I need advice or whatever, Mags is always there. Mags is my person, but we've never met in real life." I shrug, then tip my glass up to avoid further scrutiny.

"That's actually kinda sweet. But why would he think you were a letdown? You're cool and totally hot." Ana waves her hand in my direction.

My cheeks heat at her compliment. "I dont know. I've always just never felt cool or pretty or fun or whatever." I shrug, then sway slightly, but catch myself before I completely roll out of the beanbag I'm sitting in.

"Hmmmmmm" Ana taps her chin, eyes narrowed at me. Both Chewy and Pops are quietly listening. From what I know of them, this conversation is not in their wheelhouse. "Maybe it's the librarian thing. No offense, but librarian doesn't really scream cool, hot, badass." Ana points out.

I have no idea how she looks somewhat sober. She and Pops both. I'm sure they've had twice as many drinks as the rest of us. "I'm a Kiwi kid. We binge drink from the time we're like, 12." She shrugs. Whoops. She must have heard my inside thoughts.

"Librarians can be badass. Like that chubby librarian monk

from Dr. Strange," Chewy says. She's pulled her hair up into a messy bun, and that messy bun is now in Pops' face as she rests her head on his shoulder.

"Um, no offense, Chewy, but I think I have to agree with Ana on this one. The thing is, I never set out to be a librarian. I just kinda fell into it."

"You're gonna have to explain that one, sweetheart. I have no idea how anyone accidentally becomes a librarian." Pops squints at me, his head tilted at the same angle as Chewy's. The genes in this family are strong.

"Well, um, when I was younger, I wanted to be so many things, but I kinda froze up when it came to deciding. In the end, I didn't pursue any of them. Then the library job came up, so I took it because I liked kids and books and introducing them to computers and I wanted to move out of the compound. I figured it would be a good stopgap until I decided which path I wanted to take. I just never thought I'd still be there 10 years later." I look down into my empty glass, and then tip it up to my lips, trying to get the last drops. Ana takes pity on me and pours me more bubbly goodness.

"Well girl, I think it's about time you had a think about what you want to be." Pops nods emphatically.

"LIST!" Chewy screams for no reason and then she's up, stumbling around, opening and closing drawers. She comes racing back, diving onto the couch, a Hulk notepad and matching pen at the ready. "OK, tell us what you like and we'll write it all down and then me and Pops will deduce what you should be doing. Aaaaand go!"

I sit and wrack my brain for things that I like. "Well, I like kids. Especially kids who need an adult they can trust. So write that down."

59

"Needy kid with crappy parents. Got it. Next."

I watch Ana roll her eyes at Chewy. I try to hide my chuckle by clearing my throat. "Ummmm, I like computers,"

"Geeky shit. Yup, next." Chewy now has her tongue sticking out while she scribbles all this down.

Now I'm not sure. Those are the things I like and the things I know I'm good at. I look at the expectant looks on the faces of the people around me and I start feeling a little embarrassed that I can't think of anything else.

"OK, well, what kind of stuff did you like doing when you were a kid?" Ana helpfully suggests, easing my growing discomfort.

Taking a deep breath, I think back.

"Well, when I was a kid, I just loved hanging out with my dad. He would take me and Sunny along with him to train. We would play on the treadmill and he'd give us little barbells to pump. Afterwards, we would have a protein shake lunch." The goofy grin I'm sporting makes my eyes squinty.

"Hold up girl. You're trying to tell me you grew up with a bad bastard MC, pumped weights, downed protein shakes, and you came out like this?" Pops waves a tanned, wrinkled hand my way. I look down at my tee and try to figure out if he's insulting my weight or not.

"He doesn't mean your looks Rem, he means you somehow still came out like super fricking nice." Ana helpfully explains.

"Creepily nice." Chewy unhelpfully adds.

"Dad drummed it into me. I had to be different from my mother and the other women in the clubhouse. Which pretty much meant no cursing and no nastiness."

They stare at me for a moment before Chewy consults her list.

"Well, looking at this, I don't know what to tell you other than your perfect job would be to teach computer geeks with bad backgrounds how to pump iron. Is that an actual job?" Chewy looks at us with a squinty eye before tossing her notepad. "Let's go blow some stuff up."

"Oh, thank fuck! I thought you'd never ask!" Pops jumps up surprisingly fast for an older man, offering me a hand up, his bright red painted nails shimmering under the lights. I catch Ana rolling her eyes but also coming to a stand.

"Fine. But no one tell Gus this is what we did. That man is stress on legs. He's so tightly wound that sometimes he gets this throbby vein in his forehead shaped like a vag."

A laugh bursts out of me at her description and before I can bring my hand up to cover my mouth, Ana slaps it away.

"Embrace it, Rem! It'll do you good." She smiles at me, then throws her arm over my shoulder. This is what I've been looking for. Sure, I have women in my life I'm close to. I have Miss Shawna, although she's more of a mother figure. Sunny is my sister, so she doesn't really count. But this? Having actual girlfriends that aren't in any way related to me? This is something new and exciting.

"I vote Remy be the first to blow shit up!"

OK, well, maybe it'll take while to get used to.

Chapter Five

Beretta_Penn: *I'm so glad you're back home. Now I can stop worrying that you're going to get blown up all the time.*

St_Margarita: *Awwww are you trying to say you'd miss me?*

Beretta_Penn: *Of course! You're my bestie. My ride or die.*

St_Margarita: *.....*

St_Margarita: *What if I'm not the same? After what happened .....*

Beretta_Penn: *What happened to your squad shouldn't have happened to anyone. It's bound to affect you.*

St_Margarita: *Not that, what about after? You know what I helped to do. Do you think I'm a monster?*

Beretta_Penn: *You got rid of an evil man. Stopped him from hurting more people. I'd think you were a monster if you didn't do what you did.*

St_Margarita: *I can't relax. I need to know that everyone I love is safe. I obsess about it.*

Beretta_Penn: *Does it make you feel better? Does it soothe your fear?*

St_Margarita: *Yeah.*

Beretta_Penn: *Mags, I think you deserve whatever will bring you peace x*

Wire

"Yo, when was the last time you left this room?" Rhodie roughly spins what is normally Chewy's chair around and slumps back into it. "Goddamn, these things are comfortable. A bitch to put together, but the comfort almost makes the hard work worth it."

I snort because these chairs were a bitch to put together. When I first joined, Marx decided I should have the biggest suite in the clubhouse knowing that I wanted my system to be close at hand. He also figured I'd need top of the range furniture, so he found this chair, with all the bells and whistles. The salesman offered to have the delivery guy put it together for us and we took that as a personal insult. We're a group of highly trained vets, a fucking MC. We could put a pissy little computer chair together. Six hours, one black eye and one almost resignation later, we got there.

"What's going on, brother? Missing Chewy so you needed to come sit where her ass sits to feel close to her? Dude, she finishes work in like two hours. I'm sure you can last that long."

He doesn't even crack a smile. Just stares at me, eyes narrowed. "When was the last time you left this room?"

"I leave it all the time. I saw you at the bar last night when you were pining after your girlfriend."

The corners of his mouth twitch before he settles back in Chewy's chair. He regards me for a moment. "Come on. Let's go for a ride. Don't even try to tell me you're too busy. Shit can wait. There's nothing much going on at the moment. You can take a time out, brother." He tips his head at me as he stands and I know the big bastard won't take no for an answer.

I switch all my alerts to be sent to my watch and follow him out to where our bikes are all parked. Looking at my girl, I actually feel bad that I've been neglecting her. It's just when I'm on the job it's hard to switch off. I know we haven't heard the last of the auctions. Russians don't take kindly to people shutting down their businesses. It's all a matter of time before the threats rise up again and we're in the firing line. I'm the difference between us being caught unprepared or not.

Rhodie's large hand claps my shoulder before he walks the short distance to his bike and throws his leg over. I do the same, backing her out of her parking spot, then starting her up and feeling the rumble beneath me. Rhodie circles his finger in the air and I follow him out of the compound onto the open road.

The wind through my hair has me closing my eyes a little in bliss. Just feeling the warm air of Texas spring on my skin has me shaking off a funk I never knew I was in. We take the back roads through the next two small towns before Rhodie signals to pull off at a side road. I follow him as it twists and turns, climbing higher until he stops at what looks to be a rest spot. He throws his leg over and turns his body until he's looking out over a small town we sometimes pass through on our longer runs. Parking up next to him, I do the same, taking a deep breath of the clear air into my lungs. The wind therapy has definitely blown out the cobwebs.

"What have you been working on, brother?" Rhodie's voice breaks through my peace and I catalog off everything I've been doing today.

"Trying to track and trace Kovalev, Kraykowski's old boss. I know Roman says he has it in hand, but I'm not sure we can trust him. I've been supporting Lexi here and there. Making sure all our accounts are healthy. Looking at open properties for expansion, monitoring the dark web for anything that looks like could blow back at us, updating –"

"Enough, Saint." Rhodie's use of my government name cuts through and my head snaps up in surprise. "Brother, you have your finger in so many pies. It ain't good for you, man." He stares at me for a moment, a deep frown on his face. I know what he's about to ask me. "When was the last time you saw your therapist?"

I pull my shoulders back, close my eyes, and let my head roll back and forth for a moment, stretching out any kinks before taking a breath and slowly letting it out. "I'm good, brother. I don't need to see my therapist. I'm doing well. It sounds like a lot, but I have Chewy and now Remy to help. I can handle this, Rhodes." I use his name as he used mine, so he understands how serious I'm being.

His eyes bounce between mine for a moment before he slaps his hand on my shoulder and squeezes.

"I know it hit you hard when we lost –" he swallows "– when we lost the others. You stopped eating and sleeping, became hypervigilant with our safety. I just don't want to see you taken over like that again. We aren't at war, brother."

"Aren't we? We may not be in a desert somewhere, but we're still taking out bad guys."

Rhodie huffs and gives me a wry smile. "Yeah, guess you're right. Just remember, you're not alone. It isn't all on your shoulders to keep us safe and happy. Lean on us. We may not be as clever as you, but we sure can fuck shit up when the time calls for it."

He gives me a smile and a shake before letting me go, and turning back to the view. My watch buzzes and I can see Rhodie roll his eyes, shaking his head in my periphery.

"Gotta get back. Looks like your brother-in-law has had an exciting morning. The boys have towed Ana's car in and Chewy and Pops are investigating."

"Ah, shit. Let's roll out."

* * *

When we get back to the clubhouse Rhodie splits off to see his Ol Lady and I head to my room. I feel invigorated and make a vow to ride out more. Rhodie was right, getting out of the control center even for a short couple of hours has put me in a better mindset. Even the mention of what we survived hasn't sent me into a tailspin like it used to.

Sinking into my chair, I try not to think about what happened when we were deployed. Working as the intelligence specialist in our squad meant all information came to me to disseminate. It was my job to discern what was a threat and what wasn't.

I spin my chair for a moment and take a deep breath. I don't think about those times very often. Not because I don't want to remember, but because I've rehashed everything with my therapist so many times that I know now there was nothing more I could have done to stop what happened. No amount of intelligence collecting, eyes on, or comms could have changed the outcome that the enemy we were fighting was far more twisted than we could have ever imagined. Using children as weapons in your war is a type of evil that needs to be punished in the most painful way possible. Three months after we lost five brothers in arms, I helped Rhodie and what was left of our squad track down the devil and we made him pay. Not just for the lives of our fallen brothers, but for the terrified little boy he used to do his bidding.

That was the last deployment Rhodie went on. I should have gotten out then too. Instead I stayed in for longer than I should have, reliving that one pivotal moment over and over just with different teams in different places. The last time my papers came up for renewal I decided to follow Rhodie and get out. I'd seen all I needed to see to know that there was no future in that hellhole. Not one that I wanted a part of, anyway.

Do I still have nightmares about that day? Of course I do. I still wake up wondering if I had just looked harder at the Intel or from a different angle, maybe those men would still be with us. Survivors' guilt is a son of a bitch. I may not be able to change the past, but I sure as hell can make sure that it doesn't happen again in the future.

I pull up all my cameras, and as usual, I do my checks. I don't tell anyone how many times a day I watch these cameras, but it's for my peace of mind. I like to make sure I have eyes on all my brothers. Watching the cameras in the garages that we own in town, I count off the brothers I can see there. Glancing at the clock shows that it's just past 5pm, so only Squeak and Judge are in. Sniper and Tank are on a call out in the tow truck. Pulling up their GPS, I see they're on their way back. I take a quick note that their ETA should be two minutes. If they take any longer than that, I'll follow up.

Changing to our clubhouse cameras, I watch Remy for a moment. Her head is tipped forward, hair covering her face as she concentrates on her laptop in the common room. She moves in her seat a little, stretching out her back, her full breasts straining against the front of the shiny blue blouse she's wearing. My cock twitches at the movement and I have to will myself to concentrate on what I'm doing, and stop perving at Remy. She's my student hacker. She doesnt need a fucked up man like me lusting after her sweetness and yet I can't quite tear my eyes away just yet. She tilts her head slightly and I watch as she side-eyes the bunnies with a small smirk on her face. Whitney and the other bunnies are huddled over by the couches, staring daggers at Remy but knowing full well that, as our guest, she is untouchable. Like a clever mouse teases the tom cat, it would seem Remy is purposely winding the bunnies up by staking out her place in the common room. Maybe she isn't as gentle and innocent as she seems. I watch her for a little longer until I start creeping myself out. I think I need to get laid. Or have another chat with Retta. Obviously her last advice was shit if this ...feeling is still hanging around.

Giving myself a shake and a pep talk to get it the fuck together, my eyes drift around my screens until I see that the rest of my brothers are in the garage out back with the Tombs family. They had some type of drama with Ana's car, so I watch for a moment before noticing Marx on his phone. His head snaps up, he yells something, and then everyone scatters. What the fuck? Pounding footsteps coming down the hall have me spinning to the doorway in time to see Chewy and Remy come flying round the corner.

"Death Riders coming in hot, being chased. ETA 5 minutes." Chewy barks out and I feel my lips curl as I think about how similar she sounds to Rhodie just now.

"Pull up a seat Remy, shit's about to go down,"

Remy

The smell of antiseptic keeps invading my senses even though I've been sitting here in Switch's medical room for close to two hours. I'm wondering how much longer I need to sit here before I get used to the smell. Closing my eyes, I try to erase the image of watching my dad and his brothers running for their lives on Wire's surveillance. It was the one time I wished he didn't have such high resolution cameras. Watching my dad flinch in perfect clarity, and then laying his bike down as soon as he made it through the gates, had my blood running cold. If it wasn't for Ana stopping me in the doorway of Wire's control center, I would have run out into the chaos to get to Dad. Instead, she calmed me down and Wire held my hand until it was safe.

Switch pulled the bullet from Dad's chest, and now I'm sitting at his bedside, my hand gripping his much larger, rougher one. Switch said he should wake up any moment now and I want to be here when it happens. I don't want Dad to wake up in a strange place all alone.

A groan fills the silence in the room, and his hand tightens around mine. I make sure the lights are down low, so when he opens his eyes, he doesn't startle.

"Dad, Dad it's me, Remy. I'm here. Just take your time." Pressing a kiss to his knuckles, I lean forward and lightly rest my head on his beer belly.

I've been trying to keep it together, but hearing him groan and swallow and make noises after two hours of silence has the emotion welling up. The only place for it to escape is out of my eyeballs, it seems. His large hand comes up to rest on the back of my head.

"Shhh, it's OK baby, I'm here. It's all good. Shhhhh." His voice sounds rough and I can hear him swallowing from the inside, which is a little weird, so I sit up, looking into eyes that look just like mine. "See baby girl? I'm alright. I hope you didn't tell your sister. She'll come all this way to kick my ass," I snort a little and then wipe my nose on my sleeve.

"Savage called her to let her know but told her it wasn't serious enough for her to come rushing. Although she said that if you don't call her later, she most definitely will kick your ass."

We both share a smile before worry sets in again. "Who was it Dad? Do you know?"

He sighs and tips his head for me to sit down. Grabbing his hand, I clasp it in both of mine while I wait for him to spill.

"I'm pretty certain it was Hammer. Didn't see him exactly, but who else would start a nomad club in these parts?"

"Gus and Tav, Chewy's brothers, wounded and caught one of the riders. Chewy is going to torture him for information but, this is only the beginning, isn't it?" I slump a little, knowing that what I heard that day I was on the Death Riders compound all those months ago was just the tip of the iceberg.

"Hey, hey, Rem, it's going to be OK. You're safe here, remember girl? You can help Wire and that funny little lady figure out how to put a pin in all this auction shit once and for all. Once that's shut down, Hammer will move on and leave us all the fuck alone to get on with our lives."

Looking for the lie in his face, all I see is my dad's bright, shining blue eyes and the smile he has always given me when I needed it. He shakes my hand back and forth, the strength in it surprising given what he's just been through. "Trust me, girl, it'll all be fine. Now tell me what you've been learning."

And just like that, Dad makes me forget all my worries. I chat to him for only a few minutes before he drifts off again. Switch told me this would happen. The painkillers will have him sleeping a lot, and that's what he needs to do to heal. Pulling my phone out of my pocket, I pull up my message thread with Mags. I need someone to talk to.

Beretta_Penn: Hey. You busy?

St_Margarita: Not for pretty girls.

Beretta_Penn: I'm rolling my eyes. Can you feel it through the Wi-Fi?

St_Margarita: Is that what's making my balls tingle?

Beretta_Penn: You're so gross.

St_Margarita: You love it. So, what's up, babe?

Rolling my eyes, I wonder if I've interrupted something. Mags isn't usually this flirty.

Beretta_Penn: I just needed to talk to someone. My dad is in the hospital. He hurt himself and I got a scare.

St_Margarita: Oh babe! Is he OK? Are YOU OK? Do you need me to meet you somewhere?

Beretta_Penn: Wait, you'd do that for me?

St_Margarita: Can you feel my eyes rolling through the Wi-Fi? Of course, I'd do that for you. I'd do anything.

Beretta_Penn: You better stop otherwise I'll start crying.

St_Margarita: Well duh, you're a girl after all.

Beretta_Penn: And now the feeling has passed.

St_Margarita: .....

St_Margarita: ......

St_Margarita: I'm serious though, Retta, you need me, I'm there. I've got your back, for always.

Beretta_Penn: ....

Beretta_Penn: For always.

I put my phone down when Switch comes into the room to check Dad's vitals and whatever other things he felt the need to check. It was a little hard to concentrate on what was happening when there was a flock of butterflies in my stomach going crazy.

What if Mags comes here and he doesn't like me? What if I don't like him? We don't really know anything about each other. *Except each other's innermost thoughts and feelings.* Stupid inner monologue. A knock at the door has me snapping out of my thoughts to see Wire standing in the doorway.

"Do you mind if I come and sit for a bit?"

"Oh yeah, sure. Have a seat." I stand and go to move so Wire can sit, but he stands where he is, not moving, a frown on his face.

"Where are you going?"

"Oh, I thought you wanted to have a seat. I can go do some homework and stuff."

He gives me an odd look and I can feel the heat rising in my cheeks. They burst into flame when Wire lets out a deep, throaty chuckle. I'm momentarily stunned, as I don't think I've heard him laugh before. Wire is lovely and thoughtful and incredibly nice, but he also seems to be weighed down by his responsibilities. Responsibilities that seem to all be self imposed. I've noticed him checking the cameras often, noting where all his brothers are. Hearing him laugh is something new and I feel very lucky to have heard it.

"I was asking to come sit with you. I wanted to make sure you were doing OK. And I'm selfish and wanted to make myself feel better."

He clears his throat and rubs the back of his neck. Is he shy?

"My friend, she's having a rough time and I can't be with her to make it easier, so I thought I'd help another friend." His lips curl slightly and he raises his eyebrows in question.

"Oh, of course! I mean, I'm doing OK, but you can still sit with me. Dad not long ago nodded off and Switch was just in topping up his meds."

He nods at me, and then his long legs eat up the space between us. He drags a chair from the corner and places it close to mine. He settles in with a little groan, rolling his head on his shoulders for a moment.

"Tech neck?"

His lips twitch "I'd like to blame it on a badass injury where I was blown up or did it BMXing or something but yup, tech neck from sitting far too long staring at screens."

I study him for a moment, his curls are pulled up into a beanie that he wears fairly often to keep his hair out of his face. Chewy told me he's always losing his hair bands, so the beanie is the next best thing to keep his hair out of his face.

I stand up and hold my hands up. "May I?" I ask him. He looks up at me with his eyebrows pinched, head tilted in confusion. "My sister says I have magic hands. She'd ask for a massage after a workout, or after a long day at school when she was training to be a chef. Or sometimes for no reason at all."

I'm rambling now. I've just realized I've offered to massage the hottest man I've ever seen in my life. Who the heck am I right now?

"Shit sweetheart, if you're down, I'm down. Have at it." He gifts me a wide smile, his white teeth sparkling in his brown face.

I move behind him, placing my hands on his broad shoulders.

Without thinking too deep into things, I knead the muscles in his neck and shoulders. A groan rumbles out of him and my thighs clench in reply. Holy moly, the noises this man is making are bordering on obscene. I can feel my pussy pulse as my senses are filled to the brim with Wire. I'm surrounded by his scent, his groans filling the air, his hard muscles under my hands.

"Shit, Remy, that feels so damn good. You're wasted as a librarian girl," my hands bounce as he lets out a chuckle.

"Ha, that's what Sunny says."

We carry on in companionable silence until Wire takes hold of my hand and pulls me to sit beside him.

"Thanks, Rem. That feels so much better. But now it's time to look after you. It's getting late, so if you like, I'll keep watch for a little longer if you want to go get yourself ready for bed."

He is so sweet and thoughtful, and after work today and all the excitement and worry of the past few hours, I can admit that I am exhausted.

"I'd love that, but what about your cameras? I know you like to check them." A look that I can't decipher flicks across his face before it's gone just as quickly as it came.

"I'm sure it'll be fine for a little while. Besides, Chewy is in there. But then again, so is Rhodie, so maybe not a lot of camera work will go on. And they better not be fucking on my bed!" His face grows stormy, and a laugh escapes me, hearty and strong, shaking off the stress of the day.

"Thank you, Wire, I appreciate this, um, you. Good night." I give him a smile before turning and kissing my dad on his rough, hairy cheek. "Night Dad, love you."

I head toward the door, turning to check on Dad one last time to see Wire settling in next to him. His hazel eyes flick to mine as he gives me a chin lift.

"Night Rem."

Chapter Six

Beretta_Penn: *You know I kinda thought as I got older it would be easier to make friends.*

St_Margarita: *Why do you need more? I'm all you'll ever need.*

Beretta_Penn: *What about when I want to talk about periods?*

St_Margarita: *Talk away. I have a mom and three sisters. I know all about the cramps and the period poops.*

Beretta_Penn: *I have no idea why I keep talking to you.*

St_Margarita: *Because you're my ride or die. Til the bitter end sweetheart. We're BFF's for life. I'll have your back, Retta. For always.*

Beretta_Penn: *I'll have yours too Mags. For always.*

Wire

Last night I sat with Flack for a while and sent a message through to Retta, checking in on her. It kills me knowing she's dealing with her sick dad alone. Because I couldn't be there with her, I figured the next best thing I could do was help another friend who needed a shoulder to lean on. Remy looked so small and broken sitting next to Flack's bed, it broke my heart. There is just something about this woman that makes all my protective instincts flare up. And then because I'm an absolute pig, I came back to my room and worked my cock thinking of both Remy and Retta somehow rolled into one. I have no idea how it happened or what my brain was thinking, but it's fucked up.

Even more fucked up was all that happened after I watched Chewy work over one of the nomads that Gus and Tav managed to grab in the shoot out. Her new set up has her flaying skin to her Backstreet Boys mix. Disturbing? Yes. Effective? Also yes. The poor fucker was begging for death by the time he finished squealing his secrets. And squeal he did. It would seem that Hammer has himself a fairly large nomad MC and it's growing by the day. His officers are the men that sided with him when the Death Riders split, around a dozen or so men acting nomad and getting up to who the fuck knows what. I've had my system working overnight looking for anything that he may have a hand in and nothing has come up yet.

I don't know what the hell went down with the Death Riders causing the initial split other than Savage wanting to go legit. I trust my Prez and I know that he would never have allied with an MC that had shit going down, but there are some quirks about the Death Riders that have me questioning a few things. Having Remy here to learn from me and Chewy is one of the things I keep mulling over. I would have thought a brother would be more suited to the job. Even more interesting is that Remy mentioned Savage only takes his officers with him when he rides out, his most trusted men. That statement in itself didn't strike me as odd. What did was the fact that Remy knew that and seems to know a lot more about the MC than most women would. I don't want to say MC men are chauvinistic cavemen, but we all know that the inner workings of an MC are never shared with the women and children, for their protection. Deniable plausibility and shit.

"Can I ask you something?" I jump at Chewy's voice, which sounds way too close for comfort. Tilting my head, I'm met with one giant whiskey colored eye in my periphery.

"Chewy?" I whisper, because it would feel weird talking at normal volume being this close.

"Yeah?" she whispers back.

"Why are you so close?"

"I'm investigating."

"OK" I stare at her for a moment, knowing full well that she will feel uncomfortable in 3, 2, 1...

"I'm done with data collection. You seem fine. I called your name four times, and you didn't respond. I thought you may have been having a stroke or a fit. I needed to see your pupils to ascertain, and they seem fine."

She heads to her chair, kicks her shoes off, plops down and pulls her legs up. She often sits pretzeled up like that.

"Anyway, can I ask you something?"

"Chewy, you can ask me anything." I rethink that statement. "As long as it doesn't involve Rhodie's dick. Or ass." I add as after thoughts. You really need to have firm lines with this woman.

She lets out a sigh and rolls her eyes. "It's not that kind of question. I want to know what attributes elevate a person from friend status to best friend status. Me and Remy are friends, and her dad was just shot and I want to be supportive, but I'm not sure if I'm a best friend, or a normal friend."

"Does it matter?"

"Ah, yeah. They're different roles. The titles determine the level of support appropriate to offer."

"Knock, knock brother."

Chewy and I both spin in our seats to face the door, Tank filling up the space almost completely.

"You're door sized." Chewy says before looking back at me expectantly.

"Tank, you good? If it's not anything urgent, you may be able to help me explain to Chewy what makes a best friend." I smirk at him, knowing full well that he would rather get his shit done and move on to the next job, but I'm surprised when he lumbers over and rests his bulk against the desk beside me.

"OK Chewy, what do you want to know?" Tank asks in his smooth voice.

"What characteristics elevate a friend to best friend status?"

Tank and I look at each other for a moment before he beats me to it. "A best friend is someone you trust. Implicitly. With your life."

"I agree. Someone that you know always has your back. You can tell them anything and they accept you. They offer you support without you asking. And you do the same for them." I add. I can see Chewy ticking this over in her mind.

"They're also someone that you love to spend time with. They make you laugh and you can shoot the shit or bust each other's balls."

"What Tank said."

Chewy strokes her imaginary beard for a moment and then, out of the blue, she sits bolt upright and curses.

"Shit! I have been a terrible friend! I need to make this up to him." She starts madly Googling gift baskets. Me and Tank share a look, trying to figure out what the fuck is going on.

"Chewy! What the hell makes you think you've been a bad friend?" I'm leaning forward, waiting for her to tell me what's got her panties in a bunch.

Out of the corner of my eye I can see Tank leaning forward too, but with a smirk, and I just know he's waiting for whatever unhinged shit that is going to come out of her mouth.

"Marx."

"Huh?"

"Marx. From what you've just told me, Marx is my best friend."

My eyebrows shoot upwards "Wait, I thought I was your best friend?"

"Well, according to what you and Tank just told me, you're not. You tick many other best friend boxes, but you don't bust my balls." She shakes her head back and forth, "This whole time Marx was fulfilling best friend duties and I never knew. I better go tell him I appreciate him."

With that, she flies out of the room, her tiny feet padding down the hall. The sound of her voice shrilly calling out for the Pres has me and Tank doubled over in laughter. Wiping my eyes, I gesture for Tank to sit in Chewy's seat.

"Right, brother, what can I do for you?"

"There's a motherfucker that has been hanging around the towing yard. Messy, unkempt. Probably on drugs with how thin he is. Wondering if you could keep an eye on him? I scared him away the other day. He ran into that alley between us and that derelict place next door. But then Sniper spotted him again when he was leaving for a callout."

Spinning to my screens, I pull up all the cameras we have

on the yard. The tow business is always busy due to us being the only tow service in town. We have a yard attached to the main business where we keep busted cars for scrap and all that shit. Scanning the cameras, I mention to Tank that I don't see anything.

"That's because he's a sneaky fucker. We think he's getting in down the back, through the hole in the fence. We've patched it up but to be sure, do you think you could up security over there?"

"Sure thing. I'll order some of the new shit that Gus and the Tombs have gotten in. They're coming today to drop in some real slick comms watches, complete with tiny little ear pieces for us."

Tank lets out a low, impressed whistle. "That sounds like military grade shit."

I nod in agreement. I have an idea that whenever they contract to the FBI or CIA or any other agencies only known by initials, that Chewy demands they pay in tech. Thank fuck she attached herself to us because we get kick backs like all this good shit.

"Sure does. I'll get this shit handled and then I'll be out to install. Keep an eye on him, yeah?"

Tank nods and heads on out while I go back to checking my cameras in case I missed something. All I need is a clear pic of the asshole and I can run facial recognition on him. Another perk of knowing Chewy. Speaking of, I can hear low cursing coming my way and with the cadence of the steps and how heavy they are, I know Marx is on the warpath.

"I swear to all that's fucking holy, if you don't get away from me Chewy, I WILL ban you from this clubhouse."

"Aw Marx, I very much appreciate it when you bust my lady

balls."

Looking over my shoulder, I see they are now in my doorway, Marx glowering at Chewy, who is beaming up at him. I try to make my face look as neutral as possible, but I feel like I'm fighting a losing battle.

"Wire! Give Chewy a job. Any fucking job." He jabs his finger my way and I give him a half assed salute before he storms off.

"Best friend ever!"

Remy

I take a quick headcount to make sure all my afternoon kiddos are where they're meant to be. Which at this time of the afternoon seems to be sprawled all over the floor and in various bean bags looking at whatever book took their fancy today. We've already done our craft for the afternoon, we made origami bookmarks with googly eyes. At one point, one of my most mischievous boys went around and stuck them to the fronts of a few romance novels featuring couples on the cover. While hilarious, I had to scold him and try to pick them off.

I drift my gaze over the kids once more, coming to a stop at Jovie. Over the past few weeks, she has become a bright spot in my day, and hopefully I'm one in hers. I have noticed that she has been looking increasingly disheveled lately. Her curly pigtails are looking more and more askew and knotted, as if she's been sleeping with them in and she's been in the same clothes for a couple of days now. I wanted to have a word with her dad, but he seems to never get out of the car to collect her, just swings the door open for her to climb in before peeling out. If his dangerous driving didn't already worry me, the sunken in cheeks and wild eyes peering through the windscreen at me would have.

She must feel my eyes on her because big brown eyes find mine and she breaks out into a grin. Her little gapped tooth smile making me forget my worries for her and my dad. His recovery is taking longer than expected thanks to a nasty infection, but he's now getting out and about a bit more, even if it is just around the compound. I was so happy when Savage agreed to leave him at DRMC to recover. I never noticed how far apart we had drifted once I moved out. Even Sunny has come to visit a few times on her days off, much to the chagrin of two bikers who have their eyes on her.

Flicking my eyes to the clock, I see that it's time for the Library Dance party so I let my little friends know and we dance our hearts out very quietly to the three songs they all managed to agree on.

Before I know it, parents have started to trickle in, so I round up the kids, make sure they have their crafts and start with the goodbye high fives, handing them off to their waiting parents.

"You know I'm still surprised she left her with him. Why wouldn't she leave her with family?"

"It's because they have no other family. He's all she has,"

"Hmph. Can't child services get involved? We all know she's not safe?"

I listen in as two moms whisper back and forth between them-selves and I'm guessing they're talking about Jovie. Luckily, she seems none the wiser as she sits waiting for her dad's piece of junk car to drive up. He must be running late today because he's usually one of the first parents here.

"Jovie, do you want to help me do some tidying while we wait for your dad?" I offer, wanting to keep her mind off why her dad hasn't shown up yet. We make ourselves busy and soon enough the children's library section is void of my after school programme kids. Glancing at the time, I see that he's over an hour late. A small rumbling noise beside me has me glancing down at my little friend.

"Jovie, when was the last time you ate, sweetie?"

She rubs her nose for a bit and I can see she's wracking her little brain to remember.

"How about a snack, huh? Follow me. I have something special in my lunchbox just for you."

She beams up at me, and I feel like a superhero. Taking her into the small staff area, I open my lunchbox and thank the stars that I wasn't that hungry today. I get Jovie set up at the table and hand her one half of my ham salad sandwich, a packet of chips and an apple.

"There you go! Have at it. I'll wait right here with you."

"But don't you have kids to look after, Miss Remy?"

Shaking my head, I let her know I am now officially off the clock. I could have gone home when the kids all left, but there was no way I was leaving Jovie here to wander the library alone.

She digs into her sandwich and I watch her devour the lot, making me really worry when the last time she ate was.

"Jovie, what's your last name, honey? I'll see if someone can track down your dad, OK?"

She mumbles "Spencer" around her mouthful and I take note. Not just to call her father, but I'm going to do a little digging when I get back to the compound.

"Where the fuck is my daughter? She's meant to be waiting

for me on the road, not fucking around in here!" A man's voice booms and I know that Jovie's dad has finally arrived.

I gather up her things, smiling down at her when I notice that she's eaten everything I gave her. That makes me happy that at least she has something in her little tummy. Walking her out of the staffroom into the main library, I can see her father yelling at Beth on the help desk.

"She's right here, Mr. Spencer. We were just a little further back in the library. If you weren't almost 2 hours late, she would have been right where you expected her to be." I reply in a steady voice.

"Whatever. Jovie, get your ass in the car." Jovie nods, avoiding eye contact and shuffles past her father, the man giving her a little shove to get her to walk faster.

Stepping forward to get to her, I'm overwhelmed by the smell of body odor and weed. "You stay the fuck away from my kid, bitch. Unless you want to become her new mommy. I'm sure I can look past your dog ugly face for that fine rack you have on you." He leers at me, licking his lips before turning on his heel and storming out the door.

"What an asshole. Someone needs to take that kid off him," Beth says with a look of disgust on her face.

"I'm going to make sure of it," I say to her, letting her see the fire in my eyes.

I carry that fire all the way back to the compound, determined to use my newfound computer skills to help me after I check in to see how Dad is doing. I've told him about Jovie and my worries. I'm sure he'll want me to get right on to looking into her deadbeat dad, but that loser can wait for a moment. After we've had our catch up, I'll look into the few databases that Chewy showed me. It'll be an excellent test of my skills. And if

I need more skills, I'm sure Chewy and Wire will be more than happy to help me. They're good people.

In fact, the whole MC are good people. It feels like I'm fitting in a little more. I've made friends with a few more of the brothers, and I feel like I'm gaining confidence in myself. Mainly because these people want me to be heard, to be confident. It's a powerful feeling.

"You fit in well here, Rem." my dad pats my hand with his giant paw of a hand, his bright blue eyes shining at me. This is the best he's looked in a long time.

"Thanks Dad. I really like it here. Not that I hated it at home. It's just, different." I shrug, not knowing what to say.

My dad lets out a sigh before cupping my chin to look at him. "Rem. I think I may have fucked up letting you grow up how you did." I make a noise of protest, but he keeps talking. "I had nowhere else to go with you girls, no support, no family other than the men in the MC. Looking back now, it wasn't a good place for two little girls. Especially you, Rem. You're a softy, my girl. I tried to do the best I could, but it seems these men have done a better job in what is it, three? Four short weeks? Than I ever did in 18 years."

"Aw Dad, it wasn't that bad. I could have spoken up, found my place, but I was content not to make waves. It's on both of us. But I wouldn't change growing up with you as my dad for all the money in the world. I love you old man. And we are going to find exactly who did this to you and kick his butt!" I kiss Dad on the cheek and his body shakes from his chuckling.

I pull him up to standing as the DRMC cookout will be starting soon. Savage, Dex and a few of the other Death Riders are here to pick up Dad to take him back to Roxwell tomorrow. It's a good thing they plan to stay because they definitely won't be sober enough to leave tonight. I'm a little disappointed that Nat couldn't make it, but it seems our Pres and his Ol Lady are going to be parents soon and the morning sickness is kicking her butt.

"Remy! We need you in the control center!" Chewy comes flying down the hallway yelling my name, stopping for a moment in the doorway "Nomads are back, they have a sniper out the back, and the rest are coming in hot!"

My dad squeezes my hand tight in his and presses a kiss to my knuckles before pushing me toward Chewy. "Go girl, they need you!"

Chaper Seven

Beretta_Penn: *Why are you still awake?*
St_Margarita: *Can't sleep.*
Beretta_Penn: *Me neither.*
St_Margarita: *What's wrong in your world?*
Beretta_Penn: *Boredom? I just thought I'd be more. More independent, more successful. But I'm still me, just older.*
St_Margarita: *At least you don't spend all day and night thinking the worst is going to happen to everyone you love.*
Beretta_Penn: *You can't protect everyone all the time, Mags.*
St_Margarita: *Why not?*
Beretta_Penn: *Because you're not Superman?*
St_Margarita: *He's a pussy anyway.*
St_Margarita: *I just feel like I'm failing people. I don't want to see anyone I love get hurt.*
Beretta_Penn: *I know. But you can only do so much. When it gets too big you need to lean on others to help you. I'll always be here if you need me. Call and I'm there. Always.*
St_Margarita: *Only if you promise the same.*
Beretta_Penn: *Promise. We have each other's back.*
St_Margarita: *For always.*
Beretta_Penn: *Always.*

Wire

Fuck fuck fuck! I was trying to be extra vigilant with our security after that shit with the Death Riders and Flack being shot, but obviously it's not enough. How the fuck did I miss an active shooter coming onto our property? What fucking use am I if I can't even do my job?

"Get out of your head Wire, we've got baddies to fuck up," Chewy says as she strides to her chair, kicks her shoes off and plops down. She has an earpiece in already and is barking instructions.

I shake myself off. She's right. I have to get a fucking grip on myself. My eyes close and I pull a breath deep into my lungs before letting it out.

"That's it, dude, in the zone," Chewy whispers under her breath, side eyeing me for a moment.

The thud of running feet breaks through and Remy comes flying around the corner, straight to her station.

"The men have their ear pieces in. I need you to be badass, Rem, like we practiced." Remy nods her head once at Chewy, before turning to me, holding out her small pale fist. My lips twitch and I bump mine against her.

"OK ladies, let's fucking do this."

My fingers fly over the keys and I broadcast all our cameras onto the large screen in front of us.

"Remy, you all good to monitor the front gate, parking lot and treeline?" She doesn't reply and my eyes are glued to the screen, so I need her to talk to me. "Need your words, sweetheart."

"Yes, yup. I can do that."

"You'll need to warn brothers through comms too, so make sure you use your firm voice, OK?" I finally turn to look at her, her eyes are wide but I watch her steel herself, her shoulders back and stubborn tilt to her chin.

"I've got your back."

"Good girl. Chewy, you all good to monitor out the back and all the roads that run behind the compound?"

"Yeah, homie."

I ignore Remy's soft snort and check my own cameras. It takes no time at all for us three to fall into an easy rhythm. The nomad riders have us almost surrounded. By the looks of it, the shooter at the back of the compound was taken out fairly early on. Luckily for us, there is dense wood behind us with heavy duty fencing beyond that. There are some country roads that run behind us, but you'd have to be local to even know they're back there, and these guys are most definitely not local. If they were, they'd know not to fuck with us.

Scanning the screens, there have to be about 15 of the fuckers. Hammer has recruited a large crew without us or Death Riders knowing about it, which is fucking concerning. Although he obviously hadn't factored in that his men were going to be walking into a bloodbath. Yeah, they may have numbers, but they have absolutely no fucking skills, making it easy for our little IT team to bark out orders. Brothers are taking out targets as soon as we call them out. With our eyes and new comms tech we are running tighter than the units I worked with when I was deployed. Between the Tombs, DRMC and Death Riders, we have already cut a swathe through the men that thought they could attack us. Fucking idiots. I'm feeling rather confident that we'll have this buttoned up quickly, and that is when I hear Ana calling for backup. Spinning to look at Remy, she looks pale and Chewy has taken over calling the shots for her.

"Oh no! I didn't see him and now Gus has been shot!" Remy gasps. She turns her wide eyes toward me, tears pooling. Turning back to the screen, I watch as Gus seems to be moving around, even if he isn't looking too flash. The way Ana is leaning over him and gripping his arm, I can see it's not a life threatening wound.

"Hey, hey, look at me. He's fine. It's in his arm. There was no way for you to see that sneaky fuck from where he was firing from. It's OK." I make sure I make eye contact with her, so she can see the sincerity in my face. She lets out a breath and nods, before turning back to her screen.

I watch her for a moment and feel a weird tightening in my chest. I don't like it when she's upset. It screws my guts up. I don't know how it happened, but the way I feel about her is like the way I feel about Retta. Is that weird? Maybe I'm projecting my feelings for Retta onto Remy? Or the other way round? Fuck. I have no clue. I need to get both of them off my mind and concentrate on my fucking job. Two minutes ago, I was berating myself for not doing good enough.

"Aaaaand that's a wrap, folks. All nomads have been maimed or killed. I'm gonna get out there and see if I can get any information outta the injured ones." Chewy states, although before getting up from her chair she clocks something on the screens, tilts her head with a frown and then rushes out of the room.

Following where she was looking, I see Tank bringing in Gus, who looks unconscious. Remy hasn't noticed yet and I don't want her to either.

"Hey Rem, do you want to go down and see how your dad is? We'll probably debrief in the common room if you want to get ready to bring him down. I'm sure Marx will want us all there."

She gives me a small smile, nods her head and drops her hand to my shoulder, before leaning forward and brushing her soft lips against my cheek. Her floral scent swirls around me, and I wonder if it's some type of body wash or if it's her natural smell.

"Thank you, Wire." She gives me one last smile before heading out the door and turning left into the hall, and the direction of Switch's room.

I give myself a shake, taking in the screens once more. Gus is lying on a table with his shirt ripped off. Everyone looks tense as hell, but thanks to Switch's loud as fuck voice, I can hear everything that's going on and it sounds as if Gus will be perfectly fine. I count off how many brothers, including Tombs, I can see on my screens and let out a breath. Everyone is all accounted for, safe and sound.

Still feeling a little wired I quickly type in my passcode and pull up the GPS on my mom's and sister's phones. Mom is in her office in downtown Rose Grove. Eve is on shift at the hospital in Roxwell, and both Zoe and Jade are on campus around two hours away from here. I can feel myself breathing a little easier, so I log out. I told Mama I'd stopped checking on them, but what they don't know won't hurt them.

Switching my alerts to my watch, I grab my laptop and balance it on my forearm, getting everything open as I walk into the common room where I can hear Marx going off at Savage.

"OK fuckers. This is the second time we've been attacked in our own house and I dont know about you, but I've had

92

e-fucking-nough of it. Savage, this seems like your shit you brought to our doorstep, so I hope you have a fucking clue on how to fix it." Marx shoots daggers at the other man, who does not seem the least bit concerned.

"Fuck man, I would if I could, but this only happens when we're in Rose Grove." He shrugs his shoulders and looks at his SAA Dex, who nods in agreement. Everyone is quiet as that sinks in. Coming to a stop at an empty space at one of the dining tables, I place my laptop down before making myself comfortable. Looking across the room, I see Chewy in her favorite spot, perched on Rhodie's knee, squishing her lip.

"So, you've never been attacked at home?" Chewy asks abruptly, cutting Marx off. He just rolls his eyes and gestures for her to carry on.

Savage shakes his head. "The two times it's happened is when we've been here."

"Very interesting," Chewy says, stroking her imaginary "thinking" beard. "Ana, you still having shipments tampered with?"

Ana nods "Yup. We thought we nipped it in the bud when we found the men that were being paid off by Hammer, but we had another shipment arrive today that was all messed up. Roman is tightening up security. We have another shipment coming in two days that Savage and Dex are transporting, and neither of us can afford for it to be missing any product."

Chewy spins to look at Savage and Dex, making them jump with her sudden movement.

"Right, so we can assume Hammer is after you because you cut him from his own club. His men only attack us when you guys are here and I would imagine that's because DRMC and Death Riders are now allies. If he takes out both clubs, that gives him control of a larger territory and the ability to move anything he likes. The question is, why fuck with the Bratva and how the hell did he get in there in the first place?" Chewy asks the room.

I tap away on my keys, searching for any and every link there could be between the MC's, bratva, and Hammer, coming up short. Although there is something that has been bugging me since Remy landed here. After Flack got shot it was mentioned that he requested Remy for the hacker role to get her off compound because he thought shit was about to go down. He has another daughter, so why only send one?

Chewy must have the same train of thought that I do, asking Savage outright. "Last time this happened, you said that Flack had been getting paranoid. That's why he wanted Remy here?"

"Yeah. He's been antsy since we put Hammer out. We thought he was just being paranoid. Although after he was shot, we've been looking into our books and things in the clubhouse. Whatever he knows, it's enough for Hammer to shoot him and to keep coming after us. All of us."

Dayz nods once and then leaves the room without any warning.

"I fucking hate when she does that," Rider says to no one in particular. "Just leaves you hanging, no explanation at all."

"Chewy said you may need our input." Remy's husky voice quietly addresses the room. Rider jumps as she's standing closest to him and he hadn't even noticed her and her father were there.

"Fuck! You need a bell, girl." He says, his large hand splayed across his chest.

"Sorry 'bout that," she whispers. I hate when she makes herself small. Her gaze catches mine and I try to transfer my strength to her through a look. She must sense what I'm trying to do as she nods at me and gives me a small smile.

"Thanks Remy, Flack." Marx nods at them both as Chewy takes a seat in Rhodie's lap. "Savage said you had an idea shit was going South with Hammer. Was that before or after you kicked him out?" Marx says in a slightly softer voice than usual. Remy does that. She makes us less gruff and growly. Well, all of us except Switch.

Flack opens his mouth to speak, but Remy beats him to it. "It wasn't Dad. It was me. I overheard some things and told my dad about it."

We watch as she pulls her shoulders back and raises her head to look at Marx and then Savage.

"I-I don't have all the information yet, but with Wire and Chewys' help, I will. And I will kill the man that put that effing bullet in my dad."

"Good girl," Flack says at the same time as Chewy and Ana. My brothers all look a little taken aback by her words, which is funny in itself given that she said 'effing' instead of fuck, but that doesn't stop us from banging our fists on the table to give her our support. She looks around the room, a blush growing on her cheeks. Catching her eye, I send her a wink and she smiles wide.

"What do you know so far, Rem?" Savage asks her.

"Well, you know how no one ever notices me around the compound?" She says, her voice growing stronger, eyebrows raised. Savage looks embarrassed as fuck, and so does Dex. He goes to say something, but before he can, Remy puts her hand up to stop him. "It's OK, Pres, it was my choice. It's just how I am, or was." She looks around at the DRMC men and gives us a little smile. "Anyway, I never really paid too much attention to what I heard because it was always club business, so I stayed out of it. But before the stuff with Kraykowski, I overheard Hammer. Speaking Russian." She looks at me before darting her gaze back to Savage.

"How do you know it was Russian?" Marx softly asks. It freaks me out when he speaks in a soft voice like that. But I guess it's preferable to his usual way of barking at people.

She stares at him for a moment before answering. "Because it sounds a lot like when Dex talks to his mom," All the eyes in the clubhouse shoot to Dex.

"Both my parents are Russian immigrants. All above board." He grits out. Savage places a hand on his shoulder as Marx eyes him slightly before giving him a chin lift. All the brothers know that both me and the Tombs ran prelim background checks on Savage's men before they became our allies. Nothing was flagged, but it is a wild coincidence. Especially with us trying to find a link between Hammer and the Bratva.

Remy continues talking, "No one ever notices me around the club, it's just how it is. Hammer was the same. He had started taking more and more phone calls when I was around, speaking Russian. I told my dad, and he said he'd keep an eye on him."

"When was this?" Savage prods.

"Around a month before the Kraykowski thing."

"Weren't you already Pres by that time Savage?" Marx says

"We were in the transition then. Flack was the one who led the charge in getting Hammer to step down."

"No wonder you got your ass shot," Pops pipes up, tipping his chin at Flack, who just grins back. Pops' eyes then dart to Remy "Oh, sorry girl" She smiles sweetly at him, crinkles her nose and shrugs.

"So I think we agree Hammer is fucking with us all, MC and Bratva. Around the time Remy is talking about there were three Russians at play. Roman was running the Bratva here, Ushakov was pulling strings from Russia, and Kovalev was in the skin trade. Savage, your MC under Hammer's leadership were still 1 percenters, although you never traded in skin, so if he was headed down that track he could have been in business with either of them way back then, and Roman, along with the rest of us, shut it all down. That could explain why he has a hard on for us," Dayz says, looking around the room at everyone who had a role to play.

"Motherfucker. We should have just taken him out," Savage moans as he runs a hand down his face.

"We need to find who he's working with. How does he know when you guys are on a run?" Dayz looks to the Death Riders, who look at each other before muttering "Fuck" under their breaths.

"Remy, is there anything else you can remember? Names, places, dates?" Chewy asks, her eyes extra stare-y. She does that when she's in the zone.

She shakes her head for a moment, her short blonde hair whipping around her face. Her brows are pinched in the center when she stops abruptly. "Wait, he kept saying '*devushka*'. He said it more than once. I'm not sure what it means."

We all look toward Dex, who frowns. "It means 'girl' or 'the girl'. Can you remember any other words, Remy?"

She closes her eyes and I see her lips working. "'*Devushka moy*' that's what he kept saying. He was adamant. He growled it before hanging up."

Dex curses under his breath and runs his hands through his hair. " *Devushka moy* means 'the girl is mine'. What girl?"

Theories and murmurs go around the room.

Marx's whistle splits the air, gaining everyone's attention. "Looks like we have shit to sort out. Ana, if he's working with someone in the Bratva, we need to know. Savage, start cleaning house. Hammer may still have allies within your walls. Wire, Chewy and Remy, you try to figure out who this girl is. Is she someone we already saved when we shut down the trafficking ring last time, or is she someone else? Tombs brothers along with Fox, Nitro, Sniper and Tank, I need ears on the ground. What's the word on the street? We got our work cut out for us."

Chewy claps her hands, rubbing them together with a grin on her face.

"Why the fuck does she look so excited about that?" Dex says under his breath.

"Because it means me and Pops can try out some new techniques, Dex."

I watch Dex shudder and chuckle to myself.

Remy

I lean back and stretch my arms up over my head. The pull on my muscles creates a good type of ache. I've been hunched over, staring at my screen, researching anything I can think of to find even a sliver of a hint where Hammer could be hiding. Two nights ago, we found out that Ivan was Hammer's contact in the Bratva, which devastated Ana. So much so that she "went bush" as her mom says, to get her head around her friend's betrayal. Gus followed his wife to make sure she was OK, and they decided to stay a few days to decompress in Roman's cabin. Which, I have a feeling, is why all the Tombs have been hanging around the clubhouse the past two days. Gus hasn't been here to tell them to get back to the office.

With no sign of Hammer on any of the programs I am now proficient in, I instead try to relax. I've never been one to meditate, but now may be the perfect time. If I can relax my mind and think through everything I know about Hammer, I may be able to find a lead. Leaning my head back in the comfiest office chair I've ever sat in, I close my eyes and rock slightly; the movement soothing me further.

"Devochka moya, ty menya slyshish'? Ona moya" Hammer grips his phone and
growls. *"Fuck!"*

"All good Pres?"

"What the fuck do you think, Snake? Fucking Devil's Rose MC –"

I can't make out anything else because they walk the other way down the hall. I wait a moment longer, not wanting either of them to know that I may have heard them. I'm not scared of Hammer, but I've never been fond of Carter; Snake, as he's now called. It suits him. He's as slippery and as mean as a snake. I wonder if he will leave when Hammer leaves? I shouldn't know this, but my dad and Savage are going to ask him to stand down. What he's doing, the way he wants the club running, it's dangerous. It's always been dangerous, but if he's in bed with the Russians, it'll mean he wants to get into the skin trade, and I know Savage won't let him. Well, Nat won't let Savage. She'd kill him if he tried.

Deciding the coast is clear, I move down the hall, heading for the common room. As soon as I enter, Hammer steps in front of me.

"Hey Remy Girl, what've you been doing?"

"Oh, hey Uncle Hammer. I've just been in my room, reading." I

99

wave my Kindle at him and keep my face pleasant. His eyes dart all over my face, searching for the lie. When he's satisfied with whatever he was looking for, he takes his finger, his silver skull ring glinting in the light, running it through my bangs, sweeping them to the side. He stares at me as his finger runs down my cheek.

"Fuck, Rem, you look more and more like your mother every day. You ever think about growing your hair out?"

I take a step back, putting space between us. My movement snaps Hammer out of his thoughts, and he smiles at me, but not before I see something flash in his eyes.

"You'd look good with all this blonde hair out of your face, give everyone a chance to see how beautiful you are, doll."

"Maybe. Um, I'll think about it." I give him a smile, side step him and walk toward my dad, who's been looking over at us with a frown.

"You good baby girl? What did Hammer want?"

"I need to talk to you, Dad. Something weird is going on." He does the same thing Hammer did, scrutinizes my face. But where Hammer's felt uncomfortable, my dad's is out of concern.

"Sure thing Rem. Let's take a ride."

My body rocks a little longer, but nothing else comes to me, other than how uncomfortable I felt with Hammer in that moment. The only Death Rider's brother I ever had that feeling with was Snake. Hammer had always, until that moment, been an uncle to me. When I told my dad what happened, that's when the ball really started rolling. Savage asked Hammer to leave. He took half the MC with him, and then two months later I moved here.

With nothing helpful coming to me, I stretch, this time from side to side. My stomach lets out a groan and I remember I haven't had a lot to eat today. Since that day in the library with

Jovie, I've been taking extra lunch food and sharing it with her. Her dad has continued to be late for pickup, and when I asked Jovie if he had a new job or anything she told me he doesn't have a job but he's been busy with his friends. I have a bad feeling about this, but with no proof, there's nothing I can do about the situation. I tried looking online for any information on Jovie and not a lot came up. There are no records of a Jovie Spencer anywhere.

I even spoke to Mags about Jovie. Not all the details, of course, that's not how we work. But he knows enough to know that I'm worried about leaving her with her awful father. So much so he's been pushing for us to meet up and I said yes. The feelings I have for Mags are real, deep. He's my person. He always has been. But, my growing friendship with Wire, if that's what this is, has me feeling like I'm being disloyal to Mags. I'm hoping meeting up will make my feelings for both men much clearer.

I spin my seat and then decide to head to the kitchen. I'm alone at the control center and I feel like a snack and maybe some company. I've been getting a lot better at engaging the brothers in conversation, and I've been enjoying my time with them. They're all so different. Some, like Rider, are really funny and always trying to get a rise out of his brothers. Others like Tank and Sniper are quieter. They're the ones I'd say I was closest to. At the moment, though, they'll all be in Church.

The scent of brownies or cookies wafts down the hall and I follow my nose until I'm on the other side of the large stainless steel island facing Ana's mom Debs. A brownie big enough to feed an army sitting on the counter between us.

"Mmmm, they look and smell so good!"

"Well, help yourself, *kotiro*! Take one for all the hard working security team too. It'll help you relax a little." She winks at me, so I take one gratefully and let the sticky sweetness play on my tongue. It's soft, chocolatey, gooey with just the right amount of chew. In other words, it's delicious. There is an earthy hint to it as well, so it must be a secret Debs ingredient. I take another bite and try not to groan too loud. The brownie is so good I don't even realize I've closed my eyes in bliss until I open them to a glass of cold milk in front of me.

"Thank you so much, Debs. This is just what I needed."

"Been a day, huh? Tell Mama Debs all about it while I make another batch. You know what these boys are like."

I shrug, pull up a chair and tell Debs all about Jovie and my concerns. She listens intently to me, holds my hand when my lip wobbles, and gives me a hug when I tell her how powerless I feel to help. I know she's not mine, and I know I've not known her long, but somehow Jovie has burrowed her way into my heart and I really want to help her.

"Well, *kotiro*, I think you should do whatever you need to do to help that baby. If all we can do at the moment is make sure she's getting a good meal, then that's what we'll do." She pats my hand and goes to open her mouth to say something else when Chewy comes storming through the kitchen, heading straight through. She has brown gunk on her hands all the way up to her elbows, and the smell emanating from her is a mix of Port-a-Potty and roadkill. What the heck has she been up to?

Sharing a look with Debs, we both shrug at each other. Debs pops another slice of brownie on my plate before looking at me with raised brows. I take the plate, thanking her, then heading back to the control center. I have a dirtbag to look for.

Chapter Eight

St_Margarita: *Do you ever think about having a family?*
Beretta_Penn: *Kinda need a husband for that stuff.*
St_Margarita: *So do you want one?*
Beretta_Penn: *Yeah. I always wanted to have a husband who loved me, maybe some kids. Why? Sleeping with nameless, faceless women getting to you?*
St_Margarita: *Maybe. That and I can't really see myself building a life with those women.*
Beretta_Penn: *Wow, I bet they love that.*
St_Margarita: *I want someone I can have more with than just hot sex. Someone I can talk to.*
Beretta_Penn: *Have you, I don't know, tried talking to these women?*
St_Margarita: *Yes, smart ass. Anyway, I've been thinking...*
Beretta_Penn: *Hope you didn't hurt yourself.*
St_Margarita: *Har. Har. If we're both single at 29 I say we get married.*
Beretta_Penn: *You do know that we don't know anything about each other right?*
St_Margarita: *We know everything about each other. And I'm sure I can look past you being gross because I like your personality.*
Beretta_Penn: *The charm you exude is almost suffocating.*

St_Margarita: So? What do you say? Marry me at 29?
Beretta_Penn: Will saying yes make you stop talking nonsense?
St_Margarita: Never.
Beretta_Penn: Yes.

Wire

Marx slams his gavel on the table, and before he can even get Church started Rider butts in.

"Nice bracelet you have on there, Pres." He sends a shit-eating smirk in Marx's direction and we all sit silently waiting to see what he's going to do. Especially with his VP and blood brother staring at him.

"It's from Chewy. Jealous you didn't get one?" Marx smirks back, bushy brows raised waiting for the penny to drop. He watches as Rider looks around the table to see every brother, other than him and Rhodie, all have their friendship bracelets on display. Once it dawns on Rider, he splutters, and Marx's grin grows wider.

"What the fuck!? How did you all get them and I didn't? Rhodie, why the fuck don't you have one?" Rider demands, spinning to eyeball Rhodie, who shrugs.

"I'm her boyfriend. I don't need a best friend bracelet. I get blow jobs."

Rider frowns at him before jabbing his finger at me. "What about you? How the hell did you get one before me? We all know I'm Chewy's bestie!"

"Well, Marx is her ultimate best friend. This is my 'Best Tech

Friend and Almost Brother bracelet'."

Tank raises his hand. "I'm her Best Big Friend."

Followed by Sniper "Best Shooter Friend."

Soon, it goes around the room "Best Dr. Friend." "Best Road Captain Friend," "Best Group Sex friend. Although that's tied with Fox." Nitro says, before Fox holds up his wrist to show that their colors match.

"What the fuck," Rider whispers out as everyone shows him theirs. It turns out that in Chewy's world, you only have one best friend. If you like anyone else they have to be in their own category. Remy is her Best Vagina Friend which means she got a bright pink bracelet. Ana doesn't count because she's in the Best Sister in Law category.

"Rider, stop sulking." Marx shoots at him with yet another smirk on his face. "Brothers, we have a few things to cover today. First off, I'm sure you have all heard that Hammer's contact in the Bratva was Ivan. Roman dealt with him after squeezing him for information." Marx frowns and blows out a breath. "Hammer is smuggling drugs inside girls, then selling them both."

A series of curses go around the table.

"I have Wire, Remy and Chewy on it trying to find anything regarding these girls. How he's transporting them, where he's getting them, where they are now so we can rescue them." Marx looks around the table.

"I've had my ear to the ground and Jules has asked his people. No one has heard anything on our streets. I'm thinking of heading to the next towns over. See if they've heard anything. After the ass kicking we gave them, Hammer would have to be a special kind of stupid to be taking girls off our streets." Judge says.

"I agree. My team has found nothing that says he's doing anything other than laying fucking low and regrouping." I look around at my brothers, who are all in agreement.

"Take Sniper, Tank and Fox with you. Ferret out any information you can. We can't do anything to shut Hammer down until we know more. Fuck." Marx runs a hand down his face and nods once at Judge before leaning forward, resting his thick forearms on the table.

"Second point of business. Tav has spoken to me about prospecting. Has anyone got any reservations taking him on?" He looks around the table and none of the brothers look worried.

"I have no concerns. I've seen what that family can do. Tav is easygoing, and the most normal in that whole ass family. I'm good with it." Rider says, waiting to see if anyone has anything else to say.

When no one has anything to add Marx takes it as time to call a vote. "All in favor?"

Ayes go around the table, and Marx nods his head. "Good. He'll need a sponsor. Rhodie is his brother-in-law, so he's out."

"I'll sponsor him." Tank taps the table. Marx looks thoughtful for a split second before he agrees. It'll be a good match. Tav is open, thoughtful and eager to please. Tank is solid, dependable and one of the most patient people I've ever met. They'll get on well.

"Next point of business. Keep a lookout for fuckers hanging around the businesses. Tank and Sniper have caught one sneaking around the tow yard. Action plan is to grab the prick and find out what he wants. Stay alert and feed back anything that doesn't look right." He swings his gaze around the table to make sure we are all on board. "Right. We're done here."

Marx slams down the gavel, effectively dismissing us. We file out of church, pick up our phones, and head for the bar. Well, my brothers do. I head straight back to the control center. I have shit to do. It's been days with no trace of Hammer, the drugs he stole, or the girls he's trafficking. I need to find something, anything, before I go fucking insane.

Heading down the hall, I can hear Chewy chatting away. Is that Remy? The husky tone that goes straight to my balls is the same, but this voice is stronger, less of a whisper.

"- and then he felt my boob. It took him ages to find my nipples and then he twiddled them like he was tuning one of those old radios!" Chewy's laugh drifts down the hall. "He couldn't even get it up because he was too drunk, so he tried to put his soft member inside me and it didn't work. That's why I'm still a virg-"

"Whoa whoa whoa, what the hell?" I ask Remy, who goes bright red and giggles. My gaze swings toward Chewy briefly before I do a double take. "Why is your hair wet?"

Remy is boneless in her chair, her arms drooping over the armrests. Chewy is sitting beside her with wet hair. Both have a still shot of Fox and Nitro's garage on the big screen.

Chewy eyes me for a moment before shrugging. "I accidentally blew up some folks and I'm fairly certain Remy is high from Mama Debs' special brownie. Oh, and also, that skinny gross dude that works at Devil Riders Garage has been palming the cash payments."

My head spins to the screen she's pointing at, Remy lumbers forward, slaps her hand on the keyboard to hit play and I watch as this fucker blatantly takes the cash the customer hands over to him and puts it straight in his pocket.

"Fuck, I'll let Marx know and get someone to bring him in."

"CHEWY WHY THE FUCK IS THERE AN ARM ON MY ROOF?" Marx bellows down the hall. And Remy breaks into another fit of giggles.

Remy

Chewy is most definitely certifiably nuts and a genius in equal measure. After we caught that guy stealing cash, Marx sent two of the brothers to go pick him up while the rest of us stayed here listening to Chewy explain to Marx why there was an arm on the roof. And various other body parts lying around. There was science and history rolled into her explanation and in the end Marx massaged his temples and told her to clean it up and figure out a better way to get rid of bodies. One that doesn't entail them exploding.

On the upside, watching Chewy in the hot seat sobered me up fast. Now I'm standing in a rather cheery room in the back shed waiting for Chewy to question the skinny gross dude from the garage.

I have heard stories of what Chewy can do, but I've not seen it with my own eyes. Savage, Dex and Dad told me a little of what they've seen and they sounded very impressed. Maybe even a little scared. Which makes me laugh because they're all really huge tough bikers and Chewy is, well, she's Chewy.

Wire tried to convince me to stay behind, but I very strongly pointed out that I may be quiet, but I'm not sheltered. I may have also poked him in the chest. His very hard chest. He wasn't happy, but he conceded as long as I stood where he could keep an eye on me. So I'm on the other side of the room, in prime viewing location for whatever Chewy has planned.

"Chewy, for the love of all that's fucking holy, can you get on with this without us having to listen to Now That's What I Call Music?" Marx runs a hand down his face, before kicking the leg of the man tied to a chair in the middle of the room over what looks to be a drain. "Stop fucking whining."

The man snivels a little more, but at least he's doing it quietly.

"Bestie, I can definitely do that for you. Babe? Mind putting on Ultimate 2000s for me, please?" Chewy smiles sweetly at her man, tipping her head back and puckering her lips for a kiss. Rhodie obliges, pats her ass, and the frantic beats of Ricky Martin fill the space.

"Fuck me" is groaned out and I'm not sure which brother it was. I've been here for over two months now and I've gotten to know all the brothers, just not by their groans. Oh wait, that sounds wrong. Not like that. I cringe internally. I can feel my cheeks heating and hope no one else notices. Tipping my head forward, I let my hair cover my face. Thank the stars my sister Sunny talked me into getting a bob cut with a fringe. Even if Hammer didn't like it. That sends me back to my earlier thoughts, and it makes me wince. Wire frowns at me, his head tipping to the side. I shake my head at him and send him a tight smile. And a thumbs up for good measure.

Looking around the room, I catalog the men. None of them are looking at me, of course. They have more interesting things to look at, like Chewy putting on some type of Hazmat suit with Rhodie's help. The members are dotted around the room, leaning on walls or the stainless steel workbench, watching

Chewy attach something to a long chain hanging from the ceiling.

"What have you got in mind, Chewy?" Switch booms out. The big red head is almost the polar opposite to me. His voice is like a foghorn compared to my much quieter tone.

"Chinese drip torture. Although we don't have days to wait, so I'm going to speed it up a little. I just need to wait for my beautiful assistant." Chewy gives a slightly unhinged grin. I look toward Rhodie, but he's joined Judge, Tank, and Nitro on the couch in the corner.

I'm not sure who Chewy's beautiful assistant is, but I take the time to observe my surroundings while we wait. I'm not sure if it's my natural setting or whether living with the Death Riders has made me this way, but I've always preferred observing to joining in. You can tell a lot about a person by watching them when they think no one is looking. Taking a peek around the room, my eyes land on Wire. He's one of the brothers leaning on the workbench. He has his ever present laptop open and I can't quite tell what he's watching from all the way over here, but I know it'll be one of the many cameras he has around the clubhouse and the MC owned businesses in town. Sometimes I've noticed him watching a beautiful older black woman, but I've not asked him who she is. That is none of my business.

The door is kicked open, slamming against the wall before bouncing off, making us all jump.

"Don't worry everyone, I have arrived!" A gruff voice sing songs. This is met with a mix of eye rolls, chuckles, and Marx cursing under his breath.

"Sorry we're late. We had to wait for Pops to finish in the pantry." Tav says in a tight voice.

"What the hell was he doing in the pantry?" Rhodie asks,

frowning.

"Debs." Tav looks slightly green at this confession, which is really something given the Tombs family all have really good tans. Jules just looks pissed, which I've come to know is his usual setting.

"Shit Stain! I need you to wrap this belt over the cocksuckers forehead, yank his head back and fasten it to the crossbar of the chair. Got it? Or you want me to draw you a picture?"

Rhodie shakes his head at Pops, but does exactly as he is told. In no time at all, the thief's head is tipped back, looking up at the ceiling. He's stopped sniveling, mainly because it's very hard to cry with your head on that angle.

"Please! I-I'm sorry! I didn't mean to! Please!" He begs, but he isn't going to be let off just yet.

"Now, now Nigel, you should have thought about what we'd do to you before you tried to relieve us of our hard earned cash," Chewy says in a faux soothing tone.

"I had no choice! He said he was going to sell my sister and niece if I didn't pay off my debts! Please!"

That has us all stopping. There's only one person in the area who would threaten that.

Marx steps right up to Nigel, leaning in close. "Tell us what we need to know and we may look at letting you go-"

A drop of something lands right between Nigel's eyes, a splash of it hitting Marx's cut burning a tiny hole into the worn leather.

Marx's head whips around to look at Chewy and Pops, who look a little too pleased with themselves. "Chewy! What the fuck?" he yells over Nigel's screams.

"Hydrofluoric Acid drip torture. Gives us results in a fraction of the time," Chewy says in her best game show voice as Pops stands next to Nigel, waving his hands around like a magician's assistant.

Marx sucks in a breath and then lets it out. "I really want to be pissed, but it's a fucking good idea. Carry on." Marx waves her on, stomps toward the couch and stares at the four men wedged in there until Nitro sighs and gets up.

Chewy gives Marx a dazzling smile, then fiddles with the drippy thing, making her torture device drip faster, each drop hitting it's target. I'm not sure what Chewy and Pops are saying to him but their voices are kept quiet, almost nurturing as they question him. Nigel is answering as best he can while panting and screaming on and off.

Wire catches my eye and sends me a smile before looking around the room, like I had been doing. His eyes dart back to mine and he shakes his head back and forth with his lips pursed as if he wants to laugh. He winks my way, which makes my lower stomach clench and I have to look away. Luckily, I do because I manage to catch the moment Nigel's eyelid slides right off his eyeball onto the floor.

"I did not expect that. Dayzy girl, write that down in our notebook,"

Chewy salutes Pops and gets busy making notes. I was so distracted by my thoughts that I have no idea what they've found out. Hopefully, they have all the information they were after because Nigel lets out a weird rattle and then slumps.

"Tav and Jules, you're on clean up,"

Tav whistles while going to the cupboard in the corner I never even noticed and starts pulling out all manner of things.

Now that the show is over, the brothers all move toward the door, ignoring the Tombs family doing...whatever it is they do.

"Come on, Remy, let's get back to our safe zone. Away from

all these crazies." Wire says, smirking back at the Tombs family standing around Nigel's body, pointing at things.

"Hurry Rem, before he gets to his favorite part." Wire roughly whispers in my ear, gently pushing me toward the door. Before I can ask him what he means, I hear Pops yell out, "Oh wait, I love this part!"

The door swings shut on Pops, warbling out the high notes of Sisco's Thong Song.

Chapter Nine

St_Margarita: Have you ever wondered about whether or not we should ever meet up?
Beretta_Penn: Maybe. Why?
St_Margarita: Dunno. I guess I sometimes wonder what it would be like to know the real you.
Beretta_Penn: You know the real me. Just like I know the real you.

Wire

A bang down the hall jolts me awake, my neck pulling from the angle I must have dozed off on. Fuck! Blinking through the fog, I lean forward to see if my searches have thrown up anything useful. Nigel may have been a thief, but that doesn't mean his sister and niece need to be put in Hammer's cross hairs. Between him and the guy that's been seen hanging around our tow yard, it seems all I'm doing is staring at screens waiting for an answer and not getting any. That's not even factoring in that me, Chewy and Remy are all searching for Hammer and still haven't pinned him down. I've never felt this useless ever.

I scrub my hands down my face before looking at my screen. Seeing nothing of any use causes a growl to rip through my throat. Fuck this. I can feel the frustration rising and the only person who can talk me down is Retta. For 15 years she's been my other half. The person I turn to when I need an ear to listen, or a shoulder to cry on. Recently, though, someone else has been creeping her way into that space. Remy.

I run my hand down my face to clear the confusion not only in my mind but also my heart. Somehow, both Retta and Remy have been haunting my dreams. The more I get to know Remy, the harder I find it to get her out of my head. Her scent, her touch, her voice, they all haunt me. When I close my eyes, she's there, yet she isn't just her. She somehow embodies all the things I love about Retta. Her unwavering support of me. Her trust. Her geeky sense of humor. Not only am I failing at my job by not finding what we need, I'm also failing in my friendships with two amazing women. The only way I can see to move forward is to meet Retta and see if there is anything between us. It's only fair. She was in my life first. Best-case scenario we meet, decide to remain besties and I can see where these Remy feelings leave me. Because there is something there. Whether it's a real attraction connection or a more protective connection, I'm still unsure. Or maybe I am sure and am just kidding myself that we're friends. I'm sure friends don't pop a chubby everytime they see them. Fuck, I'm turning into a pussy.

"Hey Wire, whatcha working on?" Speak of the Devil, Remy pops her head in the doorway.

"Same shit as before, Rem. Same shit as before." Letting out a sigh, my shoulders slump. "I'm sure we'll get a break soon. Just frustrated is all."

"I hear ya. I've been trying to recall more from the last few times I overheard Hammer, but nothing. Although I did have an idea. His right-hand man is a guy named Snake. Carter Price. He may be easier to find? I hadn't looked into him yet because I was sort of looking into Jovie's family." I grimace at her, causing her to make a huffing sound before shrugging. "Yeah, I can't stop thinking about that little girl. Whatever is going on at home isn't ideal, but yet she still turns up every day, super positive and polite."

"I get it Rem. You just want to help her."

She gives me a tight smile before sitting in her usual spot. She spins her chair toward me so her body is facing me.

"She, she just reminds me of me when I was a kid. I had Miss Shawna. This amazing, larger than life black woman who treated me like I was her own. She's the one who got me into computers." She smiles to herself and I let her memories distract her and I take in her face. Her dirty blonde hair is looking slightly wavy today, her bangs hanging in her bright blue eyes slightly, glasses perched on her nose, giving her an effortlessly beautiful look. Like a woman you'd see in a magazine, maybe.

"Well, I think it's cool that Jovie has Miss Remy to look out for her."

Her face lights up and she gives me a smile before frowning. "Anyway, Marx asked me to come get you. Apparently, things are about to kick off?" She scrunches her brow, looking fucking adorable. I try not to stare at her too much, but there is no denying her beauty. Even in the weird slightly too long plaid skirt and vest combo she's wearing. Complete with another bookish brooch pinned to those distracting tits.

Running a hand down my face to clear my head, I push my

chair back, stand and smile at the little blonde. "Lead the way, babe."

Following her down the hall, I try to keep the conversation light. If I don't, I fear she'll turn around and clock me staring at her ass. There isn't too much to see as her skirt isn't form fitted, but a man can picture what she's hiding under those loose clothes.

We hit the common room, and it seems everyone is here, including the whole Tombs family. Debs is handing out brownies that do not contain any weed, thanks to the Remy mishap.

Everyone is shooting the shit and Ana is not so quietly asking Gus why she is missing out on her Kung Pao chicken. Tav clears his throat before stepping up to the front of the room, standing next to Marx.

"I, well, Marx has an announcement, and I wanted you all here for this," Tav says in a clear voice before stepping to the side.

"OK, listen up, you fuc-" Marx's eyes dart to Debs before he clears his throat, "I mean, you folks," He looks at Debs again, who beams at him and gives him two thumbs up. Nodding, he carries on, "I would like to welcome our newest prospect to the Devil's Rose MC family, although you all know the cheeky asshole. Welcome Tav!" He whacks Tav on the back and hands him over a cut that says "Prospect" on the front.

We all let out loud whoops, stomping our boots. All the brothers including myself head over to Tav to beat him on the back in congratulations. And to fuck with him. Takoda is lining beers up along the bar top to be handed out when we all freeze as Ana bursts into tears and Pops starts yelling nonsensical shit.

"It's obvious what's wrong with her." Pops points out, like it is, in fact obvious. To him anyway. "There are communists in the funhouse. Japan is attacking." None of us know what the fuck he's talking about and we don't know how to stop the rant. "The English have landed. Granny is coming in the red car. The painters are in. Shark week, bloody Mary, the crimson wa-"

"Fuck's sake, I'm not on my period. I'm PREGNANT!" Ana yells out, essentially shutting up Pops and everyone else in a 2-mile radius.

The room is silent for a split second before whoops and banging start up once more. Remy, bouncing next to me has me looking down at her, her hands clasped in front of her mouth as she lets out a little whoop. She's so fucking cute that she completely had me forgetting that I was in a state not five minutes ago, wanting to message Retta to talk me down. I shake my head, feeling guilty that Remy is filling in some of Retta's space within me. I need to sort this shit out. Pulling up our message thread, I type out a date and time to meet.

Saint_Margarita: Hey babe, can you meet me tomorrow at 5pm? At that lookout spot between our towns that we spoke about. Lemme know. Xx.

I watch the tiny screen for a beat but note that she's offline, so I'll have to wait for a reply. Remy rushes off to congratulate her friend, so I sidle up to the bar for a beer. I tip my chin at Takoda when he places a cold one in front of me and spin to look out into the common room, leaning my back against the bar. Marx grabs a beer and mimics my position, watching the goings on.

"Did you ever think the MC would be this big and chaotic?" I ask, taking a pull of my beer.

Marx raises his brow at me before taking a pull of his own, swallowing before answering me. "When I got back from deployment I was lost and DRMC was a dying club. It was just the old boys then, Dad and his crew but it was a safe space for me. When Mad Dog handed over the reins he told me to build something new." He picks at the label on the bottle in his hand with his blunt nail before looking at me. "I didn't think it would get this big, but I had hoped. After I got out I needed a place like this."

"So did I."

"I remember, brother." He looks at me before turning back to the room. "You're not the only one, either. Almost every brother here needed a place to land. I hoped it would be like this. But I did not foresee Tuesday Tombs and all that she brings."

I let out a snort, looking around the room until I spot Chewy. She's leaning against Rhodie, a few of the brothers are standing around her as she's animatedly talking about something. Using her hands, she mimes something blowing up.

"I can't believe she fucking blew up the nomad bodies by accident. What the fuck?" Marx grumbles. "Ah shit." Following his gaze, I watch Pops walk toward us.

"Boys. I think I'll celebrate my impending great grandbaby with a nice cold one. And then a hot one with my lady." He waggles his brows at us. Debs is walking our way with a tray of brownies, stopping to offer them to Fox, Nitro and some bunnies.

Marx watches Debs for a moment before turning to Pops. "I thought you and Rosie were a thing?"

"Who's Rosie?" Debs asks the three of us. That woman is quick on her feet and has the hearing of a bat if she heard that.

"Oh, Rosie's is the diner in town. Great food there." Pops

says, smiling down at Debs.

"Oh, I've seen that place! We should go there one day!" She presses a kiss to Pops leathery cheek before moving on to work the room with her tray.

All three of us watch her for a beat before Pops spins around and steps right into Marx's space.

"You shit stirring son of a bitch! You keep your fat trap shut, you hear me? Otherwise, I will permanently shut it for you." He mean mugs Marx for a moment, which is hard to do when Marx is well over 6 feet tall and Pops is 100 years old. Somehow, he pulls it off.

"Wait, you're not seeing the both of them, are you?" I ask. I like the old guy, but I love Mama Debs and I'm not down with him seeing two nice ladies at once.

Pops' head snaps in my direction. "Of course I'm fucking not! Do I look like the type of motherfucker that would mess with a woman like that? I'm a fucking gentleman!" He huffs, gives me the stink eye, which shows me exactly where Jules gets that look from, shakes his head in disappointment and stalks off with his beer in his hand.

"That crazy old man is scary." Takoda says, wiping down the bar top.

Marx and I share a look, and I try to hold in my smirk. This feels good. I can admit that sometimes I get a little obsessive about my job in the MC. But Remy drawing me out of my room to enjoy this with my MC family is what I needed.

The pocket with my phone in it vibrates at the same time Marx answers his phone. "Yeah?"

He stiffens, growls and then hangs up. His loud as fuck whistle has us stopping, all eyes glued to him. "We got a police team at the gate with a warrant to search the premises. Stay calm, do as you're told, and don't be fucking weird. Chewy, I'm looking at you."

She waves her hand dismissively at him. Rhodie nods at Marx and pulls Chewy's back flush to his front, wrapping his arms around her waist.

Marx turns my way, leaning in. "Call your mom Wire. We might need her."

Nodding at my Pres, I press her quick dial number. "Hey Momma."

Marx

Bracing myself for what is about to happen, I notice my men slowly corralling the women in our midst into the center of the room, creating a protective layer between them and whoever is about to burst through the doors.

A loud bang sounds out as around a dozen men storm inside. One in particular seems to be reveling in the power he has in this moment, getting in the men's faces, shoving and being a fucking tool.

"Officer Martin! The MC is cooperating. But by all means, carry on with your little dog amongst big dogs act if you want to be written up for excessive force."

Letting out a breath I didn't even know I was holding, I thank whoever the fuck is in charge that the senior ranking officer tonight is Moss Davies, a guy I went to school with and who knows the MC well.

"Pres, sorry to interrupt what looks like a nice family evening." Davies comes to a stop in front of me, waving a paper in his hand.

"Moss, I can't say I'm happy to see you, but of all the people they could have sent, I'm glad it was you. Sheriff too busy?"

Moss tries to hide his smirk but I see it all the same. "He's a very busy man. I think he's at a charity dinner in Roxwell this evening."

Figures. I have no idea how that fat fuck keeps his position. Moss runs most of the policing in our town and the bordering smaller towns.

"What have you got for me?"

"Well, besides that asshole Martin, I have a warrant here allowing us to search the premises -"

"- You know full well we don't get into any illicit substances, let alone weapons."

"Oh, I know that. That's not what we're looking for. A body was found on the edge of the towing yard. Does this woman look familiar at all? Maybe came to one of your parties? Needed her car fixed? Anything?"

He holds up his phone, the picture of a beautiful black woman. She's smiling wide, colorful braids up in a ponytail. Its a fucking shame that the light in her eyes has been snuffed out. My eyes raise to Moss's as I shake my head.

"No, I've never seen her around, I'd remember her. She's stunning."

Moss nods, looking down at his phone. He heaves a breath before looking at me again.

"Looks like she was raped and beaten, a belly full of drugs. Because it's on MC land, we have a warrant to search all your properties, businesses and compound, starting here tonight.

We'll liaise for access to the others tomorrow. The search is for any belongings or trace of this woman and backups of your video surveillance."

Running a hand down my face, I can feel my blood pressure rising. Not because of Moss, but because of the whole fucked up situation. We've had two fucking shootouts at our clubhouse recently and yeah, we may not have neighbors, but we live in a nosey as fuck town. No one called the police then did they? Someone phones in about a body and we're swarmed.

"Fuck. Moss, you know we didn't do this."

"Yeah, I know it's well outside your MO. But we had a tip off and you know we have to follow up. My guess? You pissed someone off." A snort escapes me. Yeah, we've pissed off a few someones. "Let me and my men do our jobs and we'll be out of your hair as soon as."

I tip my chin at him, and he barks orders at his men. He also sends one of his more senior officers with that Officer Martin, who I do not like the look of. Judging by the shitty look on his face, he doesn't like it either. I make a note to have Wire look into him. Rose Grove PD has never had an issue with corruption, but I don't trust the look on that dick's face. He glares at me, holding my gaze as he walks through the doorway and down the long hall where all our rooms are. We sit calmly and quietly while Davies barks orders at his men. I have to hand it to him; he doesn't like a mess. One douchebag tips up the cutlery drawer and Davies makes him put it all back in once he's finished searching.

Officer Martin comes back, clearly not finding what he was hoping to find. Instead of standing down, however, he gets in the faces of our women. Ana is scowling at him, Remy is smiling pleasantly, and Chewy is staring through him. Pissed that he isn't getting the response he's after he gets in Debs' face. She says something to him and he grabs her arm. She's squirming in his grip and I can't make out what he's saying, but whatever it is, it has Pops coming down hard on him.

"You better let her the fuck go, young buck." I can hear Pops sneer from here.

"Or what, old man? This woman," he snarls, "has an illicit substance on her. She's coming with me."

"Let her the fuck go NOW!" Pops roars and then, in an impressive show of athleticism, hits him with one of the most technically beautiful right hooks I've had the chance to witness.

"Aw shit, Pops just knocked him on his ass!" My brothers, who until now had been sitting quietly, are watching with rapt attention as another officer tries to restrain Pops. Debs clearly feels the same about Pops as he does her, because as soon as this happens, she shoves Officer Martin away from her.

"Aue! You leave my man alone you *To Teke!*" She launches herself on the back of the officer trying to restrain Pops who, for an old guy, can really hold his own. Pops has gotten out of the officer's hold and has hit him at least twice already. I mean, there's not really much the pig can do with Debs on his back. Both she and Pops are yelling, and I'm fairly certain Debs has bitten the offending officer.

Moss sighs deeply beside me. "You wanna help me with this?"

I give him a smirk and shake my head. However in the next moment that smirk slips right off my face as Officer Martin pulls out his gun and raises it to aim at Debs.

"Officer Martin! Bring a car around." Moss storms toward him, eyeballing him until he holsters his gun. He keeps on eyeballing him until Martin leaves in a huff. "Ma'am, sir, I'm going to have to read you your rights and I'm afraid you're coming with us."

Both Pops and Debs spin to look at Sergeant Davies. Pops sizing him up. "You're Flora's boy, right?"

"Yes, sir,"

Pops squints at him before nodding. He lets go of the officer that he has by the scruff and Debs slowly slides off his back. Because she can sometimes be a sweet lady she straightens the officer's collar before letting Pops take her hand, both of them walking through the common room toward the door with the officer they were fighting following close behind. Looking toward the Tombs family I open my mouth to assure them we'll have them out in no time, but, true to form the Tombs aren't worried. Not even a little. They have their phones out and have been filming the whole thing.

"Tombs -"

"Don't worry Marx. He'll be loving this," August cuts me off.

"Mum will be too. Getting arrested in America? We'll never hear the end of it." Ana beams. Fuck's sake.

"Marx, search is over. Wire has sent through footage from all the cameras covering your businesses. My men will go through it and I'll be in touch. I don't need any more women turning up on your doorstep. Or mine."

Nodding, I agree with him. Devil's Rose MC actively works against all violence against women and children. Who the fuck put her on our doorstep?

"I may need to question some of your men, especially the ones that work and run the Main Street garage."

"Then you'll go through our lawyer,"

"Lemme guess, Candice Harvey?" I grin at him while he

curses under his breath. "Great, I'll look forward to her busting my balls."

He holds my gaze for a moment, before breaking into a smile and offering me his hand. "Thanks for making this relatively painless, Johnny."

"I've not been Johnny in a long time, Moss."

"I know. And as much as I respect you and your position here as Pres, I still remember you as the star quarterback whose girlfriend I stole. The only time I ever got one over on you."

I smirk at him before shaking my head. "How'd that work out for you?"

"She left me with a set of twins I couldn't live without."

"Sounds like it worked out well, then." I slap him on his back a little too hard, and he smirks at me while walking out.

"Word to the wise? Lie low for a while."

Chapter Ten

Wire

The door barely shuts behind the last police officer before it's slammed open and the clacking of high heels on the wood floor clip clops in my direction.

"Hey Momma,"

"Hey baby."

My mom kisses me on the cheek and then turns slowly, stopping when she sees Marx. "OK, Pres, hit me with it."

Marx lets her know everything he knows, which at this point is fuck all other than the police are looking for evidence related to a body that was dumped on club-owned property. Momma takes notes in the notepad that she always carries with her, then barks questions at everyone else in the room. Did any of the officers touch us? Did they damage any property? That sorta shit.

"Your mom is beautiful. And awesome," is breathed out next to me. I don't need to turn to see who it is. My body felt Remy's presence when she moved into my orbit.

"Yeah. She's a force to be reckoned with." I smile down at

her before darting my eyes back to my momma.

She is exactly that. After Dad took off, she single-handedly raised me and my sisters. Made sure we all got the best she could give us, all while working hard to become one of the top defense lawyers in the area. When I was a kid, it was just some boring grown-up job that meant nothing to me. Now I'm an adult, I can see the determination and drive she had to have had to be a black, single mother working through all the paperwork, exams, sexism and bigotry.

"So, just so I have this straight, the only people arrested tonight were both senior citizens. And one of them is currently on holiday from New Zealand. Is that correct?" Momma frowns up at the Tombs family, who all have smiles on their faces.

"Yes, our Pops and his girlfriend." August offers.

"And they were arrested because Deborah Taylor - that's your mother, right Ana?" Ana nods. "She had marijuana on her person?"

"She may have. Or she may just have had a brownie in her pocket." Ana shrugs and my momma stares at her for a moment before looking back at her notepad.

"Riiiiight. Whatever it was, was on her person, and when restrained, Sidney Tombs then intervened. Whilst he was being restrained by another officer, Debs then called him a-" She flicks her eyes down to her notepad. "'To teke' and proceeded to attack said officer. Do I have all that correct?"

Everyone looks at each other before nodding.

"One question, what's a 'To Teke'?" Rider asks what we are all thinking. Well, OK, it may not be the only thing we're thinking. It's been a wild night. We have a new prospect, a pregnant lady and the two oldest people at the compound have been arrested because someone tipped off the police to a body on our property.

"Oh, 'To Teke' is Maori for cunt," Ana enlightens us all. Snickering can be heard from all corners of the common room. Even Marx cracks a grin.

Momma's lips twitch before she clears her throat. "So, is there a possibility their actions could be seen as self defense?"

The Tombs family shuffle around, avoiding Momma's eye contact. Tav has his palm facing toward the ground wiggling his hand as if to say it was 50/50.

"We have footage for this area. Do you want me to link it to the big screen?" Remy murmurs. A smile slowly works its way across my face.

"Yeah go on Rem." She scuttles off down the hall as I address the room. "Remy's linking the footage to the big screen."

Whoops go around the common room as we all jostle to get a good view and in a matter of moments, the chaos of the last hour plays on the projector.

"He has a hell of a punch on him. I can kinda see now how he escaped that kidnapping," Tank says. I nod in agreement as Momma's eyebrows slowly creep up her forehead.

"Well, I've seen enough. That is most definitely assault BUT I'm pretty sure I can plead mental confusion given the age of them and the stressful nature of the situation. I'll have them out by morning. In the meantime, with the police investigating this poor girl and her case, you lot are going to have to lie very, very low. They will use any excuse to bring you in. No matter how friendly you are with the Sergeant, Marx." Momma looks around the room, making sure we are all paying attention. "Lie low, do not get in trouble. I know you all want answers and by all means look, but give the information to the police. Trust me. One foot outta line and they'll come down hard."

She gives us one last hairy eyeball before coming to stand before me, placing her warm hand on my cheek and giving me a kiss. "Find the information, pass it on. OK baby?" She holds my gaze and I hold hers.

"OK, Momma."

She pats my cheek then clip clops toward the door. "Be good, lie low, and nobody get killed or arrested!" With that, the door slams behind her.

"She was BADASS! I'm going to make her a bracelet," Chewy chirps out.

Rider spins in his seat to glare at her. She waves back, oblivious.

"Maybe do that later, Chewy. We have a fucking murder to solve on top of the rest of the shit we have on our plates. Wire, I need you combing footage. How the fuck did we miss this? We also need the identity of the woman found. See if she has any connection to us at all."

Tav steps forward, his new prospect cut shining under the lights. "Pres, if you don't mind, I could ride out to the yard and have a look around. I know we beefed up cameras in that area, so I can't figure out how the tech team missed this –"

"Tech team? Our tech team? We need a name! What about the nerd herd? Ohhh, the Hackeroos? Oh, Oh what about The Com-puta's? Like puta? Cos we're whores for technology." Chewy waggles her eyebrows and I watch as Gus pinches the bridge of his nose, extending his hand out to Marx. He's taken to offering Marx antacids in times of Chewy Induced Stress.

"Tank, take our new prospect to the garage and see what you can find. Maybe coordinate with Wire's team – no Chewy! Do not say a word!" Marx eyeballs her, and she slowly closes her mouth, miming zipping her lips. "Watch them case the place in real time, Wire. Might throw up a blind spot."

I nod at my Pres. "On it. Remy also had an idea. With no sign of Hammer, maybe we should focus our efforts on his right-hand man. Guy named Snake."

"I can send you all pictures of him so you know who to look for," Remy tells the MC and Tombs family. She used her firm voice and I can see everyone shooting each other looks and soft smiles at her.

"Well, the night is young and we all have shit to do. No debauchery and fucking for your prospect party, Tav; but your grandfather got arrested, so it wasn't all boring." Marx slaps Tav hard on the back and tips his head to Gus and Ana. Before they can head toward his office, most likely to plan, Ana's phone goes off. We all freeze as she frowns at it before answering.

"Roman? Wait what?........Oh that's interesting, very interesting. Same thing has just happened to us."

At that statement Marx's brows pull down. My eyes shoot to Remy's wide blue ones.

"I'll arrange it. Watch your back Ro." Ana hangs up and looks at us. "Well, it looks like Roman got a visit from the police as well. The body of a woman was found dumped near his warehouse. Had been raped and she had a belly full of drugs." Curses go around the room. "He wants to meet tomorrow, Marx. He'll come to you." Marx rubs the back of his neck and nods. No one really like's doing shit with Roman, but it looks like yet again we're all in this together.

"Like I said, you all have your orders. We need to put this fucker down." Marx nods and then leaves, Gus and Ana following behind. Everyone starts filing out, ready to do whatever it takes to finish this.

"Com-puta's! Follow me!" Chewy yells as she storms past Remy and me, leading the way down the hall to the control center.

I have to admit, I'm glad I have Chewy and Remy by my side. It helps take the edge off. Before they crashed into my life, when shit went down I would hole up in my room, barely leaving. Sure, my brothers would stop by the check in, and I'd have human contact in the form of my daily messages with Retta; but having a team to rely on seems to keep my PTSD at bay. A little.

Taking our seats, Chewy starts putting all the tow yard footage up on the big screen, and it's a lot.

Rose Grove is a large town, with a Main Street that runs right through the middle. At one end of Main, right on the outskirts is our compound. We sit almost smack bang where the Main Street turns into highway. Around 5 minutes drive from the compound sits Devils Big Tow, our towing yard and impound lot. Tank and Sniper run the business with help from all the brothers on and off. Devils Big Tow sits between us and the older stores heading into town before you hit the main flashy shopping district with all the big name chain stores and cutesy cafes with the main businesses and shopping districts coming off that.

"Can I ask something?" Remy looks at me before turning her gaze to Chewy. "I know these cameras are always running in the background. We were raided an hour ago, so the police would have been on camera well before then securing the site. Why wasn't this picked up earlier? Surely they would have come up on the feed?"

Both Remy and Chewy look at me and I can feel the dread rising. Scrubbing my hand over my face, I mumble, "I fell asleep." Before grimacing. Fuck. Yet another thing I've missed. What the fuck is going on with me? This isn't like me to be tripping up on fucking rookie mistakes.

Remy gives me a little smile and pats my thigh, causing tingles to run through me heading toward my cock.

"Wire, you need rest. You can't keep working the way you are. You need to share the load. I can't believe I'm going to say this, but Com-Puta's work together." She grins at Chewy, who fist pumps the air.

"Also, dude. Using my superior brain and fast processing skills, -" I roll my eyes at Remy before tuning back into Chewy. "- watching this in rewind, I see no sign of cops anywhere."

Wait, what? "That can't be right. He said they found her at the yard. Go back a few hours and replay the footage."

Chewy does as I ask and we watch at 2x speed. Not so fast that we miss anything, but a hell of a lot quicker than if we were sitting here in real time. From the corner of one of the cameras, you can see movement, but checking all other angles, Chewy is right. There is no footage of police until near the very end where two officers, that douche Martin being one, and some other guy, walk past the front of Tank's office in uniform.

"That camera that picked something up on the edges. Which one is it?" Remy asks.

"That one is right on the edge of our boundary. The other side of that is the abandoned storefront next door. Been empty for years."

She nods for a moment, frowning at the cameras. Chewy pulls out her phone, punches in numbers and then places it on her part of the desk, the ring tone blaring through the speaker.

"Yo little sis. What's up?" Tav answers. He's on the move as we can hear crunching and wind blowing down the speaker.

"Are you at the yard?"

"Yup. Just arrived. Tank and I are going to check out the crime scene. The police have left their tape up everywhere."

I lean forward, slightly in Remy's space, so I can talk to Tav without yelling over her. "Where is the scene exactly, Tav? We aren't picking up anything on any of our cameras."

There's mumbling where he must be talking to Tank, some more crunching of boots on gravel. "By the looks of it, the body was between the office and the place next door."

"In that weird alley?"

"Yeah."

I remember Rhodie saying that they tried to get the building next door to expand the impound lot but the owner wouldn't sell up. Not that it's been a bother. The whole time the MC has run the yard, there's been no one occupying that building. Not that we'd know as we'd built a big fuck off fence between us and the place next door. The whole towing business, yard and impound lot is fenced in. It offers our customers peace of mind that when we tow them for whatever reason, their vehicles will be secure.

Dumping a body in that alleyway, then calling the cops, is a brave move. First, that alley and the business next door are on the other side of the fence. No one other than the building inspector, city manager and us know we legally share land rights with our neighbors. Second, the person who tipped off the police would have had to know that. Which means they've been doing their research on us.

"Tav, Tank, did you hear that noise?" Remy calls over the phone in her husky voice.

"Oh hey Remy, um, what noise?"

"There! There it was again." She looks at me with a small

smile and winks. "I think it's coming from next door. Maybe someone is in danger?"

Looking past Remy, I catch Chewys' eye and we both grin. Seems DRMC may be rubbing off on her.

"Huh? Oh! Oh, that noise. Yeah, you're right, as concerned citizens it's our duty to offer someone assistance."

Rustling can be heard along with some banging and what sounds like glass breaking. All the sounds that I'm sure Momma warned us against.

"I really hope your mom doesn't find out about this," Remy murmurs, pulling a chuckle out of me.

"Nothing to worry about. Of all my brothers, Tav is the sneakiest."

"That's interesting. I would have thought Jules would be the sneakiest," Remy comments.

Chewy waves a dismissive hand at her. "No, Jules is quieter but in these situations he's a bull in a china shop. Useless for covert."

We sit quietly mulling that over while grunts, curses and general racket can be heard over Chewys' phone.

"You still there guys? Looks like someone was here recently. Place is a total dump, dusty as hell. Doesn't look like a place where someone has been kept, its kinda open so you wouldn't bring a kidnap victim or anyone here. But there are footprints and the usual stuff you see when homeless people bunk down. I'll get Jules onto his street people. "

"Yeah, good thinking. Hopefully, they know something." Remy's heat warms my side as I stay still slightly in her space while I'm talking to Tav.

"OK, we're on our way back now. Nothing else to see here." He hangs up, and we all look at each other. Chewy starts up with her imaginary beard.

"So, we have a body dumped outside of our camera angles in an alley shared with the neighbors. An alley that fuck all people know we own half of. A tip is placed to the police. We get raided and now we're in a situation where our hands are tied. Same thing happens to Roman. I think we can all agree this is some master plan of Hammer's to legally get us out of his way."

Remy lets out a sigh. "This is typical Hammer. He couldn't get one over by brute force, so now he's tying us up in red tape."

There's something about Remy saying "us" instead of DRMC. I know she came here to learn before she takes her newfound skills back to the Death Riders, but I don't think I want her to go.

I blow out a breath and try to get my head on straight. Pulling my phone from my cut pocket, I look down to see I got a reply message from Retta. A thumbs up. I open up our message thread when a knock sounds from the door, and we all spin to see Rhodie leaning against the jamb.

"Come on baby, call it a night." Chewy beams at Rhodie before turning her body to me and Remy.

"I'm with my man. We've found nothing on the footage. We're waiting on info for next door. I can hack the police files tomorrow to see who the victim is. And I'm with Remy about looking into Snake, too. He's the one most likely to be doing Hammer's bidding while he's hiding."

Chewy then stands, puts her hand in between me and Remy, palm facing down, and then looks at us expectantly.

I side eye Remy because I have no clue what the fuck is happening. Remy must figure it out because she puts her hand on top of Chewy's, garnering her a massive grin. I place my large, dark hand on Remy's pale, delicate hand. Chewy pumps our hands yelling "Cooooooooooooom-Putas!" before raising her hand up and jazz handing it around. Remy lets out a giggle while me and Rhodie share a smirk.

"See ya tomorrow, team. Don't do anything I wouldn't do. Peace." and with that, Chewy jumps on Rhodie, wraps her legs around his waist and they head off up the hallway.

I turn to Remy, taking in her pretty face. "You may as well head off to bed too, Rem. I got this."

Even before I finish my sentence she's shaking her head at me. "No way. You won't get rid of me that easy Wire whatever-your-last-name-is. I'm here for the long haul, just like you. Let's see if we can't get a hit on Snake and start running a background on that Officer Martin guy."

I stare at her for a moment, touched that she wants to stay to help. "Harvey."

"Huh?"

"My last name. It's Harvey."

She beams at me and it makes everything feel a little less shitty. We sit like that, me soaking in her smile while her eyes roam my face, for just a moment before we both turn to our screens and get to work.

Remy

"Miss Remy, are you tired?" I tip my head at the sound, taking in Jovie's cute little face. Her brows furrowed with concern.

"You have been yawning lots." She says to me, this time raising her brows and nodding emphatically.

"I was up too late last night, Jovie."

Wire and I sat up until well past my bedtime trying to look for any lead. Other than spotting Snake at a few places around town, we couldn't find anything concrete leading us to where he and Hammer and whoever else has joined their gang are hiding.

However, at around midnight last night we struck gold. It seems the auctions are back up and running. This time it's not the Russians, whose wings were clipped by Roman and his Bratva. Which is good news. The bad news is that we don't know who is pulling Hammer's strings. Typical.

"Well, you better go to bed nice and early tonight Miss Remy." Jovie says, patting my hand and then heading off into the colorful bookshelves, no doubt looking for a new dinosaur book.

I take a quick look around and do a headcount of the children in my care, making sure I have them all. They have another 5 minutes of browsing before its dance party time, allowing me to drift back into my thoughts.

This morning, before I left for work Chewy set up a group call for the Com-Puta's. She had somehow gotten her hands on the ME and forensics report for the woman that was found at Devil's Big Tow. Not only had she been raped and beaten before being murdered; she had also been held captive for quite some time. She was malnourished and had scarring around her wrists from being restrained. My heart broke for her even more when the report stated that she had, at some stage in her life, given birth. Somewhere out there she has a baby that no longer has their mother.

I vowed then and there that I will find out who did this and I will make them pay. I know Chewy and Wire, heck, DRMC and the Death Riders will have my back on this. Hammer has lit a fire, a spark of something that I didn't know I had in me, but now I can't put out. I need someone to pay for all the awful things that have been happening. Shooting my dad, killing that poor woman, forcing others to smuggle drugs inside themselves on their way to their new owners. There is too much evil in this world and I want to fix that. What did Jovie say that day? Big things protect small things. Well, I'm going to be a big thing and I'm going to protect those who need it.

"Is it dance time yet, Miss?" Marcus, one of the boys, asks me, snapping me out of my thoughts of revenge. Shaking my head, I try not to snicker at myself. Me, Remy, the shy, invisible girl plotting destruction.

"Let me check the time, hmm?" Flicking my eyes up to the big colorful clock on the wall in the kids' area.

"You're right! It is definitely dance time. Let's round up our friends."

Between me and Marcus, we let everyone know to put all the books back on shelves, all their crafts in their backpacks, and everyone into the dance space. A smile blooms as I watch them organize themselves, using their 'airplane arms' to make sure they aren't too close. With a nod from Jovie, I start the music. One boy asked for a Backstreet Boys song his dad likes, so all the kids are now grooving to music that is at least two decades older than them.

By the time the music fades out parents have started to arrive. The kids all give me clammy high fives and a few even give me a hug around the legs. I smile and wave as they say goodbye, holding hands with their parents excitedly telling them what we did today. They all trickle out until, as has become our norm, it's just me and Jovie left behind.

"Did you eat today, Jovie?"

She pins me with her big brown eyes before looking down at her hands and shaking her head.

"Well, come on then, it's picnic time for us," I offer her my hand and then feel 10 feet tall when she beams up at me, putting her soft, little hand in mine.

I wink at Beth on the way past her front desk as she smiles at Jovie and nods my way. "I'll call you when I see his car," she mouths at me.

She's been doing that since the night Jovie's dad got aggressive. I give her a grateful smile and lead my little charge into the kitchen to gather our food before taking it outside to a little table set up for the librarian's to enjoy on sunny days. It may be fall in Rose Grove, but the weather is still warm enough to enjoy the burnished gold and rich maroon leaves.

"Wow, I haven't had a picnic since my momma was home," Jovie's face that was alight at the memory turns sad.

"Where is your momma, honey?"

She shrugs her little shoulders. "Dad said that she didn't love me anymore, so she runned away but my momma wouldn't runned away."

The thought Jovie's father saying such a thing to such a sweet little girl makes my blood boil.

"Your momma loves you. And I bet wherever she is, she is thinking about you every day." I say gently.

She smiles up at me and then takes a big bite of the brownie that Debs made. The brownie that I triple checked was OK for children.

"Rem, he's here." Beth's voice drifts through the open door and I know that she's standing just inside the hall, not wanting to leave her desk unwomanned.

"Is that my daddy?"

I nod, letting her know that he's arrived. Jovie helps me pack up the mess we made, slings the backpack that is almost bigger than her on her back and runs back inside, through the hall to the main doors, her little voice thanking me drifting out behind her.

Wire

"Brother."

Turning toward the door, I'm greeted by Rhodie frowning at me. Fuck, what happened now?

"What's wrong?"

"You. How long have you been sitting there, Wire? Seven, eight hours? And how long before that? Are you sleeping?"

Rubbing my hands down my face, I think through his questions before looking at the clock icon on my screen. Shit! It's nearing three in the afternoon and I'm meant to meet Retta in an hour.

"If you're not answering, it's because you know you've been sitting too fucking long and not sleeping. I need you to get out of here, brother."

"Well, you're in luck. I have a... thing in an hour. Chewy said she'd cover for me."

"Thank fuck for that. I thought I'd have to threaten to shoot you to get you out of here. Counselor?"

"No, just a, a friend."

Rhodie's brows climb up toward his brows but he doesn't say anything on the matter other than give me a chin lift.

"Hey hey baby!" Chewy's voice rings out down the hall and within a matter of seconds she's in Rhodie's space, slapping his ass.

"How's my man today?"

Not even waiting for an answer, she stands on her tiptoes, puckering her lips. She used to need guidance on her interactions with Rhodie. She'd hesitate with PDA, or she would go the other way and it'd be too much. Now she's much more settled and even though she's still unpredictable, she's much more comfortable in her relationship. She is Rhodie's and Rhodie is hers.

Watching the two of them together has my mind drifting to Retta. What will she be like? Will we be awkward and decide never to see each other again? Or will we be instantly comfortable with each other and fall into an easy pattern like these two in front of me?

"OK Wire, I'm here. You can leave now. You too, Rhodie." Chewy smirks at both of us and waves to Rhodie as he knocks twice on the doorjamb before throwing her a wink.

"You sure you've got this?" Chewy rolls her eyes at me before giving me a bored look. "Fine. I've been running facial recognition on Snake, and no new hits."

"Give it time, dude. And leave! Retta will be waiting."

As per usual, when she says Retta's name she says it all high pitched and super girly. She has a huge grin on her face and is waggling her brows up and down.

"What's wrong with you?" I squint at her. She seems weirder

than usual.

"Nothing. Can't I be excited for my friends?" She tries to give me an innocent look, instead her eyes are huge, and she's blinking like an owl.

"Friends?" I ask, raising my brow.

"Well, yeah, um suuuuure. You're already my friend and it turns out people seem to like me, so I'm sure I'll be friends with Retta too. Because I'm a good friend. Ask Ana." She nods once before swinging her eyes to her screen and tapping away like her life depended on it.

If I was in a better head space and not sleep deprived, I would want to figure out what she's up to. But then again, it's probably just some weird Chewy thing where she's already practiced an interaction with Retta in her mind. Or with Rhodie.

"Message me as soon as something comes through –"

"What about Retta?"

"– She'll understand. Promise me Chewy,"

Chewy gives me a weird look before shrugging. She beams 90s pop onto the big screen and slowly cranks the volume over the instructions I'm trying to give her.

"I can't hear you anymore." She yells over the music, making a shoo motion with her hands. Shaking my head, I move around to the private side of my suite and check my reflection before grimacing. I strip off my tee, put on some deodorant and a clean shirt, throw my cut over my shoulders and head out, not before mussing Chewy's hair on the way out.

Mounting my girl, I hit the road.

Chapter Eleven

Remy

"Remy? Sorry, but Jovie is back looking for you." Beth calls out.

That's odd. Usually her dad peels out like his butt is on fire and we don't see them again until the next day. Jovie's in luck. I'm officially off the clock and was about to leave. Placing my phone in my handbag, I put it down on the break room table and head out into the main area, walking toward Jovie, who is standing just inside the main doors, tears pooling in her eyes.

"Jovie, sweetie, what's wrong?" I squat down in front of her so we're level. Her little chest is heaving, and she sniffles, trying to calm herself. I wrap my arms around her, looking over her shoulder at Beth, who is frowning at us.

"My daddy said he needed to talk to you outside. He squeezed my arm hard and told me I had to get you." She looks up at me with those big brown eyes as tears well up.

She's too little to understand that her dad is an awful man who shouldn't have children. I nod at her before I turn to let Beth know where I'm going. Not that she would mind, given that I'm officially off the clock. Looking around, she isn't at her desk, so I assume she's helping someone.

"Come on little miss, let's see what your dad wants, hmm?"

Taking her hand, we both step outside the front doors. I swivel my head left and right, looking for his junker car. He normally parks right out front, however, today he's down the road a little. I have no idea why and I don't care to know why. The man is horrible.

As we walk closer, Jovie's steps get slower and slower. Looking down at her, she seems afraid, which makes sense. She's just been manhandled by someone who is meant to love her. I jiggle her hand until she looks up at me.

"It's going to be OK Jovie. I'm here and I remember a clever little girl told me that big things protect little things. Remember?"

She smiles up at me and nods. We slow to a stop in front of his car and the driver's door creaks open. Her dad steps out, looking even worse than the last time I saw him.

"Jovie said you wanted to talk to me?"

He licks his lips, his eyes looking me up and down.

"Oh, I wanna do more than talk to you, sweetheart." He roughly grabs Jovie, shoving her towards the car. "Get in there, you little shit. Just like your fucking mother." He spits as Jovie sobs and climbs into the backseat.

There is no booster seat, so she pulls the seatbelt over her shoulder, the band digging into the side of her cheek before she clips it and raises her arm up and over it, the seat belt under her armpits.

I don't know why, but this angers me to the point of no return. He may be half a foot taller than I am, but I don't care. I also don't care about the smell coming off of him as I lean into him.

"Don't you ever talk to her like that again." My voice is firm, not the quiet whisper it is when I'm trying to be invisible. Here and now I need to protect Jovie. I need him to see me.

"Oh yeah, I'm going to love teaching you a lesson," He says as he palms his privates. My eyes shoot to his leering face, his pupils blown wide from whatever he has stuck in his veins.

"I don't learn lessons from men who bully children."

"How about men with guns?" A voice whispers in my ear. I freeze. Ice flows through my veins, my gut clenching, breath coming in pants. I know that voice.

"Snake."

Wire

Checking my phone for the 500th time since I've been here, I see nothing from Retta. Fuck! Thinking back on all our interactions, I'm wracking my brain trying to think through the messages. Did she give me signals she wanted to meet or was I being so pushy she felt she had to agree to meeting me?

Running my hands through my hair that's feeling a little too long, I try to shake those thoughts out of my head. I know Retta. She wouldn't just go along with something I said. Over the years, she's gotten sassier with me. I know for a fact the Retta I know would have put me in my place if she felt I was being an asshole.

Maybe something happened to her dad? I know recently he's been unwell. Maybe there's been an emergency, and she didn't have time to message? Blowing out a frustrated breath, I take in the view and decide to wait a little longer, just in case there was traffic or some shit. Yeah, I'm whipped.

The phone vibrating in my hand has me scrambling to answer. "Retta?"

"Wire! It's me."

"Chewy? What's wrong?"

"Is Remy with you?" Pulling my phone from my ear, I look at it. "Why would Remy be with me?"

"Shit. OK. We have a problem. We need you back now, Wire."

Throwing my leg over my girl, I put on my brain bucket, then rev the shit out of my bike and peel out. I've already switched Chewy over to bluetooth.

"Give me the rundown Chewy, I'm on my way now."

"No, I will tell you in person. You might lose your shit if I tell you now and I don't need one of my besties to crash. Ride safe, Wire. See you soon."

With that, she hangs up on me, and now my gut is swirling with anxiety. I gun it down the familiar roads, making the hour long drive in close to 40 minutes. Riding up to the compound, I wave at Jimmy, the prospect on the gates, and he gets them open wide enough for me to peel through. I park my girl in her spot, take off my brain bucket and place it on the seat before heading straight in to find out what's got Chewy wound up.

Walking through the door of the clubhouse, I'm met with my brothers sitting around the dining room, Marx standing in the middle. What the hell happened?

"Wire, have you heard from Remy?" Marx barks at me before I've even closed the door behind me.

My brows pull low. "No. Why's that?"

"Fuck," He curses under his breath. Hands on hips, he looks

at the ground before looking me in the eye. "We're not sure where she is. Beth from the library called to let Remy know she left her purse behind. Saw her car in the lot and thought one of us had picked her up, but no one has seen or heard from her."

My eyes dart to the Jim Beam clock on the wall. Her shift finished at 4pm. It's now 6pm.

"I'm guessing you've tried her phone?" I ask, trying to remain calm. How in the space of an afternoon did the two women I have feelings for both go radio silent?

"Done that, brother. This isn't like her. She leads a quiet existence, goes to work, then comes home," Tank answers. He and Sniper both have furrowed brows. I get it. They're her friends.

"What about Ana? They're friends. Maybe they met up?"

"I've already checked in with Ana. She hasn't seen her since my party," Tav says. I can see the concern on his face. He's a softy.

Feet thumping down the hall has us all turning to face Chewy, her laptop balanced on her forearm.

"I have something! Beth said the last time she saw Remy she was on her way outside with a little girl named Jovie."

"Jovie's dad is a dickhead. He's threatened Remy before. She has a soft spot for Jovie. The kid is clearly being neglected." I fill in the gaps, letting my brothers know why Remy would be outside, especially with Hammer around.

The tension is starting to grow, brothers are cursing and Marx looks like he's about to lose it. Chewy grabs the remote to turn on the projector, then taps a couple of keys. By the looks of the footage it must be a lamp post camera, as it shows the shops just down from the library and a piece of shit car. We watch as Remy comes into camera with Jovie, and her fuck knuckle dad gets out of his car.

"That's the fucker that's been hanging around the yard!" Tanks yells. Chewy pauses the video so Tank can get a better look. He stands to get closer to the wall where the projector beams, squinting for a moment before shooting a look at Sniper.

"Yeah, that's him. We've chased him a couple of times but keep losing him. He's a wily little fucker."

"Meth heads always are," Rider bites out.

Chewy unpauses the video and we watch as he manhandles his kid; grabbing her roughly, pulling growls from my brothers. We all watch in fascination as Remy steps forward, getting into his space. Even though she's shorter than him, she gets in his face and I feel pride bubbling in my chest. Remy is fierce as she protects that little girl. That is until someone steps out of the shadows and holds a gun to her head.

"That motherfucker Snake!" Marx growls, teeth clenched, looking as if he's going to go on a berserker rampage any minute now.

We watch as Jovie's father pops the trunk and Snake shoves Remy in. He then turns to look at the camera, smiling wide and flipping the bird.

"The motherfucker knew we would pull footage," Rhodie shakes his head in disgust as Chewy shuts down the video and then curls up on her man's lap.

He holds her to him, murmuring how we will find her. And we will. There is no option. The feelings I have for Remy may be confusing, but they are real and deep. And I'm not letting any Death Rider motherfucker take her away from her home.

"What's the plan Pres?"

We all look at Marx, his jaw clenching hard.

"Fuck brothers. I don't know. We lost the princess of our ally club. I need to let Savage and Flack know before we do anything else. Don't forget we've been told by your momma, Wire, that we have to lie low. Whatever the fuck we do has to be stealth and fucking planned to the nth degree." He runs his hand through his hair, and then his beard. "First, we need intel. We need eyes all over this fucking town. Need to find out where those fuckers are holed up."

"Aw shit." Chewy says, staring at her laptop screen.

"What now, Chewy?" Marx asks, the look on his face showing that he is pretty fucking close to his last straw.

"The plates on Jovie's dad's car belong to the woman they found at the yard. Jayla Stevens." Chewy beams her license up on the big screen next to the frozen picture of Jovie's dad with her car.

"Fuck me. You don't think...?" Switch's voice drifts off as he too gets closer to the photos. We all stand around looking at the features of Jovie, her father and this Jayla Stevens.

"Surely that's not Jovie's mother." Rider says, eyes flicking between the photos.

"Only one way to find out. We have her home address. Who's going?" Chewy says, standing with a huge smile on her face.

I let out a deep sigh before speaking up. "I'll go."

"What the fuck Wire? I need you here," Marx orders, but I'm already shaking my head at him.

"I'm sorry, Pres, but I can get the info we need. I know the address. It's the trailer park my dad's whole side of the family live in. They'll talk to me."

Marx's brow furrows as he considers my words. "You sure?
"Yeah."

My brothers sit silent. They know what my relationship with

my father and his family is like. It may be a little distant, but everyone knows distant family has a better chance of poking around than strangers. If a stranger asks questions, they'll clam up tighter than a duck's ass.

"Chewy, you're in the control center. Rider and Rhodie, you're with Wire. That place has always been shady as fuck, and I don't expect it to be any better. Tav, you and Tank take the van. Just in case these fuckers are dumber than they look and have Remy there. Everyone else, back on the streets looking for Hammer, but do it quietly. Obey the road rules, don't speed. I don't want the wrath of Wire's momma coming down on me if you lot draw any attention to us. I have a Pres to call." Marx grimaces before nodding at us and turning to head into his office. Shoulders slumped.

"Mount up boys" Rhodie slaps me on the shoulder and leads the way.

Chapter Twelve

Remy

I can't believe that jerk Snake pulled a gun on me! Actually, scrap that. Pulling guns on people is his MO. What I can't believe is that I let myself get into this position. I should have never stepped outside of the library knowing full well what Jovie's dad is like. Now I'm stuck in his small trunk that smells like vomit as he drives like a maniac. Jovie's cries drift from the backseat to where I'm lying and I want nothing more than to reassure her I'm OK.

We turn a corner none too gently and I slide, getting my arm up over my head to brace myself before whacking my head on one side of the trunk. I wish I was more familiar with the layout of the town. That way, I'd at least know where Snake and Jovie's dad are taking me.

I know it's wishful thinking, but I hope someone from the DRMC notices when I don't return from work. Hopefully Chewy or Ana notice when I don't reply to our message thread.

Chewy has accepted me into her girl gang and I love it. I love having girlfriends to talk and joke with. We have inside jokes that I'm a part of! They let me be me, but also they help to point out that I don't have to agree with anything if I don't want to. They encourage me to have opinions and voice them. My eyes well up with tears when I think about how special they are. I make a vow in this cramped, pukey trunk that I'm going to take up more of Chewy and Ana's invitations to lunch.

We turn another corner, and this time my head isn't so lucky. I whack it on something hard, a whimper escaping my lips. I'm meant to be meeting Mags tonight, instead I'm probably being driven to my doom. My gut swirls thinking of Mags waiting at our meeting point, thinking I've stood him up.

Screeching sounds out and the car comes to an abrupt stop, jolting me once again. I lay quietly and wait. If I had a little more space, I could maneuver myself to explode out of the trunk, taking my abductor by surprise. However, at the sound of a motorcycle pulling in, I know Snake will be armed and he probably wouldn't think twice about shooting me.

The trunk makes a clicking sound, then swings open. I brace myself for the bright light. Instead, we've pulled into what looks like a dimly lit warehouse or garage.

Snake looks down at me with a leer, licking his lips as he rubs the front of his jeans. "I always wondered what you'd look like looking up at me with those big blue eyes,"

My brows pull low and I let out a snarl, surprising both Snake and myself. With a sneer, he grips my arm, roughly pulling me upright and then out of the trunk. I think he's going to let go, but his knobbly fingers tighten, gripping me even harder, his long dirty fingernails digging into my soft flesh through my blouse.

The doors slam shut and Jovie's dad has her in the same grip, the little girl fighting against him, begging him to let us go.

Seeing Jovie fight lights something within me, so I do the same. Twisting, I kick Snake hard in the knee. He buckles and I use my free arm to swipe across the arm that's holding me. Instead of knocking his hand off, it seems to incense him even more, and he recovers fast, fast enough to pull his gun from his holster and point it directly in my face.

"Hammer may want you untouched, but I'm sure he can still use you with a bullet in your leg. What do you think, Remy Girl?"

My shoulders sag and I make it appear as if I'm giving in. I'm not. As soon as the gun was pulled, I realized that if I get hurt, Jovie won't have a chance to get out of here. I need to play it safe. Which means being the old Remy. Acting timid and quiet. The Remy Snake and Hammer expect.

What they don't know is that I've spent the last two months with the Devil's Rose MC. The Remy that left the Death Riders is different from the Remy that they kidnapped. This Remy isn't invisible anymore. This Remy has a group of friends that she loves and shares her dreams with. This Remy believes she can do whatever she wants. This Remy is pissed that this is happening to her and the sweetest little girl in the world. This Remy also seems to talk in third person. I blame the adrenaline.

I let Snake drag me behind him. He uses his booted foot to kick open a door to a dark storeroom with a filthy mattress in the corner. Jovie's dad shoves her into the room, growling at her to shut up as she cries harder. Snake leans close, licking up my neck, stopping to breathe a "good girl" in my ear, causing me to shudder. He too shoves me hard into the room and I have to stop myself landing on Jovie.

"Stay put, don't make a fucking sound, and we'll be back with a little surprise. Good girls get surprises." Snake leers and Jovie's dad guffaws like it's the funniest thing he's ever heard.

They slam the door behind them and both me and Jovie hear the ominous click of the lock.

Wire

Swiveling my head left and right, I take in the trailer park where my sisters and I would spend weekends with my dad. When he remembered to pick us up, that is. It's not like he was a terrible father. He was just young and with a woman who was so focussed and driven that I think he struggled to find his place. Add to that his shit show relationship with Sandra, who introduced him to harder things than the gambling and drink he was used to and, well, let's say that my sisters and I haven't seen him for a while.

A whistle from behind me has me looking over my shoulder at Rider, who slows his bike, tips his head to us to follow, and turns down a side alley. We meander through the park, looking for Jayla's trailer.

I have to admit, the park itself hasn't changed all that much. Everything is still a little run down, although you can see pockets of pride, where people have at least tried to make what they have more like a home rather than a place to crash. A small veggie garden here, some nice deck furniture there. Following Rider, we pull up outside a tidy trailer with a bright yellow door. There are flower boxes sitting on the porch that look like they've seen better days and an overflowing trash can, but even through that, you can tell this was a home that someone looked after.

I kick down the stand on my girl, throw my leg over and tip my chin at Rhodie to follow while Rider stays with our bikes. I wouldn't trust any of the fuckers around here. There may be some good folk, but they're outnumbered. I should know.

My heavy footsteps stomp on the porch. Curling my hand into a fist, I bang on the door, Rhodie beside me, peering through the windows.

"It's a fucking mess in there, and there's kid stuff everywhere. The kid is a girl, yeah?"

I nod at him and bang again.

"What do you want?" A gruff voice growls.

Turning, Rhodie and I come face to face with a man peering over the trellis that separates Jayla's place from his. His eyes widen as he takes in our cuts, darting to Rider with our bikes before settling his gaze back on us. He squints at me a moment before recognition lights his eyes.

"Saint?"

In my periphery, Rhodie's head swings to look at me, but I'm busy studying the man on the other side of the trellis. The last time I saw him was before I deployed. At least ten years ago. Back then, he was thin, greasy, unkempt. Now? Now he's healthy, his skin a couple of shades lighter than mine, tanned, but from working outdoors rather than naturally. His blonde hair cut short instead of long and greasy.

"Dad?"

He exhales and blinks a couple of times before giving me a soft smile. "Hey, son. You look good, kid."

"You do too." A smile tugs at my lips. He does look good. In fact, probably the best I've ever seen him.

"Yeah. I, um, remember Sandra?" I nod at him. "Well, we broke up a while back. I hit rock bottom and have been working my way back up. Got clean, got a job."

My eyes flick behind him. "Got a better trailer."

He smiles, the signs of his hard life showing on some of his teeth. Even so, he looks more like the dad I remember.

"Yeah. Sure did. Got a little garden even. You should, um, come visit sometime." He rubs the back of his neck, looking uncomfortable.

I could cut him off. Tell him I'll never visit him because he was a shitty father, a shitty husband and sometimes a shitty person. But then my mind drifts to what the two women in my life would say. Remy and Retta would say that he's clearly trying to change, and that I should give him a chance.

Instead of letting him down, I give him a chin lift. "Yeah. Um, that sounds good."

He beams at me, then realizes that what is happening here isn't a family reunion. His eyes flick to Jayla's door before coming back to me and Rhodie.

"Why are you knocking on that door, son?"

"We're looking for our friend. Around 5'5ish, blonde hair, librarian. Seen her round?"

Even before Rhodie finishes the description, dad is shaking his head.

"Nah. The woman that lives there, I haven't seen around for a while now. Sweet girl, reminds me a little of your mom when we were younger," he smiles at me. "Her loser boyfriend lives there with their little girl. He said she took off on them, but I don't believe it. She was a good girl. Always trying to make this place a little better. Helped some of the older folks with their shopping, that sort of thing. The little girl, Jovie, is a sweetheart too, but I think she's been struggling to live with her dad. He leaves her alone at night. A couple of times I've overheard her crying, so I've come over to sit with her." He says, shaking his head in disgust, his expression mirroring that of me and my brothers.

Rhodie catches my eye and gives me a look. I've known him for long enough now to know that he's asking if we can trust my dad. He may have been hooked on some shit back in the day, but even then he was dangerously honest. There's no way he'd cross us. Giving him a subtle nod, he flicks his gaze at my father.

"We're after him. He's been fucking with us, and he's not fit to parent. Think you could call us if you see him?"

"Fuck yes. I've had the police out a few times, but Davey Martin just fobs Jayla's disappearance off as a druggy mother out looking to score. Jayla doesn't do drugs. Her fuckhead boyfriend does."

"Wait, Davey Martin? As in Davey who's mom is Brenda? Used to live a few trailers down from you and Sandra?" I squint at my dad.

"Yeah. That little turd grew up to be a cop. Comes around here bullying and acting like an asshole."

"Wait, that Officer Martin dickhead that threw his weight around at Tav's party?" Rhodie asks.

"Yeah. Shit, I didn't recognize him. Not even when I ran a background check on him."

"He moved him and his mom out as soon as he became a cop. He's done fuck all to help around here other than tell us Jayla is a junkie and Jovie is fine living in that trailer with her father. Do me a favor Saint? Get rid of her piece of shit father and find her a better home." His face is fierce and I know that just like she did with Remy and me, from the moment I met her, Jovie has wormed her way into his heart.

"Give me your phone." I type my number into my father's phone, call myself, and then save his number. I hand it back to him and he blinks a couple of times.

"I know I have no right to ask, but how are your sisters? And your momma?"

I study his face for a moment. "They're good. Eve is head nurse in the ER in Roxwell. Jade is doing law, and Zoe wants to be a teacher."

"Good," sounding choked up, he clears his throat. "That's good. Your momma still busting balls?"

"You know it."

Rhodie slaps me on the shoulder and heads to his ride, pulling his phone out, probably letting Tank and Tav know to stand down. Stepping closer to the trellis, I extend my hand to my father. He looks at it before nodding and placing his rough hand in mine.

"Good seeing you, son."

"You too, Dad."

Letting go, I walk to my girl, throw my leg over, rev her up.

"I'd put money on it that Officer Martin is somehow involved in this shitshow." Rhodie says quietly to me and Rider.

"Bet," I agree, and slowly pull out, throwing a hand up at my dad. We may not have found who we were looking for but we know more than we did five minutes ago and I can god damn guarantee that word will spread around the trailer park who we're looking for and there won't be a nook or crannie that this fucker will be able to hide in without someone snitching him out to us.

Chapter Thirteen

Remy

"I'm sorry Miss Remy! I didn't know the bad man was going to be there and hurt you!" Jovie sobs, her little chest heaving. I pull her into me, wrapping my arms tight around her shuddering body.

We've been in here for a while now and every time I calm her down the weight of the situation seems to press on her little shoulders and she starts crying again. It's not her fault her father is a jerk and Snake is evil.

"Jovie, have you seen Snake before?"

She runs her arm under her nose, catching the drips. "Y-yes. He's not very nice. He comes to my house, and he scares me."

"Is that why you were scared of Wire when you saw him?"

She bobs her head. "Yes, but the picture on his jacket is different and he's your friend, so I know he's nice."

I smooth her knotty hair from her face. "He is nice, Jovie, and so are all his brothers. They will help us. But we have to help ourselves a little too. OK?"

"OK."

Looking around, I see light coming out from behind a board. Standing, I run my fingers along the edge, finding a loose section. Pulling enough so I can peer around the edge, I find a window that's been boarded up.

"Jovie? I think I have a plan."

Looking around the crappy store room we're in there doesn't look like much that can be useful. I'm not even sure why there's a mattress in here but it's gross and stained and I don't really want Jovie on it but it's not like we have much choice at the moment. There's some junk sitting in the corner next to the door, so I get closer for a better look. I don't really want to touch any of it, so I shuffle it around with the toe of my shoe.

"What are you doing, Miss Remy?" Jovie whispers. Her voice is a little raw from her crying, but it seems my poking around has pulled her out of her fear for the time being.

"I'm looking for something to help me get that board off the window. If I can do that, I'll be able to help you crawl through it and you can find help."

She wipes her nose on her sleeve before nodding at me. "I can do that. I can run really fast. I'll find someone to come save us."

She crawls along the mattress until she's closer to me and peers through the dim light into the pile that I'm kicking about. Something clangs and Jovie and I both look at each other wide eyed. Getting to my knees, I feel around until I find what made the noise. It looks to be a square piece of metal, sort of the size of the grate that sits under Chewy's torture chair. It's not overly thick, so I'm sure it'll fit the gap between the board and the window and be large enough for me to pry the board off.

Jumping up, I slide the metal between the board and the window and work to loosen the nails around the rough old wood until I can fit my hands in. Getting a good grip, I plant one foot on the wall and pull as hard as I can. I'm sure the gap between the window and the boards is getting bigger, so I shake my hands out, get a better grip, and pull as hard. Feeling a tug, I look down to see Jovie is pulling me by the waistband, trying with all her might to give me the extra strength I need to rip this board right out of the wall. It must work because a long creak sounds out before the aged wood comes away and Jovie and I jerk backwards onto the mattress. We lie there for a moment; me catching my breath, making sure I didn't squish Jovie. Little girl giggles bubble up and light up my soul as I let out a guffaw before laughing along with Jovie. This little girl is the type of light that shouldn't be dimmed just because her dad is a jerk. No, he's worse than a jerk. He's an asshole.

Looking down at my little buddy, I raise my brow. "You ready to bust outta here, kid?"

"Are you coming with me?"

Eyeing the window, I know for a fact that there is no way I can fit through there.

"I'm too big to fit through the window, sweet."

She shakes her head and I know she doesn't want to go alone.

"But listen to me. I need you to find help, OK? I need you to get to my friends, Mr. Wire and the DRMC. Can you do that?"

"I-I don't know. I'm scared. What if I'm too little?" She looks down at the ground and I tip her chin up.

"Jovie, you once told me that big things have to look after little things, right? Well, this time, I need a brave little thing to look after me. I think you're the bravest little thing I know. I know you can do this."

Her big brown eyes stare up at me for a moment and I watch as she transforms in front of my eyes. Her little shoulders pull back, her brows crease together, and she gives me a nod.

"OK Miss Remy. I can save you."

"Good girl Jovie. You can do this."

I look through the dirty window and see that it's not so dark out just yet. I finish work at 4pm, and judging by the light outside I'd say it's closer to 6ish. Not so dark as to be too scary for Jovie.

"OK Jovie, when I put you through this window I need you to look for a specific person for help. You need to look for someone who looks like a mom or a nana. A lady with a bag with a long strap that she wears across her body," I show her with my hands what I mean. "Ladies with crossbody bags know everything. They'll know how to find Mr. Wire. OK? Can you repeat back my instructions?"

"Yes, find a mommy or a nana with a bag that goes across like this," she shows with her hands.

"Good girl Jovie, you are so clever and so brave. Are you ready?"

"Ready Miss Remy."

Mama Debs

"You know I can't believe it's taken me so long to come to Rosie's! This place is bloody brilliant!"

Swinging my head around I want to take in all the things. The cutesy booths, the cool decor, the biggest pepper grinder I have ever seen in my life. Sidney sits across from me with a frown on his handsome face and I have a bit of an idea of why he's in a sour mood. I assume it's because he and Rosie have some type of past relationship. I also assume it's because he doesn't know that I know all about his flirting with Rosie and he's trying to make out like he isn't the old dog that I know he is.

I should put him out of his misery but I love watching him squirm everytime Rosie comes over to serve us. Thus far she has shown no signs of jealousy. In fact, she seemed overly happy that I was here with Sid.

"Yeah, it's alright. Good food and all."

"And great service. Rosie is so beautiful. Don't you think? Such a lovely lady." I try to hide my smirk while he squirms.

He stares at me from across the booth before his eyes narrow, then widen in shock. "You're doing this on purpose! Baby, that's just cruel!"

He places his hand over his heart and slumps down like I've wounded him as I cackle my arse off across from him.

"Come on, old boy. Let's get home." He frowns knowing that he'll be dropping me off to the clubhouse where I've managed to snag a job as the clubhouse cook. I love it so much, looking after all those boys. I even have a room there, meaning Sid and I can have sleepovers every now and then. When I came to America I had no idea I'd end up living in an MC clubhouse. Ana thinks I'm crazy.

Come on Sid, I have some baking to do," I waggle my brows at him and he straightens up in his seat.

"God you know I love it when you talk dirty to me like that," He growls before dropping some bills on the table including a generous tip. I'm still confused over how that all works. We don't do that in New Zealand, but Sid is a gentleman and I never have to worry about paying when I'm out with him. That's why I love to make him baked treats.

He comes around to my side of the booth, offering me his hand like the gentleman he is. Sure he may be a little rough around the edges, and have a penchant for hurting bad guys, but he's sweet and funny and loving and at my age that's what you look for in a man. If only I can nail him down.

He tucks my hand into his elbow and he leads me toward the door, of course pulling it open and holding it for me as I pass through before him. The weather is crisp out and it's not fully dark just yet, in other words, its a pleasant evening.

"'Scuse me, can you help me please?"

Looking down at the voice I see it belongs to a gorgeous little girl who's eyes have the shimmer of tears in them.

"Oh sweetie, what happened?" I coo at her, crouching so I can be at her level.

Sid kneels down on one knee beside the girl, then tries to get me to sit on his bent knee. I roll my eyes at him knowing if I did that he wouldn't be getting back up anytime soon.

"What's your name honey?" Sid asks in a gentle voice. She stares at him for a moment before her big brown eyes move to mine.

"Miss Remy said I have to look for help from a mommy or a nana. A lady with a bag that goes across like this one." She points to my cross body bag.

"Miss Remy? We know Miss Remy. She's our friend. And she's right. Mama Debs is a mommy and is almost a nana. I'm a poppa so we can both help you. Do you need your mommy? Or the police?" Sid asks again.

I don't know whether she notices or not but she's now got her little body leaning on Sidney while she holds my hand. This little baby is just searching for comfort.

She shakes her head at us "No. I need to go to the DRMC. Miss Remy said to find Mr. Wire. He will help."

Sid and I share a look as I gather this little sweetness in my arms. "Well sweetheart, let's get you to Mr. Wire and DRMC."

Wire

After finding nothing at the trailer park other than a promise to call us if Jovie's dad surfaces, I spiral. I need to get back to my control center. It's my safe space. Once I'm there, I have eyes everywhere. I can do my checks. Make sure Momma and the girls are safe. Make sure the MC businesses and all my brothers are safe. And hopefully I'll be able to track down Retta. With Remy missing, I need the anchor that Retta will provide me to help me get my head screwed on right. That way I'll be able to find Remy, Snake and that fucker Hammer. I need to end this.

Following my brothers into the clubhouse, I'm hit in the legs by a weight that almost knocks me straight on my ass.

"What the fuu-" Looking down, I'm met with big brown glistening eyes.

"Mr. Wire! You need to save Miss Remy! She said you would save her!"

"Jovie?" I stare down at the little girl for a beat before my knees hit the ground and I pull her into my arms. Looking up and seeing the common room packed.

Savage, Flack, Dex, Savage's Ol Lady and a woman I'm

guessing is Remy's sister are here. So is Roman, his husband Sasha and the whole Tombs family, including Pops and Debs. Debs comes over to take Jovie by the hand.

"She found Sid and I in the street, said she had to find Mr. Wire." Debs says as she smirks at me. "Come on baby, time to finish your dinner, yeah?"

"OK Mama Debs." She hugs me before looking up at me. "You have to save her, OK?"

I watch as Debs leads her away into the kitchen before looking to Marx for guidance.

"Snake and Jovie's dad kidnapped them, which we knew. Jovie said that Remy and her were put in a little room that had wood over the window. Remy managed to get the wood off and got Jovie through the window to find help."

"Why the fuck didn't she escape too?" I tug at my hair, trying to understand.

"The window was too small. Jovie said she told Remy she'd be brave and find you and your brothers to save her."

Rubbing my hand down my face, it almost takes my breath away how brave Remy and Jovie are.

"She say where they were kept?"

"Said it wasn't far from Rosie's. She ran until she saw people. Debs said she wasn't out of breath when she approached them, so close by."

Nodding, I eye my Pres. "I need to be in the control center. Give me 20 and I'll have something."

He nods once, giving me permission to go somewhere and lose my shit for a minute before coming up with a plan. Everyone else in the room watches as I leave. Flack looks like he's barely containing himself, but at this point everyone knows there is nothing we can do until I have a location. Add to our problems the fact the police are still investigating us and we don't actually know which cops we can trust, it's a fucking tense time for all of us.

Stepping into my room, I take a deep breath to center myself before sinking into the familiar leather of my chair.

"You OK?" Chewy says from her spot, her eyes not leaving her screen as she runs searches.

"No Chewy, I'm not. Remy went missing and now Retta isn't talking to me." I feel exhausted. Retta quiets the noise in my head. When shit is bad, Retta is there to talk me down to help me focus. Without her, I'm worried I won't find Remy.

"That's because Retta was kidnapped."

"What?!" My head snaps to look at Chewy.

"What?"

"What do you mean, Retta was kidnapped?" My breaths are coming in fast. How the fuck do the two women I care for both go missing? I need Chewy to elaborate, but all she's doing is staring at me like I'm an idiot.

"Retta is Remy. Remy is Retta. Didn't you know?"

I splutter. What does she mean they're the same person? The person I've been writing to for 15 years is the woman who has been sitting next to me all this time? What the fuck?

Using an even voice, I ask, "Chewy, what makes you think Retta is Remy?"

"Trolls."

Staring at her, I circle my hands, trying to get her to explain. She blows out a long breath, rolls her eyes, and looks at me like I'm an idiot. Maybe I am.

"I was with you when you bought and sent a troll to Retta," she says slowly, as if by doing that I'll understand what the fuck she's talking about.

"Yeah?"

"And then last week, Remy and I went to town to have lunch with Ana. She stopped by her post box and there was a troll in there. She was super giddy and when she showed it to me, it smelled like you."

"It smelled like me?"

"Wire, come on, you know my flavor of autism means having the nose of a bloodhound."

Yeah, actually, I did know that.

"Wait, I'd fucking know if I was sending something to a post box in town. It's probably a coincidence."

"That's what I thought too." She turns her body toward me, pointing at me. "Until she told me that Flack was a nomad for years before becoming a dad. He had all his mail sent to an aunt four hours away. She'd forward it to a post box. It became normal for all their post to go to her. Remy's still does. Now her aunt forwards it here to Rose Grove. After that I did a little digging and saw all your messages to each other. Then I checked through Remy's stuff and the turn of phrases, grammar. It all matches. Remy is Retta."

I'm glad I'm sitting down. What Chewy has just hit me with is fucking huge. My head spins as I try to process that the two people I've been having feelings for are, in fact, the same person.

"Wait, you went through my messages?!"

"Look, before you get all butt hurt about it, you're my best friend. I know that I've organized my besties into categories, but it doesn't mean anything. The feelings are the same. I have your back, through thick and thin, and I'm not going to sit by and watch my best friend fall in love with someone online only to find out that the woman he loves is actually a big, toothless

169

black guy from Minnesota. Not that toothless black guys don't need love, just not with my best -"

"Chewy?"

"Yeah?"

"I'm going to hug you now,"

"Oh, OK,"

I stand and wrap Chewy's small body in my arms. This woman, who blew into our lives and has made shit bright and colorful, chose me as her bestie. Yeah, OK, she went through my messages and is snoopy as hell, but it's for a good cause. She pats my back awkwardly, and I let her go.

"So, best friend, wanna help me find my girl?"

"Fuck yeah!"

Chapter Fourteen

Remy

Voices echoing from outside the door have me pressing myself back into the corner of this gross room. Since hoisting Jovie through the little window, I've been going through all my options. There isn't really a lot other than to fight with all I have. I'm not sure exactly where we are being kept, which means I'm not sure how far Jovie had to go to look for help. I can only hope that she found a nice mom or nana to take her to safety.

The voices get closer to the other side of the door, and I realize one voice sounds off. Moving toward the door of my prison, I press my ear to the door, hoping to hear a little better.

I think the voice sounds off because it's on speaker phone. The other voice sounds a lot like Jovie's dad. I can't quite make out all the words, but Jovie's asshole father sounds even more unhinged than usual. The lock clicks and the door is thrown open before I can get to a safe distance on the other side of the room.

"What the fu-" He looks around the room, eyes darting to

the now uncovered window before it dawns on him that Jovie's not here.

"Where the fuck is my kid, bitch!?" He snarls, getting in my face, his big hand grips me, squeezing my cheeks tightly, so even if I wanted to answer I couldn't, anyway.

Getting annoyed with my lack of response, he shoves me backwards onto the mattress. I jump up as fast as I can, but he kicks my legs out from under me, then wrestles me onto the mattress, his gross boner digging into my thigh.

"Keep fighting bitch, I love it when bitches fight. You should have seen Jovie's mom when I sold her. Fought for all she was worth, and she still ended up dead." An evil grin covers his scabby, scarred face.

Instead of lying dormant I pull my head back as far as I can and then slam my forehead into his nose, blood exploding over both of us as he rolls off me, covering his face and screaming obscenities.

My vision blurs slightly from where I probably got a little too much of his forehead in that hit, smooshing my glasses into my eyes, but I don't care. I get up and kick his balls before jumping over him and making a run for it. Pumping my legs as fast as I can, I'm able to see what looks to be the door. I head in that direction only to have my head snap back when something grabs the back of my short hair, pulling me down to the ground.

"Now, now Remy girl, where ya heading to? We're only just getting this little party started."

Snake grins down at me and even though my hair is burning as he drags me back into the little room, I don't go easily. I scratch and kick, twist and try to bite.

"Shit, Remy, I don't know where all this piss and vinegar

came from, but Hammer is going to love to fuck it out of you. I will too. You know how Hammer loves to share."

He smirks down at me and I seriously wonder if vomiting on the guy will gross him out enough to loosen his grip. He throws me into the room, where I land on the gross mattress for the fourth time in one day.

Jovie's dad is cursing his head off and instead of beating on him, Snake grabs him, looks deep into his eyes and says, "Find that girl. Her buyer will be here in two days."

I can feel the bile rising along with my anger. That bastard sold his wife and now he's sold his daughter. I get the urge to launch myself at him again, but that'll do me no good. I need to regroup. Be smart about this. I have hours before anyone will be able to locate me, probably. Like I told Jovie, sometimes we need to help ourselves. I may not be able to stop Hammer right now, but with enough time I will be able to stop Jovie's dad. And maybe even Snake. All I need to do is bide my time and try to get as much information as I can.

"So what's the plan? Sell me and Jovie? How much did we make you greedy bastards?"

"Whoa! Look at little Miss Remy with the bad language," Snake grins at me like I'm a silly little girl.

"There's more where that came from, asshole," I mutter to myself.

Snake's grin drops and he crouches down, crawling towards me, crowding me until I'm pressed up against the wall. He's straddling my legs, pinning them to the mattress so I can't kick out. He sneers down at me, his nose touching mine.

"You want to know the plan? That sweet little girl you were protecting will be sold to a man in South Africa. He loves little biracial girls. Eats them for breakfast. Like's breaking

173

their spirit until they're nothing more than broken little dolls littering his basement." He licks a stripe up my neck, making me shiver in disgust before whispering in my ear, "As for you, my sweet, well, Hammer has owned you for years."

He pulls back, smiling in glee at the horror he must see on my face. Not for me, but for Jovie.

"Hammer doesn't own me. No one does." I have no idea how I push the words out without stammering. This can't be real.

He clicks his tongue "Oh, but that's not true, little miss. Hammer bought you from your slut mother when you were 3 years old. It was even better when Flack took you from her and brought you home. He could watch his investment grow. Who do you think told your dad that cursing wasn't ladylike? Hammer has been in Flack's ear, shaping you to be his perfect woman since you came to live with us. Who you are today is because that's who Hammer wanted you to be."

I recoil in horror, the back of my head hitting the wall. The extra attention he'd paid me as I was growing up never quite made sense. Sunny never got birthday presents from Hammer. I just thought the Pres was being nice. My hand covers my mouth as the gravity of what Snake is telling me sinks into my brain. I shrink back onto the mattress and ignore Snake's laughter as he walks out, closing and locking the door behind him.

What the hell? Is it true? Did my dad know? Surely he didn't. Flack may be many things, but he is a good father. I mean, he led the charge to get rid of Hammer. He sent me to DRMC to learn. And to keep me safe. It dawns on me then. He got rid of Hammer. He sent me away. I thought it was because of what I had overheard. Because of what I told him. He knew months ago and set everything in motion, but he never told me. Always protecting me and in doing so, he made me weak. I will not be that weak, invisible person anymore. I'm going to be like Chewy and Ana and Nat. I was raised as the daughter of the VP of a 1% club. I'm my father's daughter. I will tear Hammer and Snake apart with my bare hands if it means mine and Jovie's freedom.

Wire

With Chewy by my side, I storm down the hall with a plan of attack. We have narrowed it down to three buildings where Jovie could have run from. It might not be accurate given that the brave six-year-old was terrified and it was nearing dark, but it's all we've got.

"We have got three locations where Remy could be-"

"And you're going to tell the police those three locations, aren't you, baby?"

My head snaps up, clocking my momma, standing full force in the middle of the room.

"Momma, what are you doing here?"

Momma squints at me, lips pursed. "I'm here updating everyone on the investigation. Sergeant Davies was lovely enough to call and let me know that tomorrow morning, Tank and Sniper will be interviewed by the police. I will be there with you both." She says as the eyeballs them until they nod. "Oh, also, he wanted to know why the hell three DRMC riders were seen at The Grove trailer park earlier this evening when I remember telling you all to lie low. Care to explain?"

"His Ol Lady has been taken. We have to get her back. They were canvassing the last known address of the kidnapper," Chewy casually throws out there.

Judging by the intake of breath from my brothers, the Death Riders, Roman and the Tombs, I doubt anyone saw that coming.

"Remy?" Jules asks, with a squint. I nod in return. "Figures. It was only a matter of time."

"Your Ol Lady, huh? And when were you gonna tell your momma?"

"After I told her?" I end on a question and watch momma's eyes widen in shock.

"What about your internet friend?"

"Well, that's the kicker. It's the same person!" Chewy crows.

At this, my momma's face softens. She knows what Retta means to me.

"Hold up, you're Mags?" Flack comes to stand in front of me, eyeing me up and down.

"Yeah. Chewy figured it out when both Retta and Remy went missing."

"Well, I'll be damned. You were the best thing that happened to my girl. Helped her through a shit ton. I'd be happy to welcome you to the family. Not as great as this one -" Savage's snort interrupts him "- but it's still family." Flack slaps me way too hard on the back before heading back to the Death Riders' table.

I look at my momma expectantly. She purses her lips as she thinks, looking around at the large group gathered around that are waiting for her to say the word.

"You said there were three locations?"

"Yeah."

"And you're serious about this girl?"

"Yeah" I can feel a small smile playing on my lips

"And you'll one day give me grandbabies from this girl?"

Flicking my eyes at Jovie, who is sitting with Debs, I can see that happening sooner rather than later.

"Yeah."

Momma narrows her eyes even further before turning to Marx.

"Marx, call in a favor from your old friend, Moss Davies. Let him know you're sending out three pairs of men to do a quick grid search of the streets. Quietly check the locations Wire and Chewy found. If you think she's being held in one of them, radio or phone or whatever, to the other two teams. The other two teams will call in the police to check their locations, drawing the heat off whoever has found her. The rest is up to you to decide."

Momma looks around the room to make sure we all understand her instructions. My brothers all nod, smiles growing on their faces.

"I'm going. Behave, don't get arrested or killed."

Momma kisses my cheek before gathering her briefcase, waving to everyone and then clip clopping out the door.

"Well, it looks like Wire's momma has solved our problems with how the hell we're gonna be able to ride out without getting arrested. Fox and Nitro, you take one location. Rider and Savage, the next. Wire and Flack, the third. Chewy, you're eyes until Wire gets back." Chewy salutes him, because of course she does.

A throat clearing has us looking at Gus. "We'll each follow with an SUV. We don't know what we're walking into, whether there are others that need help."

Marx gives him a nod, his shoulders relaxing some. "Go and bring back our girl."

Chapter Fifteen

Remy

I've spent long enough in this shitty room to realize that my choice of weapons is very limited. I have no idea what time it is, or when Snake, Jovie's dad or even Hammer are going to arrive. What I do know is that I'm not going to go quietly. I've spent my life doing that, and no more.

I gather up the metal plate I used to pry the board off the window and wonder if I can sharpen it enough to use as a slicing weapon. I rub it on the rough concrete and then realize that is probably a waste of my time and energy. Turning my attention to the window, I decide that may be my best bet.

Taking off my sweater, I wrap it around the metal plate and gently hit the window. I don't want to smash the whole window out, I just need it to break enough so that I can use a shard. The glass makes a cracking noise; the fissures working their way out from my fist. I press gently until some of the glass breaks away and falls to the ground on the other side of the window. There are some long, jagged pieces left sitting in the caulking in the windowpane, so I wriggle one out in my sweater covered hand so as not to cut myself.

Tearing a piece of fabric from my blouse, I wrap it around the bottom of the shard, giving myself a handle, a safe way to wield my weapon. I dare those bastards to come at me now.

Squatting down on the mattress, I swing between biding my time and making more weapons. I decide to get crafting, mainly because if I sit with my thoughts and feelings, I'm liable to lose the small edge I'm carving out for myself.

Finding the board with the nails sticking out of it, I figure it'll be a good enough weapon to hit someone with. Getting whacked with a hunk of wood with sharp metal sticking out of it is sure to stop a man like Snake in his tracks. It'll definitely take out Jovie's crackhead father.

With my protection placed strategically around the room, I sit on the mattress and wait. I wonder what the DRMC is doing? Have they realized I'm missing? Mags will have noticed that I stood him up. My stomach lurches at the thought of Mags waiting for me. I love him, in only the way you can when you have known someone for so long. I sometimes wonder if I could love Wire the same way. There are so many things that are similar between the two men. The way they make me feel comfortable and not like a shy burden. They want to know my thoughts on things. I can be sassier than I ever am with the both of them. I even noticed when I picked up the gift from Mags in my post box that they even smell the same! Maybe that's why I felt so comfortable with Wire? I've fantasized so many things about what would happen if I met up with Mags in real life, but since I've met Wire every time I picture Mags, he has Wire's face.

Sighing to myself, I realize all this fantasizing is going to get me nowhere. Men like Wire don't end up with women like me.

They end up with badasses like Nat and Chewy and Ana.

The sound of a motorcycle getting closer echoes through the warehouse until it's a dull roar near where I'm being held prisoner. I listen carefully to it idling, noting the small tick that it makes. I breathe out a breath I didn't know I was holding. That bike is Snake's, and at this point I'd rather face him than Hammer. Especially after what I've just learned.

Making sure my weapons are close at hand, I decide to go stand closest to where the door will open. That way, Snake will have to move into the room to look for me. It's dark so he won't see me immediately, giving me time to hopefully knock him out.

Pressing myself against the wall, I breathe deeply, trying to calm my racing heart. This will be my one shot. Snake has a wicked temper and if I don't take him out, he'll make me pay.

The snicking of the lock is almost drowned out by my heart beating in my ears and I wait for what feels like years before the door swings open, almost hitting me.

"What the fuck?"

Heavy boots thud on the concrete floor until Snake's body is almost blocking the small amount of light coming in through the window. Raising the board above my head, I step forward and then bring it crashing down with all my strength straight onto Snake's head. He crumples immediately, knees hitting the ground first before his top half flops forward onto the mattress. I stand frozen for a moment, staring at him like it's a trick. Well, that and I've never actually purposely tried to hurt a human being like that. Looking at this one, I find I actually like the feeling.

Looking around, I weigh up my options. The first one would be to run outta here like my ass was on fire. The second is to restrain Snake and poke at him until I find out useful information. Like where the hell is Hammer and what are his plans?

Looking through the door to the warehouse once again, I see the door to the outside. Snake's bike is parked up. I could ride that out of here. Striding to his pride and joy, I go through his saddlebags until I find all the things I need. Taking them with me into the storeroom, I lay them out on the mattress. Rope, knives, cigarettes, a gun. Glancing back at the exit door, I decide my next move. Snake and I are here for the long run.

Wire

Racing through the streets, I can hear both Marx's and my Momma's voices in my head to not draw attention. Well, fuck that. I need to find my girl. And then convince her to be my Ol Lady. I'm fucking terrified that she'll reject me, but then I remember I know this woman. I've known her more than half of my life. She's the other part of me. Surely she feels it, too.

Flack pulling up beside me has me shaking off my thoughts to concentrate on the task at hand. Our destination is an empty warehouse looking place. It used to be a furniture consignment store that moved to a larger, flashier building nearer the shopping center, leaving this place empty but close enough to Rosie's for a little girl to run there.

I tip my head at Flack, signaling that he follows as we pull into the parking lot. There is fuck all here, but I have a feeling about this place. Like I sense her in there.

Before we dismount, I take a look at the outside. I checked to see where the cameras were placed before we left the compound, however now that we're here I can see there are none. Probably a good thing if the inside is being used to keep women and children.

Getting off my girl, I creep up to the door, Flack following close behind. Before I twist the handle to the door, a scream sounds out and all my good sense leaves me. I throw the door open and storm in, hoping that Flack will have my back in case I'm storming into a bloodbath, and that's exactly what it is.

A gasp rips from Flack's throat and I stand frozen as I take in the sight before me. Remy has Snake sitting upright on his bike. His hands are tied to the handlebars. His feet tied to his bike at an odd angle, too far back. That is until I notice the sweet, steaky scent of burning flesh in the air and realize that Remy has tied his feet that way so that his legs sit either side of the pipes. The pipes that get fucking hot.

Snake has blood dripping down his face, likely from a head wound. He has burned flesh on his calves, and there seem to be lacerations on his chest. Remy is standing over him, her hands covered in blood and a pissed look on her face. I'm unsure that she's even noticed that we're here.

Turning to Flack, the older man is frozen in place, his face a mix of shock and sorrow. I get it, his baby girl was kidnapped. Innocent sweet Remy has been replaced with a valkyrie and that is making my dick pulse in my jeans.

Stepping closer, I gentle my voice so as not to startle her.

"Retta,"

Her head snaps toward me, a slight frown pulling her dark brows together. "How do you know that name?"

I can't stop the sheepish grin on my face. "I'd like to say I figured it out, but it was Chewy,"

"Wait, what?" She drops the glass shard that she's been using on Snake and steps away from him. Snake relaxes in relief, which is a pity for him because while Remy has been walking toward me, her dad has been stalking toward him.

As they pass each other, he reaches over and strokes her cheek, "I love you, baby. I'm sorry this happened to you."

"It's OK, Dad. I used everything you taught me. I'm not weak. I'm the daughter of the VP." She smiles brightly at him and he kisses her on the head before she looks at me and steps closer.

"Um, can you explain to me how you know my Shadow Wrath name?"

I blow out a long breath. "Beretta_Penn is your avatar name. Your avatar is a large green troll, with piercings and long black hair. You've been playing since you were 13 years old. Your first day you joined a campaign with an elf, Saint_Margarita. You would spend all day at the library because you had stuff going on at home. I would spend all day online because my parents were breaking up. Girls picked on you at school. I slept with all the girls at school." Her eyes grow wide and glossy and her perfect lips open on a shocked o. "I skipped prom to hang out with my older guy friends while you went to prom and some douche got too drunk to take your virginity like you wanted. You messaged me every day while I was deployed and put me back together when I got home. You're my conscience, my hope, my other half, and I'm yours. I have your back for always."

Tears freely roll down her cheeks as she whispers, "For always."

Beaming up at me, she does something that I never thought

she'd do. Stepping closer, she runs her hands up my chest, her touch sending little electric shocks of awareness through me. Sliding her hands behind my neck, she tugs me closer until my face is so close her beautiful sky-blue eyes are all I see. With a sweet exhale, her soft lips touch mine in the gentlest of kisses. Sliding my hands into her silky hair, I cup her face and deepen the kiss, swiping my tongue across her bottom lip asking for permission. She sighs and her tongue comes out to glide across mine.

We move and taste each other, the desperation of the last few hours leading us to grasp and grip at each other, at what we could have lost.

"Listen kids, I'm glad you've found each other, but mind if we get this fucker back to the compound?"

Remy tears her lips from mine, looks over my shoulder at her father and bursts into giggles.

"Fine, come on then. I wanna show Chewy what I did!" She claps her hands and beams like escaping a kidnapping and then torturing the fucker who did it is a completely normal thing to do.

"She's been hanging out with your lot too long," Flack grumbles as we watch her run to Snake, untie him, and push him off the bike onto the ground.

"Is that a bad thing?"

Flack turns to look me in the eye. "It's bad because I fear I'm losing my little girl. But the woman I see before me now is someone she should have always been."

He dials his phone and barks at Tav to bring the van around to collect Snake.

"You two go on. I'll wait here for this piece of shit's ride."

I grin at Flack, excited that I finally get to feel my girl on the back of my bike. Waiting patiently for Remy, my brows pull into a frown.

"Um babe? We need to get out of here, and I need you on the back of my bike."

"I want that too, but tonight, I'm going to be riding my new bike home." She smiles widely at me as she throws her leg over and sits her pretty little ass on Snake's bike. Well, Snake's old bike, her new bike. Starting her up, she cackles as she slowly glides her way to the roller door.

"The DRMC created a monster," Flack laughs as we watch the woman we love wait for the roller door to open before riding out.

"Come on, slowpoke!"

She revs her engine, and I run out to catch up.

Chapter Sixteen

Remy

As I ride to the Devil's Rose MC compound, I use the time to clear my head. I could have easily jumped on the back of Wire's bike, held him close and breathed him in. But I earned this bike fair and square, so the ride is giving me time to come to terms with everything that's happened. I was kidnapped. I got Jovie out of there all to learn that Hammer bought me when I was a child. I fought back against someone who scared the living crap out of me and harassed me most of my childhood. I spent a little time torturing him all to be found by my dad and Wire, who then reveals that this whole time he has not only been my perfect man plaguing my nights but also my best friend. All this time I'd been flip flopping between wanting Wire and feeling like I was cheating on Mags when they were one and the same.

The wind through my hair seems to help with some of the shell shock, but heck, this is a lot to process. From the corner of my eye I can see Wire pulling level with me. I turn to face him, and the brilliant smile he gives me settles the turmoil whipping around inside of me. He sees me, he's always seen me, just like I have always seen him. Pulling into the compound, I just know that everything will be alright.

I idle on Snake's, no, my bike until Wire parks his, then I park up next to him. We both dismount and stand facing each other, the toes of his big shit kicker boots touching the toes of my sensible, black wedge shoes. Looking down, I take in our feet and let out a giggle. Tipping my head to look at Wire, I can see that he's noticed the same thing I have. He looks at me and we both share goofy smiles.

"Fuck, is it bad that I don't know what to call you anymore? You're my Retta, but you're also Remy."

I shrug. "I'm probably going to call you Wire to your face. But you'll always be Mags or Maggie in my messages."

His eyes narrow. "You know I've always hated that."

"Yeah, I know," I grin even wider at his disgruntled look before frowning. "You're not disappointed, are you? That I'm Retta?"

He cups my face in his large hands. Somehow they seem rough even though I know he works on a computer all day.

"Before I found out, I was all twisted up. Retta has my heart, but Remy was quickly worming her way in there. To find out that you're the same person, that the different things I loved about both women were actually wrapped in the one, it was like all my Christmases come at once."

He steals the space between us by covering my lips with his, nibbling at my mouth until I groan, wanting more, wanting everything.

"Soon baby. I want you in my bed, where I can love on you all night." He pulls away and then pecks me once more. "But first, there's a little girl in there waiting for Miss Remy and two surly bastard Pres's looking for answers."

I groan before taking a deep breath, pulling back my shoulders and start walking toward the door. Before I can reach for the handle, Wire pulls me to a stop.

"First, I gotta know. When did you become such a badass?" His lips curl as I roll my eyes.

"These past two months with DRMC have shown me I can be opinionated and strong and still be me. So when those assholes -" Wires brows shoot up at my cursing, "took me, something snapped. I was no longer content to just go with the flow and be invisible. Then they told me they were selling Jovie, and I was pissed. I'm going to bring them all down."

Wire adjusts his erection and I get a little thrill that I did that to him. He throws his arm over my shoulders and then we step through the door to be met with the sounds and smell of home.

"Remyetta! Holy shit, I saw you riding that hog on the cameras, you looked like a total bad bitch! Also, whose blood is that?" Chewy yells at me in excitement before stopping in her tracks, tilting her head at the blood covering my top.

"Snake's," I answer and then watch as her wide eyes scrunch up because of her wide grin.

"Fuck yes," she whispers at me before stepping forward and awkwardly patting my shoulder.

"Move, Dayz," Ana says before pulling me into her embrace.

I hug her back, before turning to look at the next people in line wanting to hug me.

"Nat! Sunny!"

"Fuck yeah girl, there was no way I was going to let Savage leave our asses behind when our girl was out there on her own." Tears well up at Nat's words and I hug her before falling into my sister's embrace.

189

"You OK Rem?" she gently asks as she wipes the happy tears from my cheeks.

"Yeah. I'm perfect."

"So's your man," she smiles at me before tipping her head at Wire, who only has eyes for me.

We share heart eyes until I hear my name being squealed "Miss Remy!"

Spinning, I look for the little tornado that stole my heart. Crouching low, I wrap Jovie up and hold her tight while she whimpers against me. I soothe her until her body grows heavy and her breaths even out.

"She wouldn't sleep until Mr. Wire saved you," Debs says, brushing the hair out of Jovie's face. "Do you want me to take her?"

"No, I want to hold her a little longer, if that's OK?"

Debs' smile softens even more. "Anything you want, baby girl." With that, she kisses me on the forehead like I always wished my mom would have when I was little.

Wire pulls a chair out for me and I take a seat with Jovie on my lap.

"Right people, we have our Remy back and scumbags to fuck up. Remy, tell us what you know."

Nodding my head, I take a deep breath, blow it out, and then go through exactly what happened and what was said. I could feel Wire grow more and more tense when Hammer selling Jovie and buying me was mentioned, but he kept his temper in check.

That's not what I'm concerned about, though. What I'm worried about is what happens after this. When we go to his room, will we make love and then I'll fall asleep while he spends hours brooding and running himself ragged in front of this computer? Will he start watching everyone more than he does now?

Now that I know that Wire is Mags, I understand his behavior better. I understand how his PTSD rules him most days, even if he doesn't see it himself.

Well, I'll just have to distract him with my body then, won't I? I snort at my little joke, knowing full well that I'm a virgin and he's a man whore. A moment of unease unfurls in my belly, thinking that I won't please him, but then I remember I know this man better than anyone. I have all the hacks to make Wire happy, and I will make sure I use every one.

"DRMC and Death Riders, I'm calling church for 10am tomorrow morning. Savage, Roman, Gus and I will come up with our next steps. We have Snake now trussed up in the back shed. Thanks Flack," Dad tips his chin and grunts at Marx. "We have Jovie's dad to find and end. We have a little girl we need to keep safe somehow, and we have Hammer to find, all without drawing heat from the police. Especially that Officer Martin dickhead. It's a fucking shitshow and we're all in the middle of it. Get some rest." Marx gives a nod and everyone disperses.

Debs comes and takes Jovie from me, telling me she can sleep on the little pullout bed in Debs' and Pops' room tonight. I want to fight with her, but her gaze flicks to Wire and then back to me before raising her brows. I can feel my cheeks heat, especially when Sunny snorts and laughs at me.

"We'll catch up tomorrow, OK Rem? I want all the goss! When you left, you were an L7 Weenie. Now you're a badass who almost cusses and you beat and stabbed a man." Sunny waggles her brows before pulling me in tight and whispering in my ear, "Fucking proud of you, little sis."

She kisses my cheek and steps back so Nat can repeat the same thing. Looks like I'm having a girls' day tomorrow.

"Come on baby, I'm exhausted and I need to hold you." Wire takes my hand in his and we walk hand in hand to his control center.

Stepping over the threshold, he looks at his computers with longing, and I just know that he won't settle until he checks on everyone.

"Do your checks. I'm going to get in the shower. Wash Snake off me,"

His eyes darken for a moment before he nods and pats my ass. Before I get all the way into the bathroom, he hands me one of his shirts and I almost squee like a little girl. Grinning big at each other, we at least try to play it cool. Well, I do, until the bathroom door closes behind me and I dance around like a little girl, all the while muffling my happy squeals in the shirt that smells like the man I've spent over half my life falling for.

Wire

I'm a fucking loser. My girl, the one I've been wanting, is within my grasp, soaping herself up in the shower and I'm here. My big ass sat in my ergonomic chair thinking about checking my cameras.

Roughly rubbing my hands over my face I decide fuck it, Chewy and my brothers are all in the compound. The Death Riders and Bratva are all here. I'm sure they can cope for one night without my eyes on everything.

Pushing myself out of my chair before I have second thoughts and start logging on to my cameras, I gently twist the handle on the door and push it open. Remy is dancing around on her tiptoes. My shirt scrunched in her hands in front of her face, her eyes closed, and a weird muffled scream coming out of her.

"Fuck baby, are you OK?" I immediately go toward her and am stopped by a punch to the gut.

Air rushes out of me and Remy's wide, light blue eyes stare at me wildly.

"Oh my god, oh my god are you alright?" She pats me, my shirt forgotten on the ground.

"I'm OK, are you OK? You were screaming when I came in."

A blush creeps up her neck until it blooms across her cheeks. Her eyes dart everywhere as she chews her lip until I'm forced to cradle her face, my thumb pulling her lip from between her teeth.

"Talk to me, Rem. You know you can tell me anything."

Her gaze settles on mine. She swallows before whispering, "It seems different when you're right here in front of me. Online, I could write whatever I wanted, and I never had to see your reaction. Now I can."

"How do you think I'll react to whatever you're going to tell me?"

Twisting her lips, she lets out a sigh. "I think you'll think I'm a dork." She tips her head up to the ceiling before letting out a huff. "I was sniffing your shirt and dancing, because it smells like you and I like the way you smell and you're like, my *boyfriend* now. It's a lot, OK?"

By the time she tips her head forward to look at me, she has a frown on her cute face that makes me smile. She looks even more disgruntled, and I can't help the grin that grows on my face until she rolls her eyes and I let out a laugh.

"Babe. Retta. Remy. I already know you're a dork. You play Shadow Wrath. You want to go to Comic Con dressed as your troll avatar. Speaking of dress ups, you dress as Where's Waldo for Halloween most years because it makes you laugh. You love Dad jokes and you think I'm the coolest person ever. None of that makes me want you less. In fact, I think it makes me want you more knowing that you're so excited to be my girlfriend that you'll dance in a steamy room sniffing my shirt."

She stares up at me, a smile playing on the corners of her lips. "Your girlfriend, huh?"

"Yup. This has been years in the making. You can't get rid of me now."

Leaning down, I brush my lips over hers, a whisper of a kiss, before pulling back to look at her. Cupping Remy's face in my hands, I hold her gaze, her hands coming up to grip my wrists as I lean down, this time angling her face to fit mine. Her lips part as we kiss, cradling my bottom lip between hers before my shy little minx sucks gently, causing my restraint to snap.

Deepening the kiss, my tongue sweeps against her bottom lip before tasting her, my tongue gliding across hers. Her kiss is inexperienced, raw, making me want to pull out all the stops to show her how much pleasure I can give her. Her small hands release my wrists, resting on my chest, before moving lower to pull my shirt up and over my head, our lips parting for mere moments before attacking each other again. She fumbles with my belt, her hands desperate to get me out of my jeans, a little growl escaping her.

"Get naked!" she growls, not removing her lips from mine.

Chuckling into our kiss, I rid myself of my belt, unbutton

my jeans and shove them and my boxers to the floor. I break my lips free long enough to get her shirt up over her head, bra unclasped and then attack her mouth again as she unzips her jeans and pushes them down. Her generous breasts press against me, her tight nipples poking my lower chest. Ripping my lips from hers, I grip hold of her shoulders and push her back. I want to get a look at what my girl has been hiding under all those ill-fitting librarian clothes.

"Holy shit, babe."

She's fucking breathtaking. Standing on the white tile, steam swirling around us, stands my Retta. My Remy. My dream girl. Her skin is flawless, so pale and smooth. The thought of my brown hands on her, my cock gliding through her pink pussy, has my dick leaking. Her breasts are a thing of absolute beauty. Perfect teardrop shape topped with candy pink nipples that just beg for my hands and my mouth. Her soft belly leads down to a thatch of blonde hair nestled between her thick thighs, waiting to have my face between them. Remy is a fucking goddess, and it's my job to worship her for the rest of our lives.

My eyes take her in from top to bottom and then back up again. That's when I notice my girl is squirming under my gaze and praise, her thighs rubbing together as she takes in my body hungrily. Her hand reaches toward me before pulling back.

"I'm yours sweetness. I belong to you. Yours to touch, yours to do with what you please."

Her eyes flick up to mine before settling back on my cock. Her little pink tongue pokes out of her mouth and her brows furrow as her hand wraps around my steel, so gently that if I wasn't watching her intently, I'm sure I wouldn't feel her touch.

Remembering that my girl doesn't have any experience at

this, I wrap my large hand around hers, showing her how I like to be touched. When it's my turn to touch her, I'll ask her to show me how she likes it. This is about communication and feeling good and learning each other's bodies.

Retta is such a quick learner that after a few strokes she takes over, pumping my cock like a pro, pulling a groan out of me. All the anxiety I had about my cameras and my brothers safety has left my body and my head falls back on my shoulders as I pump my hips slightly. Hot wetness touches the head of my cock, causing my eyes to fly open. Looking down, Remy has that pink tongue on me, tasting me. I angle my hips away and smirk as she pouts up at me.

"Baby, I want nothing more than to see those gorgeous lips wrapped around my cock, but I'm in charge and I want to take care of my girl. Will you let me do that?"

Remy's eyes narrow at me for a moment before she nods. Then I take her by the hand, lead her into the warm water, letting it beat down on us as I soap up my hands and run them over my girl, feeling every inch of her.

"That feels so good. Don't stop, please," she gasps as I tweak her nipples lightly before letting my slick hands drift away, moving down to cup her ass, pulling her cheeks apart before letting them go and doing it again because I can.

My hands drift between her thighs, gently caressing her folds, drifting away to massage her inner thighs and then going back for more. Sucking on a spot below her ear, I draw a moan out of her as I let one of my thick fingers sink into her tight little hole, pulling out to spread her moisture around her lower lips, and then sinking back in again. I know my girl is untouched, and as much as I would like to sink balls deep and fuck her until I'm imprinted in her little pussy, I know I need to be gentle with her.

"Mags, Wire, whatever, I need you. I need more, please!" Her begging gets more desperate until she's gasping at me, and I can barely think straight other than to stop the water, wrap a towel around her and carry her into my room.

Dumping her on the bed, she throws her head back and laughs, all the while looking at me through hooded lids, her blue eyes dark with lust. My Retta is bold and brave and yet even in this wanton state the Remy I know still looks back at me, a shy blush covering her cheeks even as her legs are parted wide, with her pink lower lips spread and her swollen clit on display. I have no idea how the fuck I got to be this lucky, but I'm not looking a gift horse in the mouth. Or the pussy.

Starting from what look to be her bumble bee inspired toes, I trail kisses up her toned, pale legs, her little gasps spurring me on, until I get to her pussy and show it no love by skipping straight past and kissing down the other leg. I know that she's noticed I did that on purpose because her head lifts off the bed and she has a small frown, which disappears as soon as I lean forward and suck her clit into my mouth. Gently working her nub with my tongue, I pull back enough to run my tongue down to her tight hole, circling where my cock will be soon, lapping up her cream as she writhes beneath me.

"Please Wire, I'm close, please, I need you!"

Cupping her pussy, the heat of her has my cock leaking like a faucet. I ease my thick finger into her, testing to make sure she's ready for me. I'm not a cocky son of a bitch who brags about how big his dick is, but she's never done this before and I really don't want to fucking hurt her. I want this to be the best experience of her life.

Moving between her spread thighs, the weight of my pelvis

against hers has her eyes flying open, holding my gaze.

"Rem, I haven't been with a woman in a long time. I've been tested, I can show you on my phone, if you like. I just, I want to feel you with nothing in between us."

"I-I'm on the pill. I trust you."

A blush covers her chest, building until it's all over her beautiful cheeks. She's smiling up at me in wonder, I think. Until I sense amusement and her lips curl up, before a snort escapes and she starts to giggle.

"Um, babe, what's so funny?"

A wheeze escapes her, "I don't know. I've pictured this before and I really want to come and then I look up and it's, it's *you* and you're all just there with your big dick," she whispers this part for some reason, "and then I got all nervous." She looks up at me through her lashes and I can't help but chuckle at how fucking cute she is.

"Nervous giggles?"

She nods, then blows out a breath. "OK, I'm ready now. Enter me, St Margarita,"

Staring down at her smiling face, I watch as she purses her lips; the corners curving up. I know that she's fighting nervous giggles and I don't want to make her feel self conscious or embarrassed. I know from our messages that when this happens she can't control it, so I choose to ignore it and notch my cock at her entrance, hoping that will distract her.

It doesn't. Instead, the giggles get worse, until she's snorting and I'm starting to soften.

"Quick Wire! I'm dying here! I need to come and you're taking too long!"

"Dammit, Remy, I can't do it if you keep laughing!"

"I can't help it, you ass! I'm nervous and I'm horny and I

198

don't know what to do!" In that one sentence she goes from anger, to lust to frustration so I press my lips to hers, kissing the living daylights out of her as I press forward, the crown of my cock breaching her entrance, both of us tearing our lips apart as we groan at the feeling of becoming one.

She's tight as hell and I have to think about my cameras and my brothers and my family to stop from blowing my load. Pulling back, I rock in and out of her heavenly pussy, getting deeper and deeper until I'm fully seated, my balls nestled against her luscious ass.

There are tears pooling in her eyes, and my stomach clenches, thinking I've hurt her.

"Baby, are you OK? Do you need me to stop?" I'm resting on my elbows, my large dark hands cupping her pale face, my thumbs brushing tears from her cheeks.

"No, it's perfect. You're perfect." She cups my face and beams at me, pecking me on the lips before pulling back. "Now fuck me."

Chapter Seventeen

Remy

I'm not sure exactly what happens but I think Wire hearing me cuss snaps what little restraint he's been holding on to. I'm not some delicate flower, even though I know that's how a lot of people view me. I may be a virgin, but it's not like I don't own my own toys. I've been using them religiously since I met Wire.

He pulls out until it feels like I'm going to lose contact and then he thrusts back in, my boobs bouncing in a way that pleases him because he smirks down at me, swivels his hips and then does it again, and again, until I feel like I'm going to go crazy. My vision is hazy, my head in a fog of lust, the slapping of our bodies driving me higher and higher toward my peak, but I'm unable to fall over the edge just yet.

"God damn baby, you feel so good wrapped about my cock. Look at that perfect pink pussy taking me. Look baby, look at us,"

Wire's words break through the fog and I open my eyes, tipping my head up to look between our two bodies. Wire cups the back of my head, pulling me up to almost sitting so I can see the darker skin of his cock gliding in and out of me, covered in my juices. It's so obscene and hot that I can't tear my eyes away.

"Do you like watching me claim you? Do you like knowing that my cock is the only one that's allowed in this little pussy?" He pulls his cock out, grips the base and slaps it against my clit before sliding it up and down between my lips. My hips buck of their own accord and I try to angle them to draw him back where I need him, where he belongs. I must time it right because on his next glide between my lips I lift my hips, angle them up and over and capture him exactly where I need him.

We both groan in pleasure as he sinks deep inside me again. Raising my leg, he places one, and then the other, on his shoulders, leans his weight forward on his hands beside my head and powers into me, my body nearly folded in half. The mushroom head of his cock is hitting me exactly where I need him, over and over until I'm hurtling to my orgasm, lights dancing behind my eyes and a wail ripping from my chest.

My legs shake as I try to catch my breath, but it's no use. Now that I've fallen into the abyss, Wire is on a mission to join me. His hips stutter, his rhythm grows jerky as he lets out a grunt and then a deep moan, but he doesn't stop pumping his hips. He glides in and out of me, getting slower and gentler with every pass, the noise of our combined juices making sounds that would normally make me giggle if I wasn't so spent. After long, leisurely moments, my legs slide off his shoulders and he lands gently beside me on the bed, his large palm spread on my stomach, as if he doesn't want our connection to break just yet.

"Fuck baby, that was incredible,"

I roll my head to look at him beside me, a silly grin on his face and his eyes hooded.

"I bet you say that to all the girls," I tease, but his face darkens at my comment.

Raising up to his elbow, he looms over me and I notice just how large this man is. He seems gentle, less imposing and dangerous than some of the other brothers, but that's just because of his nature. I'm sure if Wire needed to, he'd be able to use his size to his advantage. But not with me, never with me.

"Rem, all those other girls, they meant nothing. They were nameless, faceless pussy. A vehicle to scratch an itch. I know that sounds fucked up, but it's true. You, Remington Wright, you own a part of me that no one else ever has. Our connection, that's what made our fucking incredible." He gazes down at me, willing me to believe his words, and I do.

"It felt the same for me. Although, I haven't had a lot of nameless dick, so maybe I need to try some out just in-" A squeal is pulled from me as Wire rolls me over and slaps me on the ass before rolling me back toward him.

"No fucking way. You're mine," he growls in my ear, causing my body to go soft against his.

Dropping a kiss on his chest, I look up at him. "And you're mine."

"Let's get cleaned up, then you need to sleep. You were up late last night, had a long day at work, were fucking kidnapped, saved yourself and then you had your first taste of dick. You need to rest so I can mess you up all over again."

Pulling my boneless body up from the bed, he slaps my butt on his way to the bathroom, checking the water temp before we get messy all over again.

***

Something hot, damp, and thrashing wakes me with a start, and it takes a moment to register where I am. The smell calms me immediately, the rich and slightly spicy scent of Wire. His body is taut on the bed next to mine. He tosses, turns and moans, as if fighting an invisible enemy. I imagine most women would panic, they'd lay hands on their men and try to wake them, but I know Wire. I know that waking him in that way will cause him to lash out at me, then he'll be riddled with guilt. I've known about Wire's PTSD since he came back from deployment years ago. He's shared with me his dreams and his nightmares and how his PTSD affects him. For years he's asked over and over if that makes him weak, or scares me. But I've known this man since we were kids, so instead of getting upset or looking at him with anything but love, I sit here, next to him, and recite one of my favorite stories as a kid. Keeping my voice in calm, hushed tones, I wait for him to work through the scenes in his mind, until after however long he opens his eyes and gazes at me.

He looks haunted and vulnerable, much like Jovie did earlier. And like I did with her, I lie with him wrapped in my arms, my hands in his hair, his hands stroking my back. His heart rate is still rapid, but he's breathing easier now.

"I bet you want to run for the hills now, huh? No one wants a broken man with nightmares."

"Well, that's where you're in luck. My perfect man has girly curls, a jacked up back from sitting too long, and can't sleep through the night. So, it looks like you're stuck with me."

He huffs a breath at my joke, but his shoulders are still tight with tension.

"Wire, did you check the cameras before you joined me in

the shower earlier?"

He goes quiet and I now know that he didn't. I thought he came to shower a lot quicker than I expected, so I'm guessing he skipped his usual routine.

"Why don't you jump up and we'll look at them together, yeah? I know that I'll rest a little easier knowing that everything and everyone is all good."

He raises his head to look me in the eye and I raise my brows back at him, like I do to the little boys at the library that don't really want to do something, but will do with enough egging on.

"Fine. I'm not sure I like this bossy Remy,"

"You love her," I say as I slap his ass on the way to put on his oversize tee. Just because we are in our private space doesn't mean that we have to have our naked bits on the seats.

I sit in my chair next to his, pull my legs up and wrap my arms around my knees to watch my love.

"Can I ask you something?"

He turns his gorgeous hazel eyes on me. "Of course, ask away."

"Why is your Shadow Wrath name St Margarita?"

He throws his head back and laughs, the rich sound washing over me. "My first name is Saint."

My bow furrows. "Wait, what?" Thinking back to what I know about Wire, it suddenly clicks. "You were born on Christmas day!"

He rolls his eyes. "Yup. And because Momma is creative, or nuts, she decided she didn't want to name me Nick. So I got Saint."

"Wait, but what about the margarita part?"

"You know my last name."

"Yeah, it's Harvey."

"My dad used to say that it was his great grandfather that made up the Harvey Wallbanger. So I just chose the only other cocktail name I knew of at 13 years of age."

"Wow, we were really basic as little kids, huh? Mine is an exact word substitute for my real name."

I watch as Wire's perfect man brows furrow a moment, his lips moving noiselessly before his head snaps up, and he laughs again.

"Fuck, how the hell did it take us so long to figure it out?"

"We didn't. Chewy did."

"And she'll hold that over us for the rest of our lives, you know." He grins at me, and I can't help but cup his cheek. He leans into my touch for a moment before pulling away, shaking himself off and making his nightly checks.

He's beautiful and thinks he's broken. That came through loud and clear in our messages over the years, but to me he's not broken. Just a little bent. And with love, care, and security cameras and gadgets, we can work through this together and create something amazing. I know because the more cameras he checks, the more his shoulders relax, the tension in his face eases and the stress in his body melts away.

He turns to look at me, his eyes darting around my face before settling on my eyes.

"I love you, Remy. For always."

"I love you, Saint. For always."

And just like that, the last of the tension fades away as we laugh at how dorky we are.

Wire

The sun peeking through the curtains that I never shut properly shines onto Remy's beautiful face as she sleeps soundly.
She's bound to be exhausted after everything that happened
yesterday. And last night. I didn't want her to know the extent
of my PTSD. Usually, I don't have night terrors, but I think
forgoing my usual routine to join her in the shower last night
triggered something inside me. It's hard to tell. It's been years
since I left that hell hole and yet every night before I go to bed
I do the same routine. My nightly checks help me sleep better.
Of course, I told Retta all about my problems over the years,
never thinking we would ever meet. Retta was the faceless
person who supported me through the ups and downs, good
and bad. She knows me better than I know myself, so I should
have known that Remy would know exactly what to do. Instead
of waking me with a start, she sat and spoke to me until her
husky voice pulled me out of the hell in my mind until all I
could hear, see, smell and touch was her.

After that, she worked her magic again. Not berating me for
not doing my checks, instead making out like she would rest
better if she could see everyone was safe. Any embarrassment
that I had about my needs evaporated at that moment. She sees
me, the real me, and that's who she loves.

Looking at my watch, I note the early hour, and slide quietly
out of bed, trying my best not to wake my girl. She had a fucking
nightmare of a day yesterday and then had me sinking into her
tight, wet pussy two more times after we got back into bed last
night, so she needs her rest.

Pulling on my jeans and a clean tee, I sneak to the other side of the room divider and wake up my screens. Flicking through the cameras, I see Tav sitting on the back deck watching the sunrise. I can't tell by his body language what his exact mood is, but he definitely looks more gloomy than usual.

I complete my checks and decide to head to the kitchen and get my morning cup of coffee out of the way early. Doctoring it just how I like it, with lots of creamer and a little sugar, I head out the back.

"Mind if I have a seat?"

Tav's head swings around and he smiles up at me before tipping his head to the chair beside him.

"Busy night, brother?" Tav asks, a smile playing on his lips.

"A little. You?"

He looks out to the back shed thoughtfully before shaking his head. "No. Nice and quiet. Waiting to hear from a girl."

"She special?"

Tav sighs, "I'd love her to be. But she keeps pushing me away."

He turns to look at me, and I circle my hands, to encourage him to keep speaking.

"She's a few years older than me, has kids. So we have to think of them, take things a little slow, which is cool. I'm good with that. But she does something funny to my chest. I want to be with her all the time, but she's not as all in as I am. She was weird about me joining the MC."

I frown at that. Tav is good people. So is everyone in this MC. "She got something against MC's?"

He snorts, "Weirdly enough, she seemed happy I joined. She's different from every other woman I've ever been with, but she's skittish. Grew up in Louisiana, so I think she has some weird religious or voodoo hang ups." He shrugs and looks toward the shed again. "Maybe I'm just moping because I haven't watched Chewy torture someone lately."

"Oh yeah, that'll be it." We share a smile as I drain the last of the dregs in my cup.

Standing, I drop a hand to his shoulder. "Look man, if this girl is special to you, and not weird or blind, she'll know what she has in you. Sometimes this good shit takes time. Look at me and Remy. That was 15 years in the making."

He nods at me and then grumbles about not waiting 15 years for his girl as I walk back through the kitchen to my room to snuggle with my woman. Now I know why Rhodie went soft. When you find your one you want to spend all your time with them.

I have even more of an urgency with my woman. Knowing full well that Hammer put things into Flack's ear to groom her over the years, I know he isn't going to just give up on her. That makes him even more fucking dangerous than usual.

Sliding under the covers, I wrap my arm over Remy's waist and pull her into me, the little spoon to my big. Taking a deep breath of her hair, I close my eyes. Bliss is more than just being buried deep inside my woman. It's also having her here, in my arms. I don't have to message her anymore! We can talk to each other. I can see her reactions to my jokes and I can see her reactions to my teasing.

Although at the moment it's Remy doing the teasing. Her luscious ass is gently moving against my hardness, her heat making me harder still.

Pressing my hand against her soft stomach, I try to hold her in place.

"Baby, you need more rest. I kept you up last night. Let's just sleep,"

Instead of stopping, she moves even more, almost twerking on my cock, making me hard enough to pound nails with the fucking thing. I could tell her to stop again, but I'm clearly a weak-willed man. Even as the thought crosses my mind, my hand slides down her stomach into the front of her drenched panties, through the fine hairs on the top of her mound until I'm circling her swollen clit.

She opens her legs, lifting one up over my hip so my cock can access her heat. Tugging her panties to the side, I notch the head of my cock at her entrance and slide in deep in one thrust. We move together like that, lazy, gentle soft movements, not the frenzy from the night before where we needed to ground each other. This one is for us. Softly, gently, we reach our peak together, whispering to each other, promises, memories, plans for the future before dozing off again, only to be woken by banging on the door.

"Oh Remyetta!! We're all out here waiting for you! We have a little girl to shop for!" Chewy's voice calls out, only to be interrupted by what sounds like her sister Sunny.

"And we need to know what that dick do!"

Giggles drift through the door and Remy's body shudders next to me as she tries to hold her giggles in.

"OK! Gimme 10 minutes!" She calls out and then rolls toward me for more cuddles.

"You do know that if you aren't out of here in 10 minutes, Chewy will bust in here and drag you out." I raise my brow at her while she rolls her eyes.

"I know. I just wanted one last cuddle with my man."

I drop a kiss to the top of her head. "Take my card. You'll need it for all the things Jovie will need."

"I have my own money, you know."

"I know, but what about little girl bedding and toys and stuff? She can't keep sleeping in a biker's room. She needs a little girl's room."

Remy frowns at me. "What are you talking about?"

I sit up, taking her hands in mine. "Remy, Jovie's mother, was the body the police found. She's dead, and very soon her father will be too. Jovie doesn't have any other family. My dad, he lives in the trailer next to theirs. He told me he used to sit with her sometimes, when her father went out. She's a good kid. I know that this is new, you and me, but I don't think I can in good conscience put that little girl into foster care. Can you?"

She pulls back a moment, her frown even deeper as her eyes flit all over my face. "Are you saying you want to keep her?"

I swallow. Maybe I'm wrong in this. Maybe I'm pushing Remy into something she doesn't want, but Jovie is a fucking cool kid and I don't want to see her lost to a shitty system.

"Are you saying you don't?"

Tears pool in her eyes and I think I might have read the situation wrong. "I've wanted to wrap that little girl up and bring her home since the moment I first met her. Are you sure Wire? Because I can do this on my own if I need to." Her eyes flit between mine, as if trying to find any uncertainty.

"No need. We have a huge fucking family to help us. We have my brothers. We have Mama Debs, and I can't believe I'm going to say this, but Pops as well. Jesus, my mother is going to go wild."

My eyes must go huge because Remy sniffs and then giggles her ass off. "I cannot wait for your momma to find out. I better get ready before Chewy's girl gang kicks the door in."

She bounces out of bed like her ass is on fire and quietly

shuts the bathroom door behind her. As I slowly descend into a panic about how the hell I'm going to tell Momma that I have a girlfriend and a kid. Shit.

Chapter Eighteen

Remy

After the quickest shower in the world, I bounce out of Wire's room and head to the main room. The early morning buzz drifts down the hall and the smell of bacon wafts toward me. Hitting the mouth of the hall, I look into the room and take in my family, both old and new.

Savage, Dex, Bones and my dad are all mixed in with the DRMC brothers. My sister and Nat are hanging out with Ana and Chewy. Grabbing a seat next to Chewy and the girl gang, I take in the very domestic scene. Tank and Sniper, my usual breakfast table buddies, give me grins and chin ups. Mama Debs and Pops are in the kitchen serving and my heart almost beats out of my chest and flutters into my stomach when I see Jovie in Wire's powerful arms. She may be six, but she looks tiny perched on his tattooed forearm as he points at all the breakfast options.

"That's a mighty fine looking man, huh sis?" Sunny whispers as she nudges me with her elbow.

I can't even speak, so I just nod wide eyed at her.

"It's black magic, Rem. As soon as you put a kid in a man's arms, they get 1000 times hotter. My cooch is gonna combust when I lay my eyes on Savage with our little nugget," Nat says, rubbing her non-existent baby belly.

Wire leans down and gently puts Jovie on the floor, who squeals and comes racing up to me as soon as she sees me.

"Miss Remy! Wire said I can have three pancakes for breakfast. Look how big the stack is!" Her eyes are huge and full of excitement as she dances in place.

Wire drops a kiss to the top of my head and Jovie's, then places Jovie's food in the empty spot next to mine as I pull her chair out and help her up.

"There you are Princess Jovie, now remember, if you eat it all you might grow up to be big like Tank over there,"

Jovie's head swivels until she spies Tank, her eyes grow huge, and she bursts into little girl giggles as if Wire is the funniest man on the face of the planet. He winks and smirks as I roll my eyes back at him.

"I like your name, Jovie. I don't spend a lot of time with kids, but you seem cool." Chewy says to Jovie. Rhodie smiles softly at his Ol Lady and I try to cover my smile, but I'm unsuccessful as I catch Ana's eye and she smiles back at me.

"I like your name too. Chewy is a funny name. Do you like dinosaurs?" Jovie says all this with a mouthful of chewed up pancake.

The look on Chewy's face is priceless as she stares at Jovie like she's a foreign creature.

"What's your favorite dinosaur?" Chewy asks with suspicion.

"Ankylosaurus,"

"Second favorite?"

"Parasaurolophus,"

Chewy's gaze finds mine. She narrows her eyes and nods approvingly at me before looking back at Jovie.

"We're gonna get on well, kid," Chewy tells Jovie, who couldn't really care less as she smears maple syrup across her cheek.

"Ooookk, well, now that Chewy has bonded with Jovie, let's get this show on the road, ladies! We have shopping to do. Jovie, you're coming with us for some new clothes and bits and pieces and then Mama Debs will bring you back here for a rest, OK?" Ana announces.

"Wait, what are we doing after Jovie's shopping?" I ask.

"We're going shopping. Me and Nat need stretchy underpants to accommodate our growing bellies and asses, and you need a new wardrobe befitting of the badass you now are."

"What about Hammer?" I know he's still out there, and I'm wondering why the heck we're being allowed out instead of on lockdown until the threat is neutralized.

"Tombs Security is on the job. Because they can't possibly let us traipse the streets without big manly men." Chewy says while rolling her eyes.

Ana snorts because we all know that of everyone in this room Chewy is probably the most dangerous of them all.

Mama Debs comes bustling over with a cloth to clean Jovie's hands and face and then does the "Chop Chop" motherly thing to get us all moving into the SUVs. I help Jovie into the car seat that somehow materialized, before getting in the back with her, Sunny next to me and Nat in the front with Gus. Pops is bringing up the rear with Mama Debs, Ana, and Chewy. Jules and Tav are on their bikes and we make quite the imposing convoy as we ride to the big box store on the other side of Rose

Grove.

Piling out, we grab trolleys and lead Jovie to the little girls' section. Instead of going wild like most kids her age, she freezes in place. Tears building in her eyes.

"Jovie, sweetie, what's wrong?" Kneeling next to her, I gently stroke her hair from her face. I notice Mama Debs had brushed it this morning, but given the texture of her hair, I suspect she probably needs some good shampoo and treatments and maybe even a protective style. I make a note to ask Wire what I should be doing to care for it.

The rest of the ladies gather around me and Jovie. Well, all bar Chewy who has wandered off and is currently opening and sniffing jars of silly putty.

"I, I don't have any money. I don't know where my daddy and my momma is. Who will buy my clothes and look after me?" Her large dark eyes stare into mine and I pull her into my arms. I can't answer just yet, my throat is clogged up. If I ever get my hands on her father, I'm going to take his balls.

The girl gang feels the same. I can tell by the murderous looks on their faces. Well, all of them except Chewy, who is now opening packets of fidget toys.

"Where do you want to live?" She asks, not even looking at Jovie.

Jovie looks at me, her lips wobbling before whispering, "I want to live with Miss Remy and Mr. Wire."

A smile grows over my face as I squeeze her tight..

"And it shall be so, child," Chewy says with a flourish like a small, murdery fairy godmother.

Pulling back from Jovie, I wipe her little face. "Right, so that's settled. Ready to get some new clothes and some stuff for your bedroom at the clubhouse?"

She nods her head emphatically before taking mine and Sunny's hands and leads us to the kids' section, packed full of clothes, toys, and stuff for Chewy to touch.

After a solid hour of buying everything that Jovie sets her heart on, Pops arrives to escort Mama Debs and Jovie home while me and the girl gang decide to get a bite to eat and coffee before moving onto the next phase.

"Are you serious about keeping Jovie, Rem?" Sunny asks, settling her big sister gaze on me.

"You've seen her and spent time with her. She's a sweetheart who drew the short straw. She needs this, and I-I think I need her." I stare at my sister, her eyes identical to mine and our father's. I let her see everything I can't verbalize.

She stares at me before blowing out a breath. "Yeah, I see that now. She'll heal that timid little girl inside of you, and you'll help her find her voice." Sunny nods, leaving it at that. She's accepted it and now she's moved on.

"And I'll help with her papers. By the end of the day, you and Wire will be the proud parents of one little girl." Chewy says, before taking a very loud, long chug of her water.

"Yes, she drinks like a toddler." Ana says to us all before turning back to her sister-in-law. "What do you mean by 'I'll help with her papers'? What papers?" Ana asks, eyes narrowed at Chewy.

"Birth certificate. Social Security. That sort of stuff. By the time I'm done, she will have always belonged to Wire and Remy."

"Wait, if you could do that, why did I marry your brother? Why the hell did we have to go to that mean counselor when you could have just given me my green card?" Ana frowns at Chewy, who looks blankly at her.

"Huh. Yeah, I could have done that, too." Chewy shrugs her shoulders, dismissing her sister-in-law's grumblings. "I can do a quickie divorce if you like?"

"Hell no! I love that big, bossy bastard."

"I heard that!" Gus grumbles from somewhere nearby.

"Love you!" Ana coos back before turning to us. "Me and Nat need stretchy pants. What are you tramps shopping for?"

Sunny and Chewy decide they need lingerie and then they zero in on me.

"You're a badass now. You need to not look like that," Chewy points out. In a loving way, I'm sure.

"What's wrong with the way I dress?"

Everyone grows quiet and some, not Chewy, avoid my eye contact.

"Rem, is that what you wanted to wear, or were you groomed to wear it?" Sunny asks gently, resting her hand on mine.

My mind flashes back to when I was younger and Hammer would buy me dresses for my birthday, or when he would tell me I looked nice in long-sleeved shirts and trousers. Nothing creepy at the time, a quick "Looking good Rem," here and there. But knowing what I know now, my skin crawls under my ill-fitting conservative clothes.

"That's it. I need a new wardrobe. Let's go ladies."

In no time, I'm in my underwear surrounded by women.

"Holy shit, Remy, I can not believe you were hiding this banging body under all that tweed!" Ana says.

"I told you she had good boobs!" Chewy crows before poking the girls. "And those legs!"

"Do you really think I have that good a body?" Looking up at them all, nodding wide eyed at me like I'm a blind fool. Turning to look in the mirror, I hear a screech and spin back around.

"That's the flaw ladies! She has no ass! Thank god. I was worried with all that tit and those thighs that we were done for. But the woman has no ass, so we're fine. We're gonna live to fight another day." Nat says, wiping her brow as the other women cackle around her.

"Well, Wire seems to like my less than round ass, so I don't care what you say." I flip the bird, spinning back to look in the mirror and catch them all smiling goofily at me. "What?"

"Nothing, Remy, you're just, you're you, but the you I always knew you could be if you could find your spine." My sister. "No more hiding, yeah?" Sunny says, reaching for my hand and holding it in both of hers.

"No more hiding."

Wire

As soon as the girls leave, Marx yells for Church, so we all dump our phones with Takoda, who's on phone duty, as we file in. We have three Death Riders and two Bratva with us too, so they file in behind and take up whatever space we have left at the table.

"Let's get this started. I think we know now that we need to put down Hammer as fast as we can. With Snake hanging in our shed, I'm hoping Rhodie or Chewy will get something out of him."

Marx looks around the table, everyone nodding at our Pres. Hammer has been a thorn in our side for too long. The only problem is, unlike the Russians that caused us problems last time, Hammer seems to be a lot fucking harder to catch.

"Whatever you need from the Bartashev Bratva, we are at your service. Usually I wouldn't get involved," everyone rolls their eyes at this statement. Even Roman's husband Sasha. "However, he had the police crawling all over my business, so he needs to die."

"He fucked with my family. He bought my fucking baby. He will die, but not before I make him pay," Flack growls, fire in his eyes.

Marx regards him for a moment. "You never knew this whole time?"

Flack bristles, "If I knew that my fucking Pres was grooming my baby because he *bought* her from her slut mother when she was a toddler, I would have put them both down years ago. As it stands, that bitch will get a visit from me very soon."

Marx nods at Flack, before glancing at Savage to make sure the man hasn't taken his questions as a dig at them.

"Look, you know full well the problems Hammer has caused us. Not just with Remy and the trafficking, but well before then. We had good reason to get rid of him, but none of us knew he was in this fucking deep." Rubbing his hands down his face, he looks back at Marx. "Look, man, Death Riders MC is on its last legs. I have a total of ten members, most are retirement age and want a quieter life. We took a vote and all agreed to disband. It's a fucking sad day for the legacy members but Hammer royally fucked what we had and he just keeps on fucking us."

Looking around at his brothers - Dex and Flack, Savage looks at all my DRMC brothers before returning his gaze to my Pres.

"We're out of the Death Riders, but we're not ready to give up the life just yet."

"You asking to patch over? We're a small MC. We're not looking to charter." Marx explains as he leans back in his chair.

"We're looking to move. We all know Remy won't be coming home. If Flack wants to be closer to his girl, he's going to have to move."

"What about your businesses? You've only just opened them."

"The tattoo parlor and restaurant will be run by the brothers as they lean into their retirement. Although I imagine we'll need a new restaurant manager and chef cos I'm sure Sunny will want to move to be closer to family."

Marx runs his hand down his beard as he nods thoughtfully.

"We've been looking to expand into more businesses, but the bulk of the brothers are tied up running our garages and towing yard. I'm sure you boys have skills we can use as we expand. How are you going to feel giving up Pres?" Marx pointedly asks Savage.

"Honestly? It'll be a fucking relief. I have a pregnant Ol' Lady and I just want to take care of her and our baby."

He looks around the room, and I can tell he's sincere. Shit, if I were him I'd want to chuck it all in too.

"You understand we'll have to put it to vote?"

Savage offers a chin lift. "Yeah, we understand. If we get the vote, we can be here within two weeks. Nothing holding us back."

Marx nods and moves on to planning what the fuck we're going to do. There isn't much we can do other than wait for Rhodie and Chewy to work their magic on Snake. Then, we need to find Jovie's father and tie up that loose end.

"I have something I would like to put forward." I say, clearing my throat. "I'm just putting it out there that I'm claiming Remy,"

My brothers all bang their fists on the table. Flack jumps up and slams his big hand on my shoulder before roughly shaking me before returning to his seat.

"Also, we have decided that we want to keep Jovie. She's a sweet kid, and neither of us wants to see her in the system." I hold my breath and wait for the reaction.

I'm not sure what I was expecting, but it wasn't all my brothers talking over each other about who will be the favorite uncle and plans for her own little trike to ride on.

"Well, brother, congrats on becoming a dad." Marx grins. "DRMC members, stay behind so we can vote on Savage's proposal. Savage and Roman, we'll all reconvene once we have more info from Snake."

Both nod before they and their men get up to leave, until only DRMC members are left to determine Savage's fate.

"Brothers, we have a vote to make. I feel Savage, Flack and Dex will make good brothers. They've tried to turn that shit show of an MC around, but that shit's been poisoned from the start. So, what do we think? Wire you have all their backgrounds?"

"Yeah, they're all safe. Savage and Dex both have time served in the army. Flack is, well, he's pretty much a less crazy, more refined Pops. He's all good."

"Of course you'd say that about your father-in-law," Rider says, rolling his eyes and then ducking as I swing on him.

"From the businesses they have opened, or were looking to open in Roxwell, they have skills we don't have. Having them will widen our business portfolio," Sniper offers.

"That's a good point. We don't have a restaurant. They've already opened and run a successful one. We could do that here with their experience." Tank shrugs.

"Dex is a personal trainer. We've spoken about buying that gym space in town, but none of us have the know-how to run it properly," Fox says before Nitro butts in.

"Yeah. We can offer MILF classes." He wags his eyebrows while we all roll ours.

"So, what's the vote?"

We all look at each other before Rhodie starts the vote with an "aye". Then the ayes go around the table until it's unanimous. Savage, Dex and Flack will patch over. But they'll be given the big talk from Marx. If they fuck with us, they're dead men. You know, the usual welcome spiel.

"That's that then. Fuck off the lot of ya and get to work or whatever you were doing. Scratch that, go clean out the room next to Wire's for my new niece." Marx grins as he slams the gavel down and we all file out the big doors in high spirits, regardless of the shit swirling around us.

Grabbing my phone from Takoda it vibrates in my hand, my dad's name flashing across the screen.

"Dad?"

"Son, Jovie's asshole sperm donor came around all frazzled, looking for her. I told him I heard word that she was at your club. The idiot is heading your way."

A chuckle rips out of my throat at how dumb this fucker is. "Thanks, Dad. I owe you one."

Hanging up, I holler to Marx, interrupting him just before his beer touches his lips.

"He's coming here? Here, to the compound? How dumb is this cocksucker?" Marx's frown is in full force, overshadowing the confusion in his voice. "What in the absolute fuck?"

"Dunno Pres, but he can't be the sharpest tool in the shed.

He got mixed up with Hammer, for one thing, and kept Remy and Jovie in a room with a window. Clearly, we aren't working with a genius here."

Marx scowls harder before waving his hand at me. "Well, we better get out the welcome mat."

Smiling big, I take a seat at the bar with a good view of the front door, grab the beer Takoda hands me, and even before I can take the first sip the door is booted in and the greasy little worm is shoved through it by Pops.

"Any of you boys order a tweaker with a death wish?" Pops booms kicking Jovie's dad in the back of the knee, making him crumple to the ground.

"Where in the hell did you find him?" Rider asks as he stands over the dickhead, poking him with the boot of his toe.

"Would you believe he was out the front demanding entry to come get his kid?"

"And what the hell happened to his face?"

"Would you believe he fell? Many, many times?" Pops asks with his most innocent face.

Rider lets out a snort before kicking Jovie's dad again.

"I have to go get my girls. I told them to wait in the car while I dealt with fuckhead here. Jovie was upset so I'll bring her in the back way." Pops nods and then heads back outside, leaving the fucker on the floor surrounded by bikers, all standing over him.

Does that make him rethink his life choices? Hell no.

"Gimme my kid! I want my daughter!" he yells, struggling to get up due to all the boots shoving him back on his ass.

"You know boys, that's exactly what I was saying yesterday when some greasy fucker took my daughter!" Flack roars in his face.

Instead of shrinking back, the meth makes him brave, so he yells in Flack's face again until a well-thrown punch knocks him out.

"Rider, hang him in the shed next to Snake. Wire? Get a hold of the women. I need my best enforcer - no offense brother,"

"None taken,"

"I also have a feeling Remy might have something to say to this one," Marx says as he gives him a swift kick with his boot, before spitting on him.

"Ew Pres, I have to touch him and I don't want your germs on me," Rider whines, then trots away trying to dodge Marx kicking him in the ass.

"You know, every interaction I've had with you lot, I always thought it was nuts because it was stressful and shit was going down. But you're like this all the time, aren't you?" Dex asks, wide eyed.

"You get used to it," Rider shrugs before grabbing Jovie's dad by the foot and dragging him behind him out the door.

Chapter Nineteen

Remy

"Oh, we gotta roll, ladies." Chewy announces as she whips back the dressing room curtain, wearing a red lingerie number that makes her ass in the mirror look phenomenal.

"Huh? Why?"

"Jovie's dad just turned up at the compound. We got both those assholes and we're needed back for a little show and tell." Chewy smiles, all crazy like, waggling her eyebrows.

We rush to grab our purchases and haphazardly put on any clothes we weren't wearing when Chewy ripped open our curtains. I should feel flustered, instead I'm on fire. I cannot wait to stand in front of those two men and watch them beg for mercy the way Jovie did when her dad hit her and threw her into that little room. I think I may also want to have a little go at making them beg myself.

We load up and speed back to the compound, walking in to find everyone waiting for us.

"Baby, you need to go comfort Jovie a little. She saw her dad turn up and I think he may have been ugly to her before Pops put a stop to it. She needs you now, then after that you can come and help in the shed, OK?" Wire stoops a little to hold my gaze. When I nod, he kisses me on the forehead and then taps my butt. "Go on then, babe. We'll wait for you."

"We'll go get dinner started. You do what you need to, Rem," Sunny says as she, Ana, and Nat all head toward the kitchen.

Quickly moving down the hall, I stop at the room next to Wire's, which the MC designated as Jovie's new room. Knocking gently on the door, I push it open. All the rooms in the MC are painted the same beige grey color, this room is no different, however it's also had a major injection of little girl. There's a pink glittery canopy over the twin bed, girly artwork on the walls and stuffed toys on almost every surface. I know for a fact that we didn't buy all of this on our trip this morning, which means somehow the MC brothers have had stuff delivered. Looking around to find Jovie, my gaze freezes on Mama Debs sitting on a fluffy pink rug on the floor next to a Rug Rats pop-up tent.

My hands fly to my mouth and I remember my days spent in my little hideaway. Mama Debs reaches her hand out to mine, drawing me closer to her. Kneeling next to her, she smooths my bangs out of my eyes.

"She's in there, all tucked up, but she's been waiting for you. You check on her and I'll be up there, on the comfy bed. I'll sit with her while you unleash hell on those people in the shed."

Mama Debs heaves herself up muttering about being too old to be on the floor, as I gently call out, "Knock, knock."

"Come in," a little voice answers.

I push the little flap open and crawl in next to Jovie, pulling her onto my lap.

"Hey brave girl, whatcha doing?"

"I'm hiding in here. It's my fortress. Takoda got it for me from his momma's house. She kept it for him since he was little," she says as she rests her head on my shoulder.

"When I was little, I had one like this too. It was my fortress as well and no baddies could get me in here."

She beams up at me, bright eyed and full of life. "Are you going to make the bad men go away?"

"I am."

"Good. You can go now. I want them away. I'll be safe here in my fortress." Her face brightens. "And Mama Debs is my guard. She will keep all the baddies away."

"Damn straight, baby," Mama Debs' voice calls from her comfy spot on the bed.

"OK sweets, I'll be back. After that, do you want to have a Remy Wire Jovie night and we can all watch a movie together?"

"Yes!" she yells and throws her arms around my neck, hugging tight before pulling back. "OK, you can go now."

I try to cover my smile as I crawl out of the little tent. Standing, I look back at it and think of all the times I hid in mine, my hand coming to my chest as my heart aches for the little girl I was, knowing that the little girl behind me will have a much different life. One where she will rule the roost, making all these strong men bend to her will.

"Thanks Mama Debs, I'll be back in no time." Leaning down, I drop a kiss to her cheek.

"Take your time. I think I might need to make some movie snacks. If only I had someone to help me...."

A squeal sounds out behind us and we smirk at each other before I turn and make my way through the clubhouse to the shed. With every step I feel more and more wild. The rage builds until I feel like I can barely contain it. But I will. I want to see these men suffer, and they can't do that if I go wild in there and end them too soon.

Standing before the door, I'm unsure whether to knock. The Remy that thought she could just kick the door in has reverted to the old Remy. I raise my hand and before I can bring it to the scarred wood, the door swings open and Wire stands there, so wide he almost blocks out the rest of the room.

"Coming, Retta?" He holds his hand out to me and I take it.

"Thanks, Mags." We share a secret smile as he leads me further into the room.

Chewy and Rhodie have been busy. Snake is strapped to a St Andrew's cross, which shocks me somewhat because I only know of those from the smutty books I've read.

"Is that a St Andrew's cross?" I whisper to Wire.

Before he can answer, Tav speaks up. "Yes. Yes, it is. Somehow, this place got both sexier and grosser." He has a disgusted look on his face as he watches Rhodie straighten his sister's safety goggles before grabbing her ass.

Jovie's dad is dangling from a chain, and Pops has just wheeled in an assortment of things on a stainless steel table like a nurse's aid.

"What are we gonna do with this one? We can't remove his teeth. The meth already got them." Pops says as he wrestles one of those mouth stretcher things the dentists use into his mouth.

"I'm not sure yet. Strip him naked. I need to see his dick. I have plans." Chewy says before giggling like a coy woman, rather than a maniac.

Jules shrugs as he and Tav step forward and cut Jovie's dad's clothes off.

228

"What is your name, by the way? We can't just keep calling you 'Jovie's cocksucker dad'" Chewy says, doing something with a container of goop to his privates.

Because Pops has shoved that thing in his mouth, whatever he says comes out all garbled.

"Ngarain,"

"Huh?"

"Ngarin,"

"Garin?"

"Ngarrin,"

"Nope, still not getting it."

"NGAR-"

"Fuck's sake, his name is GAVIN." Marx growls out, obviously at the end of his rope.

"Oh, well, you should have just said that then," Chewy says as she rolls her eyes and huffs before eyeing him up, handing over the container of goop to Pops. "Are we doing the usual set up? Bratva, Death Riders, then DRMC all take turns with the torture?" Chewy looks around as all the major players in the room look at each other.

"I'm happy to sit this one out. I only need the information. If Sasha wants to play, he can," Roman says as he unbuttons his suit jacket, flicks the flaps back and takes a seat on the leather couch.

Savage looks at Dex, then Flack and then me.

"I'm leaving Gavin up to the Wrights. I have a feeling both Flack and Remy will have something to say to that fucker."

My dad nods. "Lemme fuck him up a bit, just to get the edge off. I'm sure you have a much more painful way of dealing with things, Chewy."

Chewy nods at him as he steps forward, adjusts his favorite

knuckle dusters and makes a few choice hits. Once he's done, he turns to me but I shake my head.

"No. I'll wait until he's begging like Jovie did when he threw her in that room." I stare at *Gavin* as I say this, letting him see how little I care about him.

"We'd like to have a go at Snake when the time comes," Savage adds, nodding toward Chewy, who smiles brightly back.

"Well, I'm guessing Gavin's the weak link, so I say we freeze some fingers and toes off while we question him. If he doesn't answer with that incentive, then I have a little bit of a new idea I want to try out." Chewy says and everyone groans. The last time she had a good idea, the compound ended up raining body parts.

She and Rhodie whisper amongst themselves a moment, while Pops and Tav whisper to each other while mixing something at the table. Rhodie hits a couple of things on his phone, starting the neon lights and Chewy's soundtrack of choice for the night.

"Now *I've had the time of my life,*"

A dozen or so heads swivel in horror at Chewy as she cackles.

"It's perfect because *nobody* puts Jovie in the corner!"

We all groan collectively, however that's drowned out by Gavin's screams as Chewy methodically starts freezing his toes off.

Wire

It's times like this that I'm fucking glad Chewy is on our side. So far, Gavin is minus all of his fingers and toes, and Chewy is fizzing to try her new idea out.

"So, I actually have two great ideas. I'm going to put the first one into action, mainly because I feel like Snake has been missing out," she pouts at the very thought.

Looking toward Snake, I've noticed he's gotten more and more panicked looking the longer Chewy has been interrogating that piece of shit Gavin.

"Earlier, before we snapped off his phalanges, you may have noticed I spent a little time with his junk. That's because I made a mold of Gavin's penis." She says 'penis' all prim and proper. "And we all know that I have experience taking peen molds. Whilst I was busy, my beautiful assistants here -" she waves in Tav and Pops direction as Marx rolls his eyes and runs a hand down his face, "They were fashioning me this!" She produces a lackluster looking dildo, made from the mold of Gavin's junk.

"What the fuck are you going do to with that?" Tank asks, scandalized.

"Jules," Chewy clicks her fingers as her brother rolls his eyes before wheeling a rolling stool with some weird-looking contraption on the top. Almost like one of those machine massage gun things, but not quite.

Roman and Sasha sit forward with interest as it rolls past. Gus looks his cool, calm, collected self, although I notice his jaw clenching slightly.

"What. In. The. Fuck. Is that thing?" Switch booms out. I'm

sure as a doctor, some things he sees Chewy do must turn his stomach.

"This, lady and gentlemen, is a thrusting dildo sex machine! Or a fuck gun. Whatever." She shrugs. Rhodie drops a kiss on her head, looking proudly at her.

"Tell them what your plan is, baby."

"I'm going to mount that guy's cock on here, and while I finish Gavin off, pun intended, Snake over here will have his ass breached. According to his file, he enjoys having non-consensual sex, so, let's see how he likes it huh." Chewy's eyes gleam as Snake starts struggling. "Flip him over, boys. I need access to that ass."

Glancing around, I notice the Death Riders all watch in horror as Rhodie and Jules manhandle Snake, turning him around, then re-cuffing his wrists and ankles to the St Andrews Cross. Chewy gets all her things into position, looks at the lube in her hand before shrugging and tossing it aside.

"I'm going to start her off nice and slow, OK? I need you with me for when it's your turn to talk." She says sweetly, before patting Snake's ass and turning the machine on to the setting she described as "gentle."

Snake's ass and jaw both clench and he makes a grunting noise. His arms and legs are shaking and sweat drips down his back, but the tough fucker refuses to make a noise.

"Who would have thought he was that fucking loyal, huh?" Flack says with a chuckle. "Take it all, boy, you deserve it."

Chewy gets all our attention by clapping her hands together. "Remy, I have one last trick. If you had to choose who was going to feel your rage more, Gavin or Snake, who would you pick?"

Remy looks between the two men. On one hand, Snake used

to torment her as a girl. He'd corner her and leer at her. But Gavin is the fucker that not only kidnapped her, he sold Jovie's mom, got her killed and then sold his daughter. I know which fucker I'd choose.

"Gavin. I want Gavin."

"Excellent choice! Here are the options." Chewy claps excitedly and then leads Remy over to her table of tricks.

"I don't think I'll ever get used to watching this shit," Dex grumbles.

"You better, you boys are DRMC now," Rider says before cracking up.

Remy turns, her eyes scanning the group before landing on me. Tipping my head forward, I stare at her a moment, wanting to know where her head is at. A slow grin covers her face and I know she's good.

She steps up to Gavin, and instead of raging at him, she leans toward him. Her lips are moving and yet none of us can hear what she's saying. She leans back, smiles and then circles to stand behind him. She squats a little, eye level with his ass, then she does something that makes him squirm and cry out.

"What in the fuck is she doing to him?" Fox asks, frowning at the man as he struggles to move away from her.

"Expanding foam. In his ass. That stuff is gonna expand until his colon blows up." Pops answers, grinning wide. There is something seriously wrong with his particular gene pool.

We all take two steps back and I don't know about anyone else, but I'm unable to tear my eyes away. Gavin's stomach is starting to swell from the inside out. I'm not sure if he will actually explode, but the noises he's making are fucking awful. Shuffling sideways, I angle myself behind Tank. He's fucking huge, so he'll protect me from a lot of the fallout.

I may be hiding, but my girl isn't. She's standing in front of Gavin, watching him squirm in agony. Once he begs for mercy, she smiles. She keeps smiling as she holds the can up to his wailing mouth and presses the button. The foam expands until it fills his mouth, his throat bulging with the stuff. She watches as he struggles to breathe, as he turns blue and as his body shuts down, slumping in front of her.

"Good fucking riddance," her husky voice says loud and clear as she tosses the can on the ground and makes a beeline toward me.

"Snakey, looks like it's your turn!" Chewy coos out.

Remy walks right into my arms. I hold her to me, rubbing my hand through her silky, soft hair.

"Take me to our baby, Wire. I want us to get into our PJs and settle in for a movie with our girl."

"Whatever you want, baby." She pulls back and gives me one of her beautiful smiles, letting me lead her out the door while Snake screams behind us.

Chapter Twenty

Remy

By the time we tear Jovie away from the kitchen and all her new "aunties", bathe her, shower ourselves and get into our PJ's, the interrogation is over and all the brothers decide that the movie night should take place in the common room. Jovie has gone from being a neglected little girl to a little girl with three new grandfathers, two new grandmothers, and at least two dozen aunts and uncles.

Jovie is now perched on a plush pink bean bag watching Nitro, Fox, Rider and Switch argue over why we should watch their choice of film. All little girl safe, of course.

"Jovie, princess, don't you want to watch a really cool film about two best friends, who are toys that come alive when their boy is asleep or at school? There's a sausage dog in it," Nitro says as Fox nods behind him.

"Look, Joves, that's a good movie and all, but what about one with a badass little Scottish girl with hair like mine?" Switch says, somehow using a quieter voice than usual. Rider is behind him, nodding emphatically.

Wire and I watch as the little girl who burrowed into everyone's hearts taps her finger on her chin, her little brows furrowed before smiling up at Switch and yelling "Badass ginger!"

She bursts into giggles as Rider and Switch tease Nitro and Fox, but she's a soft-hearted little thing, so she pats Nitro's hand.

"It's OK, Uncle Nitro, we'll watch your one tomorrow."

He smiles down at her and musses her hair. Which reminds me, I need to know how to care for it.

"Hey babe -"

"Already on it baby,"

"I didn't even say anything!"

"No need. I know you."

Letting out a sigh, I snuggle deeper into his arms. "Thanks for having my back."

"For always, Retta."

I smile at the nickname and look around at the family we have in the room. When I left the Death Riders, I did so, knowing it was only for a short while before I'd be back to help my family. Instead, I found a new family here, one that accepted me and helped me grow. Now, my closest Death Rider family are moving here over the next few weeks, starting new lives.

It's crazy how much has changed in such a short time, including me. Not only did I buy a completely new wardrobe that I'm excited to wear, but today I also did something I would never have had the confidence, or lady balls, as Chewy says, to do. I called Rose Grove Library, and I told them that unfortunately, due to what happened, I will not be returning. Did I love my job? Yeah. But the part I loved the most was seeing Jovie, and now I get to see her every day. I'm not sure what I'm going to do for work just yet, but I'm sure I'll find my path soon.

"Psst, Remy." Turning at the sound of my name, I see the girl gang and Sasha all waving at me.

Wire turns to look over his shoulder, sees what's happening, grins down at me and tips my head to go to them. Smiling, I drop a kiss on his lips and then quietly tiptoe into the kitchen, so as not to disturb all the big, burly alpha men watching a little kid movie.

We all lean against the counter, looking through the window part of the kitchen at the scene.

"Look at them all. Who would think that's what all those tough men get up to?" Nat says, smirking.

Even Marx, who is sitting at the bar pretending that he's not watching, is watching.

"Looks are deceiving. Do I look like the type of person who goes around punching bad guys starfish?"

We all turn to stare at Chewy. Ana's eyes narrow as she mouths "punching starfish". Sasha must know what the term means because he's trying hard not to laugh.

"Butt fucking, ladies. Keep up."

"It's hard. You have such a wide vocabulary," Nat says, deadpan.

"It's one of my autism super powers. It really must suck to be walking around with a neurotypical brain." Chewy shakes her head, genuinely looking sad for us.

"Anyhoo, how are you holding up after your time in the shed, Rem?" Sunny asks, in her big sister mode.

"Honestly? It was kinda gross, and I feel bad that I killed a man. But at the same time, I feel... powerful. I managed to slay a demon today." I smile at my friends. "But I don't want to do

237

that again. No offense, Chewy, but you can keep your job."

"Of course, I'm by far the best enforcer this MC has."

"Even better than Rhodie?" Ana asks, a twinkle in her eye.

"We have different specialities. He's brute force. I'm more, delicate." She says as Ana snorts loudly.

"Anyway, ladies and man. I think we need to organize a Girls' Night. What do you say?" Sunny says. Sunny loves a party.

"Oh! I know how to girls' night. I have a good idea for one too. Can I do the entertainment?" Chewy has her hand up. The rest of us all look at each other before shrugging. "Yussss!"

"Well, then. That's sorted. I better get my man and get going. Growing humans makes me tired." Ana says on a yawn as Sasha adds, "And gassy," under his breath, dodging her ill aimed punch.

"Hear, hear sister! I'm gonna grab Savage and make him rub my feet," Nat cackles as she heads into the common room, the rest of us following.

Instead of heading straight to Wire, I take a detour to the bar.

"Hey, Takoda."

"Hey Remy."

"Um, I just wanted to thank you for the Rug Rats tent. Jovie loves it."

"Oh, it was nothing. It was just sitting in a box of stuff my mom had in the attic from when I was little." His cheeks pinken a little as he busies himself with wiping the bar top.

"Well, it means a lot. When I was a kid, really little, I had the same tent. It was my safe space. I could hide in there and no one could get me. You brought back a lot of memories for me, and I'm so glad that I can share that with Jovie, so thank you, Takoda. It means a lot." I lay a hand on his and give it a squeeze. He gives me a small smile and nods his head before I let go and he goes back to his work.

Smiling to myself, I turn to look at the room and all the people in it

"It's a good sight, huh?" Marx's rough voice rumbles next to me.

"That it is, Pres. Although, I have to ask, why are we all in here relaxing when we could be chasing down whatever info you got out of Snake and Gavin?"

I follow Marx's gaze to the little girl that's now snuggled on Wire's lap.

"We've been wading through shitstorm after shitstorm for months now. No matter how many men we put down, more rise to make the world a fucked up place. We could all be out there, chasing down leads and working off the tips Snake gave us, but that shit will still be there tomorrow. Tonight is about welcoming a little girl into our family. It's about spending time with our brothers, old and new. And taking a little time to count our blessings that tonight, we are all happy and whole. Tomorrow we'll call a meeting and go through what we have, but for tonight, let's just enjoy each other."

Looking up at Marx, who I initially thought was scary and gruff, I see a man who cares deeply about everyone in his clubhouse.

"Thank you, Marx."

The big man shrugs. "It's what we do."

I feel Wire come up behind me. Turning, my heart turns to mush as he stands there, Jovie crashed out in his big arms.

"Ready for bed, baby?"

Smiling up at my little family, I follow Wire down the hall as the manly men watch the end of Brave.

Wire

Tightening my arms around my woman, I snuggle my face deeper into her hair, breathing her in before I get my big ass up and ready for the day. She had a late night last night, what with me fucking her mercilessly after we put Jovie to bed in her pink glittery room.

Dropping a kiss to Remy's naked shoulder, I gently untangle my legs, sliding my arm out from under her, so as not to wake her. Pulling on a fresh henley, jeans, socks, boots and my cut, I creep out into the control center, quickly doing my morning checks to make sure all is good in my world. Well, as good as it can be before Marx presents Chewy's findings this morning and fucks up our world all over again.

Shuffling has me turning toward the door in time to see two white bunnies standing in the doorway.

"Hey, good morning sleepyhead," I coo quietly, "Did you sleep well?"

Jovie shuffles closer to me, turning slightly as she reaches me, standing between my legs, allowing me to pick her up and place her in my lap before giving her a morning cuddle. I never knew I'd have such strong feelings for a kid I'd met at the library, but this kid is absolute magic.

"Morning Wire."

"You ready to get dressed and have some breakfast? We'll let Remy sleep a little longer, OK?"

"OK." She nods and places her head in the little crook between my shoulder and jaw, just like Remy does when she snuggles.

Lifting her in my arms, I carry her back to her room, sitting her on the bed while I look for clothes for her.

"Huh. Where did your aunts hide all your clothes, Jovs?"

She giggles before sliding off the bed and leading me to her closet. Opening the door, I can see all her new clothes hanging. Looking down at her, I raise a brow. This is quite a different wardrobe to what my sisters had growing up. Instead of a row of dresses, I'm met with a row of shirts, all with dinosaurs on the front. Under the dinosaur shirts is a row of cargo pants and shorts, all in different colors. Under that, a couple of pairs of little biker boots. Huh.

"Jovs, how come no dresses? I thought you'd have a wardrobe full of them to match your princess room."

She giggles at me. "Wire! My princess room is pretty. But you can't play in dresses. The poofy's get in the way."

I shrug at her. I mean, she has a point. "Fair enough kid."

I hand her all the items she wants, and she goes about getting dressed. I only get the urge to punch things three times, each time when I see a different bruise on her brown skin. I'm glad Remy ended her father. If she didn't, I would have.

"Take a seat kid, let's sort this hair, yeah?"

Spraying her hair down with water, I then hit it with the detangling conditioner before combing it out with the wide-toothed comb my sisters recommended. Once it's detangled, I work all the different creams and oils through it like I did when my sisters were little.

"Right little miss, how do you want your hair today?"

She looks at me before a smile splits her face. "Like yours!"

Grinning, I pull it into a bun on top of her head, securing it with a scrunchie before doing her edges. She rushes to her little mirror, looking at herself from all angles before she claps and dances her way back to me. Throwing her arms around me, she

241

kisses me on the cheek.

"Thanks Wire! I love it sooooo much!"

I grab her, toss her in the air and carry her giggling into the common room, ready for breakfast.

My brothers all call their good mornings to her, holding out big fists for her to bump, or teasing her about falling asleep through the movie last night. She giggles with them all before wriggling down to hug Mama Debs and Pops good morning.

"Looks good on you brother," Rhodie says as he stands beside me, sorting his breakfast.

"Thanks, man. Feels good too."

"How's things?" He raises his brow. I know what he's asking.

"Not as suffocating. I feel peaceful. Like, I'll still be an asshole about safety, but it doesn't feel like such a burden anymore."

His hand slaps my shoulder as he grins at me. "Good, brother. That's good."

Choosing a seat, I place my plate down with Jovie's next to mine. She comes running, climbs up and starts digging in. My kid is a good eater. I'm about to dig into my own breakfast when I freeze at the vision in the mouth of the hall.

There's my girl, but she's not the Remy we're used to. Gone are the tweed and frumpy skirts and blouses. In their place is a pair of jeans that look like they've been sprayed on, highlighting Remy's thick thighs and shapely legs. Instead of those old lady shoes, her feet are in a pair of black motorcycle boots. Instead of an ill fitting silky blouse with a book brooch, she has on some type of sweater that pulls tight across her amazing tits and accentuates her smaller waist. Instead of letting her jaw length hair sit straight as it usually does, she has pulled it up in a short ponytail, letting her beautiful face be seen.

"Holy shit, it's like when Sandy in Grease got that makeover," Judge whispers and I spin to growl at him.

Jovie sees what I'm looking at and claps her hands. "You look beautiful, Remy!" She throws her a thumbs up before putting another fork full of pancake in her mouth.

I want to stand and go to her, but I'm still in so much shock that before I even blink, she's standing right here in front of me.

"Fuck me, baby, you look, fuck, you look stunning." I wrap my hand around the back of her neck, pulling her down to me so I can claim her mouth. Pulling back slightly, I remember to mumble, "I loved you before, but this, fuck." I claim her mouth again until she pulls away, giggling.

"Tav!" I roar out. He stops in the kitchen hatch, assesses the situation, grins at me and disappears for a moment before coming out with a box in his hands, passing it to me.

Handing it over to Remy, her eyes dart between me and the box before she places it on the table. Gently removing the lid, she gasps softly, tears pooling in her eyes as she removes the cut I had made for her. Holding it up so all the ladies can oohh and ahh over the patch that says "Property of Wire." Slipping it over her shoulders, she runs her hand down the soft leather.

"You're a fucking vision, Remy."

"I love it." She beams at me.

"That's all that matters, baby. Sit down, I'll get your breakfast." I cut off her protests with a kiss and go to serve my woman.

Chewy and the other women let out whoops and "hot mama's" I even hear a "hubba hubba" from somewhere, but I ignore it because the look on Remy's face is all worth it.

"Alright, settle down you animals," Marx says, throwing a wink at Remy. "Now we're all here, including Roman and Sasha." Shit, I didn't even notice them come in. I knew the Tombs were all here. They're always here. "We can work through what we learned last night. Mama Debs?"

Debs steps forward, taking Jovie, who has finished her pancakes, by the hand. I can hear them planning out their morning, so I know they'll be busy for the next hour or so.

"Chewy, do you want to do the honors?"

Chewy steps up to Marx and then performs a deep bow before straightening up.

"Sure thing, bestie." She claps her hands while Rider growls. "Right. Gavin didn't have too much to offer other than he had been lurking around a bar in Roxwell and had overheard some of Hammer's nomads talking. He sold Jovie's mom to them, saw how much meth he could buy with the proceeds, and then sold Jovie. It just was a coincidence that the after school library program Jovie's mom had signed her up for was being run by Remy. Gavin, along with Snake, then hatched the kidnapping plan. Apparently Hammer had been trying to find a way to get to Remy. Her relationship with Jovie made it easier for them to get to her."

A round of cursing goes up, as well as many brothers shaking their heads.

"Did you find out why the fuck he was lurking around the yard?" Tank asks.

"He knew that they needed a place to keep Jovie and Remy so he was staking the place out. Officer Martin, who knew Gavin from growing up in the trailer park, told him that the yard and alley were owned by the MC, so choose somewhere else. When

Jovie's mom Jayla died before they could sell her, Hammer told them to dump her in the alley and called in the tip. Did the same thing to Roman with another girl that also died in their care."

"Fuckers," Pops curses.

"Snake had even more for us to work with. We already knew that Hammer wasn't working with the Russians anymore, thanks to you, Roman." Chewy nods her head at him. "He also currently isn't in Texas anymore. He's been hiding out in Louisiana, working with a family there. Their reach and influence makes them hard to pin down."

Roman sits up. "Interesting. The Cajun Mafia stick to drugs, not girls."

"What about girls with drugs inside them?" Judge asks, his brow raised.

Roman shakes his head. "Not their style. Not the Orleans Mafia style either."

"Wait, those aren't the same families?"

"No. Different families. Our territories all butt up against one another. We know who is dealing what at all times. It's a sign of respect. Any slight against that would start an all out war and presently, none of us want that."

"You make it sound like you're all just out here doing legitimate business," Rider snorts.

"We are. We even have a WhatsApp group to make sure we aren't stepping on any toes." A few eyebrows fly up at this information. "So I can assure you, Hammer isn't working with the mafia."

"Roman's right. The name Snake gave me isn't mafia. It's Landry. I did a little research on them this morning. They're super religious types."

"Mormons?"

"Oddly, no. From what I could find out online, the patriarch touts himself as a prophet. And as with all self professed prophets, he has a shit ton of wealthy benefactors all paying for salvation. He has 13 wives that were too young to legally agree to marrying him and a large number of children. He's elderly and, from what I could find, unwell. Once he dies, his brother is next in line to lead the flock."

Marx frowns, rubbing his beard. "What the fuck would a religious sect want with trafficked girls?"

"I say we ask them. Valor Landry, the prophet's nephew, is in town this afternoon for a little Preach'n'Tell. He also has a van and was meeting Snake with Remy and Jovie." Chewy shrugs and then looks shocked when everyone shouts, wanting to know why she didn't just lead with that.

An ear-piercing whistle shuts everyone up and we all reclaim our seats while Marx glares at us.

"Look fuckers, we can't all ride out because that dick Hammer has us locked down with the pigs on our backs. Chewy has Snake's phone. She'll confirm that he's good to meet at the warehouse where they kept Remy and Jovie. Savage, Roman and I will meet with Landry. Gus, Jules and Sniper will be in position watching the warehouse's exits. Everyone cool?"

We all nod. We have a few hours to kill before the meet, so Remy decides to spend a little time with Jovie while I work with Tav at getting cameras set up in the warehouse. I need to have eyes on this.

Marx

"Everyone in position?" Wire asks through the headset.

The crackling voices of Gus, Jules and Sniper all sound off, one at a time, letting us know they're ready. Savage and Roman sit with me in the SUV around the corner from the meet. I'd much rather be on my hog, but we have to at least make it look as though we have girls to hand off to the sick fuck. So I will sit here and be suffocated by Roman's cologne.

"How much longer?"

"He's just packing up his soapbox," Remy's voice says into our earpieces.

"Wow, the librarian has a pleasant voice for these sorts of things," Roman says with a smirk.

A growl comes through the line, and we all know it's Wire. That just makes Roman chuckle.

"Car is on the move. ETA will be 2 minutes," Wire barks down the line.

I settle back into my seat; the leather creaking around my bulk. Valor Landry expects us to be waiting for him. Fuck that. We'll unsettle him by arriving after him. We watch a slick gunmetal gray van drive past, slowing to pull into the open garage door of the warehouse. Savage and Roman sit quietly with me, each of us busy with our own thoughts.

"What the fuck?" Wire's voice says in our earpieces.

"Wire? What's happening?"

"Holy shit! We got a third player, just pulled in on a Harley." This time, Chewy.

"Marx, get in there now. Something's going down," Wire barks.

Starting the SUV, I throw it into gear and gun it into the warehouse. Pulling in through the doors, I screech to a stop, throw open the door and duck behind it, in case of gunfire. Instead, we're met with a short, curvy woman, with cropped, dark hair standing in the back of the van, a body slumped behind her. And she's pointing a gun right at us.

"Who the fuck are you?" I demand.

Instead of answering me, she jumps down, walks a few steps closer before stopping again, eyes on me the whole time.

"I'm the bitch who will end you if you have little girls in that car." She flicks her gun toward the SUV.

Narrowing my eyes at her, I realize she isn't a threat. I'm not sure what she is exactly.

"We're here for Valor. Want some answers. Like where the fuck his business partner Hammer is. And why the fuck he was buying my new niece and sister."

She chews her lip for a moment before lowering her gun. "Who are you?"

"I'm Marx, Pres of Devil's Rose MC."

"DRMC? You know Tav?" She tips her head to the side.

Savage and I side-eye each other before nodding, her lips tipping up slightly in the corners.

"This is Savage, and Roman Bartashev -"

"Bratva. Heard you lost some drugs?"

Roman just stares at her as she shakes her head at us. "Valor isn't going to talk. If you want Hammer, he'll be scuttling back to these parts soon enough."

With that, she walks off, her boots thudding dully on the concrete floor. Savage looks at me before walking to the van and peering in.

"Fuck. Valor's dead. Single gunshot to the head."

Turning back to the mystery woman, I whistle to her as she throws her leg over a softail Harley. She freezes, her dark eyes glaring at me.

"Who are you?"

"Blanche Landry. Say hi to Tav for me."

Epilogue

Wire

In the month since Remy got kidnapped and then filled a man with expanding foam, shit has gotten real quiet. Contrary to the mysterious Blanche Landry's warning, that Hammer will be back, we have had nothing to back that claim up. Which has had me on fucking edge.

"I thought I'd find you here," Arms wrap around me from behind and Remy tucks her nose into the crook of neck. "Found anything?"

Tipping my head to the left, I let my head rest on hers. "Nothing yet, baby. It's just so quiet."

"Well, let's look at this logically. We know who he's doing business with. So far, the Landrys have stayed quiet. Their prophet is on his deathbed and until he dies, his successor, Royal Landry's hands are tied. We've been monitoring missing women reports from Rose Grove and the towns within a 50 miles radius, so far there have been none. No one has seen Hammer's nomad MC either, which is a good thing."

I grunt at her laying it all out like that. Before Remy I'd obsess over finding crumbs to follow. I'd pull all nighters trying to find something, anything to settle the thoughts in my mind. I'd wake in the night with nightmares of my brothers and family all dying. Now, I have Remy to keep me calm, and Jovie to focus on. She needs the very best father figure, not someone who's broken mind is elsewhere thinking up scenarios.

"Look, babe, we can't borrow trouble. Not for the moment, anyway. It'll find us, and when it does, we'll be ready. We're stronger now. You have three new MC brothers and we have more badass women."

And hell if she isn't right on that point. Savage, Dex and Flack moved to Rose Grove two weeks ago, bringing Nat and Remy's sister Sunny with them. Since then, Chewy has been in girl gang heaven and my girl has been going from strength to strength. She's even started a new job; working in Dex's gym alongside him, running the self defense program for women and children who have escaped family violence. She's thriving. And so is our sex life. I never thought much about women's workout gear before, but holy shit, Remy in tight leggings and a tank top, all flushed and a sheen of sweat on her pale skin has me bending her over any available surface. Which is why I'm currently banned from visiting her at work. That doesn't stop me watching her on my cameras though.

"I hear what you're saying, and I know you're right, but," A loud sigh escapes me, "I have so much to lose, baby. You, Jovie. I can't lose you. You're my world." Lifting my head, I spin in my chair and pull her into my lap, her ass parked on my thighs while her legs hang over the armrests of my chair.

"How come we haven't fucked like this?" Remy asks, her brows furrowed.

I go from 0 to 100 immediately. Hearing Remy say shit like

that always has me ready to go off. Looking down, I take in what she's wearing. A tight, navy blue bandage dress with a mouthwatering amount of cleavage on display, her milky globes almost spilling out over the top. With her legs splayed the way they are, the bottom has ridden up and I can see her trimmed thatch of blonde hair atop her glistening pussy lips. Running a finger down her slit, her head drops back to her shoulders, and she lets out a low moan writhing in my lap.

"You are so fucking perfect, Retta, so perfect, pink and wet for me."

Leaning forward, I suck on her cleavage, leaving wet kisses across the top of her large tits before licking up her neck and claiming her lips, thrusting my tongue between her lips.

Her hands wind around my neck as my hands push her dress up her thighs, gripping her ass.

"How much time do we have before girls' night starts?" I whisper, not even bothering to remove my lips from hers.

"You have about 10 minutes before Chewy comes looking for me,"

"That's doable. I'll make it up to you later."

"Shut up and put your fat cock in my pussy right now."

Smirking at my girl I rub my thumb over her bottom lip, letting her suck it into her mouth and lave it with her tongue. Pulling it from her lush lips with a pop, I press my thumb to her clit, enjoying the little whimper that escapes her. Sliding lower, rubbing it around her tight hole, her wet pussy sucking it in, I pump it in and out, gathering her cream. She writhes on my lap as her hands work quickly to get my jeans undone. She takes out my rock hard length, smearing my precum around the head before positioning me where she wants me.

"That's it baby, fuck, you're so wet for me."

Raising her hips slightly she lines up, and then sinks down slowly. I can't tear my eyes off her pussy lips spread wide as my cock disappears into her hot cunt. Once she's seated she rolls her hips, the base of my cock massaging her swollen clit. She does this over and over, scooting back and forth in my lap, her moans getting more and more frantic. I watch as her movements grow faster and then stutter, her pussy gushing on me as she grunts out my name. Knowing that she has reached her peak I grab her ass in my big hands, raise her up slightly and drop her down into my lap as I pump up into her. I do this over and over until she creams all over me again and I roar out my own release, pumping her full of my cum hoping that maybe we made another beautiful daughter to add to our family.

"Holy moly babe, how does that get better every time?" She asks breathlessly, her head in the groove between my shoulder and jaw, right where she belongs.

"I dunno babe, must be that magic pussy of yours."

She snorts into my neck before sighing. "How much time have I got?"

"Probably 3 minutes before the stampede comes."

She groans and then slowly slides off my cock. "I'll clean up, you run interference if they turn up."

"I've got your back babe, always."

Once Remy's cleaned up I kiss her thoroughly and we head to Jovie's room. Our little girl, just like Remy, has been thriving. She's also been collecting family members like they're going out of fashion. Not only were my momma and sisters over the moon to meet their new grandbaby and niece, but somehow this little ball of light and love has brought together a family. Dad comes to visit his grandbaby often. The first time he and Momma crossed paths, we were all prepared for a scene.

Instead, they commented on how good the other looked and then they focussed all their energy on Jovie, who lapped up the attention.

Heading to Jovie's room, it looks empty, until we hear her little voice chatting away. I share a look with my girl and we both get to our knees, crawling to Jovie's fortress.

"Knock, knock baby girl,"

The flap is pulled back and our daughter beams back at us.

"Hey Retta and Mags, I was just reading to Bumpy." Jovie points to her Stegosaurus toy. She has been calling us Retta and Mags for a few weeks now. Those are our special names for each other.

Not long after Chewy completed Jovie's paperwork to make her our daughter, we sat her down and told her the sad news that her momma had passed away. We reminded her that not only did she have Remy and me, but she had a huge family of people that will take care of her and love her as well. After that she decided she wanted to call us Mom and Dad, but in her words, her Dad was bad and she doesn't want to think about him. Remy also told her that her momma Jayla was an amazing, brave woman and she wouldn't feel right taking her name. Just because we have Jovie now doesn't mean that we don't honor her momma. We found out all we could about her. Me and my brothers went by her trailer and took anything we thought Jovie will want as she grows older. Jovie's room is covered in pictures of her and her mom and she has some new pictures of her new family popping up as well.

"And is Bumpy enjoying the book?"

"Yup. I think he likes dinosaurs as much as me and Chewy do."

I can feel the smirk on my lips. Even though Chewy probably

isn't really kid friendly, she loves that Jovie loves dinosaurs. Which means Jovie pretty much has a whole ass dinosaur library and somehow even owns a dinosaur fossil.

"Well, Mama Debs will pick you up for your sleepover, so let's make sure you have all your things, yeah?"

She nods at me and crawls into my lap. Standing, I cuddle Jovie and Remy at the same time before patting her ass and telling her to get to her girls before they come looking for her. She walks off, that tight dress stretched across her ass, and I have to talk my cock down while I help my daughter pack for the night.

In no time, Mama Debs whisks Jovie away and I head to the common room for a little quiet time with my brothers.

Instead, I find the place covered in pink streamers, strobe lights and the bunnies looking sour.

"What in the hell is going on in here?" I ask no one in particular.

"Well, apparently no bar wanted to host their girls' night. So Chewy decided to have it here. Which is probably a good thing because it means I can somewhat relax instead of stalking my pregnant wife around a bar all goddamn night," Gus grumbles before taking a pull of his beer.

Savage tips his at him, as does Rhodie. I just shrug. I know how hot my girl is. I don't want any fucker eying her up, either.

We shoot the shit, gradually watching Remy, Chewy and Sunny get more and more messy. At one point, they all start trying to twerk before collapsing into giggles.

"You look happy, brother." Marx says as he watches the antics.

"Very happy. I'd be happier once we put down Hammer."

"All in good time, brother."

A hand lands on my thigh, drifting up to my dick. Recognizing the long, red nails, I grab Whitney by the wrist, ripping her hands off me, disgust rising at the audacity of this bitch. Before I can open my mouth, Whitney's ripped away from me violently.

"Don't you dare touch my man you bitch!" Remy yells before punching Whitney in the face.

Everything goes silent before a screech is heard and all hell breaks loose. The four bunnies we have are all in some type of fight with the girl gang. There is hair all over the place, a lot of screaming, and Chewy is wielding her heels like daggers. Marx's phone goes off.

"Not a-fucking-gain!"

The door opens and about six police officers rush in. They take one look at what's happening and the one that looks like he's in charge brings his bullhorn to his mouth.

"Freeze!"

Like magic, the girls go silent. Remy has her hands in Whitney's hair, wide eyed. Sunny has Mariah in a headlock, Nat and Ana are both sitting on Chelsea and Chewy has her foot on Kelly's hair extensions.

"You're all under arrest!" The asshole with the bullhorn says.

"What the fuck for?!" Marx roars back.

Officer Bullhorn looks him up and down. "For being too sexy."

Dance music starts up and the officers start gyrating. As soon as the first shirt is ripped open, Chewy throws her hands in the air and yells "Girls night!" at the top of her lungs, the girls all cackling and high fiving while my brothers, MC and Tombs sit speechless.

"What in the fuckery is going on?" Marx whispers. Gus reaches out his hand with his roll of antacids, but Marx shakes his head, unable to pull his eyes away from the scene in front of him, puts his hand in his pocket and pulls his own roll out.

"Good man," Gus mumbles.

"I'll let them have half a song before I'm kicking these fuckers out," Marx grumbles.

He doesn't even make it to half a song. As soon as the snap pants get torn off and thrown on the floor, Marx bellows for them to all fuck off. But not before Nitro sticks a dollar bill in Officer Bullhorn's G string.

"Well, it was good while it lasted, ladies," Nat says, her face flushed from dancing.

"If I'm being honest, I never thought we'd get that far through the show. I figured the men would have shut that shit down immediately." Ana chimes in.

"Shock and awe technique," Chewy grins proudly, and they all high five each other.

Remy walks straight into my outstretched arms, standing between my spread legs.

"How was girls' night, baby?"

She pulls back to gaze up at me, her eyes shining brightly. "It was the best. Time. Ever."

"Even half a strip show?"

"Pshh. I have a much hotter man in my bed every night. It was just fun because it was with my girls, surrounded by my family. This is what I've been looking for, Mags. A family like this with the love of a boy I met when I was 13 years old. And I got it!"

"Yes, you did, baby. I love you, for always."

She beams at me before gently touching her lips to mine.

"For always."

Tav

"**D**ude, what the fuck is wrong with our sister?"

Turning, Jules' grumpy face comes into view. I can't tell if he's grumpy because that's his natural setting, or because the bunnies are so beat up none of them want to fuck him and Fox and Nitro. I have no idea what they all get up to together and I don't want to know.

"Are you asking as a serious question or just venting?"

He stink eye's me as I shrug and get back to work. I have to admit, working the bar has its perks. I can watch everything that's going on, and a lot of the time it's a comedy of errors. Prospecting has been one of the better decisions I've made. Don't get me wrong, I love working at Tombs Security, but I need people. And the excitement of never knowing what's going to happen next.

Actually, that's not quite true. When it comes to my love life, I'd love to know what's going to happen next. Blanche still isn't fully on board. I know she wants me. She's told me. She just has business that needs to be finished and the kids to worry about. I haven't told Marx and the brothers that I'm in love with the woman that took out Valor Landry. They know we know each other, and I told them the truth. We met at a security conference six months ago. And every day of those six months I've been trying to convince her to be my Ol Lady. She's the one. I know it.

"Tav, Jimmy says there's a bunch of kids at the gate asking for you." Rhodie calls out, his phone against his chest.

Frowning, I glance at the time. 9 o'clock is late.

"They asked for me?" Pointing to myself in case Rhodie has gotten me confused with someone else. He's great and loves my sister, and because of that fact, I'm unsure how clever the man actually is.

"You're the only fucking Tav Tombs we've got, dickhead."

"He say how many?" Brow furrowed, I check my messages and see nothing to note. Pulling up my tracking app, I check to see where my girl is. I'm not surprised to find she's turned her phone off.

"Four kids, ranging in size from Jovie to small man sized."

My lips twitch. Jimmy, the prospect who does gate duty, has a fun way with words. "I know them. I'll go out."

"Prospect," Marx barks, "It's 9 o'clock at night. Some kids asking for you means they need help. Rhodie, get Jimmy to bring them in."

Rhodie nods and says something into his phone. All the brothers are looking at me. So are the girl gang, but they look more nosey than anything.

"How do you know these kids, Tav?"

"I've been dating their mom."

"Wait, the skittish woman?" My brother asks. I know he and Jules have been concerned about my girl not wanting to be all in with me, but there are reasons for that.

Marx nods, and Jimmy walks through the door, ushering the kids in.

"Tav!" Cove yells out, running up to me. I pull her into my

arms instinctively, her slightly older brother, Elio crowding my legs.

Niko steps closer to his sister Sage, eyeing up my club brothers.

"Hey, it's OK. You're safe here. This is my club Pres, Marx." Marx steps forward and smiles gently at the kids. He's met with a scowl from Sage. "The rest of the men here are my club brothers. Their wives and girlfriends are over at the table there."

Thankfully, the girl gang has settled down. They smile and wave at the kids.

"Tell me what's going on."

Niko eyes everyone before setting his dark eyes on mine. "Mom went hunting. Told us that if she wasn't back in 12 hours, we had to come to you. You'd keep us safe."

"She's damn right. Nothing is going to happen to you, OK?" I look down at the little one hugging my legs.

The girl gang gets to their feet, Nat taking the lead. "We'll get rooms set up. One for the boys, one for the girls." Marx gives them a nod and I shoot them a smile in thanks as they all traipse off down the hall, whispering about how cute the kids are.

"Can you tell us what your mom was hunting for, kid? We can get a group together. Some of us are ex army search and rescue. We'll find her."

The older kids, Niko and Sage, stare at me, unsure how to answer Judge. Tipping my head at them that it's safe to tell these men, Sage turns to look at Judge.

"It's not what she's hunting. It's who."

A sharp intake of breath can be heard along with a few "what the fuck's?"

"OK kid. Who is your mom hunting?" Marx asks, being infinitely more patient than I'm used to.

Niko looks at me before looking at Marx. "Royal Landry."

"The prophet's brother?" Wire asks. I know that he and Remy have been watching the family closely since finding out that Hammer is working alongside them and their trafficking business.

"Tav, would you like to please enlighten us who your girl-friend is?"

Snuggling Cove closer to me, I look at my brothers before setting my gaze on Marx.

"Her name is Blanche Landry. And she will be my Ol Lady."

About the author

Cleo Browne is the pen name of a neurospicy geeky girl from Aotearoa New Zealand. As a child, she realized very early on that she wasn't a people person, so she would spend all her time reading and writing her own stories. These stories usually ended with the line "and then they died." As an adult, she has gotten slightly more people-y (not much) and better at not killing all her characters off when she writes.

Cleo loves to write about women who don't need a man to do their dirty work and the hot alpha men who turn to mush when they watch their women handling business.

When she's not writing romance novels about strong, curvy women and the men who adore them, she hangs out at home with her hubby, her boys, and her ancient greyhound who likes to creepily watch her write.

Acknowledgements

First off, I'd like to thank all the wonderful readers who continue to keep taking chances on a kooky little woman from New Zealand. Without you all reading my books and loving my characters, I would have just faded away into obscurity, never to be seen or heard from again. So, thank you. I appreciate you all.

Second, I'd like to thank my author bestie and all round good biartch Shaye Torrel. Thank you so much for talking me off the cliff when I would freak out that I didn't know what I was doing. I still don't, but at least I'm not freaking out about it. I wouldn't be here without you, chick!

Thanks to the amazing Gabi Brockelsby who caught perhaps the most hilarious typo ever! Thanks for catching that one Gabi!

And finally, thanks to my partner PN. Without his constant words of encouragement, "I really didn't think MC books were a thing," I would never have finished this book. Thanks also go to my boys. Ronnie, for being completely disinterested, and Louis for your two hour long phone calls that would eat into my writing time. Love you guys.

Thank you for reading!

Thank you so much for choosing to spend a little time with the characters I made up. What a wild ride!

If you want to know more about me or what I'm reading you can find me all over the place –

Follow me at my author page on Facebook

Friend me on Facebook

Join my group Cleo Browne's Babes

Follow me on Instagram

Keep your eyes peeled for upcoming books in the Devil's Rose MC Series, The Tombs Security Series, and a new series, because I can't just write two concurrently, The Davies Family Series - Small Town Romance set in Rose Grove. There may even be cameos from some of your fave characters.

Cleo Browne Books

Rhodie – Devil's Rose MC Book One

August – A Tombs Security + Devil's Rose MC Crossover

Wire – Devil's Rose MC Book Two

Tav Devil's Rose MC Book Three
In progress

Devil's Rose MC Christmas Novella
In progress

www.ingramcontent.com/pod-product-compliance
Lightning Source LLC
Chambersburg PA
CBHW020913130726
47904CB00006BA/1907